Quinn breathed against her neck. "Just by how you smell. Usually it's so subtle I hardly notice it, but sometimes, like right now"—his lips grazed her throat—"it's unbelievably overpowering."

Then she felt the wet heat of his tongue slide along her neck, and something happened that she didn't like at all—something that scared her more than anything else that night.

Her damn knees weakened.

She was crushed up against a wall by a hungry vampire, who apparently already knew what her blood would taste like, and it was *turning her on*.

How completely embarrassing.

"You want to bite me?"

He groaned. "Oh, yes."

"Bite me. Just . . . try not to take too much."

His breathing became even more erratic. "Oh, my God. This isn't right. Go, Janie. Just go." He pulled away. But she wasn't going to let him die just out of principle and misplaced morals. She slipped off her jacket and pulled her tank top off until she was standing there in the dark in her tight black jeans and lacy black bra, her neck and shoulders completely exposed. She grabbed Quinn's face, pulling it down to her neck.

"Bite me or I'm going to kick your ass."

*Please turn this page for praise
for Michelle Rowen's previous novels.*

Praise for the novels of Michelle Rowen

FANGED & FABULOUS

"Rowen once again presents an exciting, action-packed, and . . . humorous tale."
—*Romantic Times BOOKreviews Magazine*

"Rowen has done it again . . . wonderfully amusing . . . terrific!" —**RomanceReviewsMag.com**

"A laugh a minute . . . Quirky vampire chick-lit at its best!" —**FreshFiction.com**

"A funny and witty tale . . . I laughed out loud all through the book. The dialogue by this bestselling author is sarcastic and hilarious and the characters will leave you waiting impatiently for the next installment."
—**ArmchairInterviews.com**

BITTEN & SMITTEN

"Campy and vampy . . . This is what makes it so much fun." —*Shelf Life*

"Four stars! Fun and clever . . . this novel is bound to appeal to those who like their romance a little offbeat and definitely humorous."
—*Romantic Times BOOKreviews Magazine*

"Rowen's sense of humor is just too good to pass up."
—**RomanceReaderAtHeart.com**

"A study of contrasts: frothy chick-lit wrapped around a grittier reality and a flip side featuring a modern heroine paired with a Brontean hero. Let us welcome this fresh voice to the genre." **—Booklist**

"A terrific vampiric chick-lit tale filled with biting humor." **—Midwest Book Review**

ANGEL WITH ATTITUDE

"4 Stars! Rowen does a delightful job mixing things up with her sassy and sexy characters. She has her own unique spin on life and the afterlife and good and evil, which makes for downright fun reading." **—Romantic Times BOOKreviews Magazine**

"Divinely funny . . . A subtly provocative paranormal romance that shines a new light on angels and demons and witches, oh my! Michelle Rowen . . . has more than earned her 'wings.'" **—Heartstring Reviews**

"Fun and fast-moving . . . Valerie is a wonderful character. Kick off your shoes on a cold winter's night and relax with this. You'll be glad you did." **—Mythprint**

"Anyone who reads a Michelle Rowen romance is bitten and smitten to obtain more of her works. An amusing, heavenly romance with a hell of a price to pay for not reading it." **—Midwest Book Review**

"You have to read this book! It is quirky, funny, and sweet. If you love original and hilarious, you have to pick up *Angel with Attitude*."

—FallenAngelReviews.com

ALSO BY MICHELLE ROWEN

Angel with Attitude
Bitten & Smitten
Fanged & Fabulous

ATTENTION CORPORATIONS AND ORGANIZATIONS:
MOST HACHETTE BOOK GROUP USA books are available
at quantity discounts with bulk purchase for educational,
business, or sales promotional use. For information,
please call or write:

Special Markets Department, Hachette Book Group USA
237 Park Avenue, New York, NY 10017
Telephone: 1-800-222-6747 Fax: 1-800-477-5925

Lady & the Vamp

Michelle Rowen

FOREVER

NEW YORK   BOSTON

This book is a work of fiction. Names, characters, places, and incidents are the product of the author's imagination or are used fictitiously. Any resemblance to actual events, locales, or persons, living or dead, is coincidental.

If you purchase this book without a cover you should be aware that this book may have been stolen property and reported as "unsold and destroyed" to the publisher. In such case neither the author nor the publisher has received any payment for this "stripped book."

Copyright © 2008 by Michelle Rouillard
All rights reserved. Except as permitted under the U.S. Copyright Act of 1976, no part of this publication may be reproduced, distributed, or transmitted in any form or by any means, or stored in a database or retrieval system, without the prior written permission of the publisher.

Art direction by Mimi Bark
Cover photography by Herman Estevez

Forever
Hachette Book Group USA
237 Park Avenue
New York, NY 10017
Visit our Web site at www.HachetteBookGroupUSA.com

Forever is an imprint of Grand Central Publishing. The Forever name and logo is a trademark of Hachette Book Group USA, Inc.

Printed in the United States of America

First Printing: April 2008

10 9 8 7 6 5 4 3 2 1

Acknowledgments

Thank you to Bonnie Staring, Laurie Rauch, and Heather Harper, who gave the book a good read-through and made sure it all made sense. You guys so rock!

Thank you to my editor Melanie Murray, who reads my stuff and sends me her notes, and I just sit back and think . . . well, of course! That's what it's missing, or that's what needs to be taken out to make things better. The woman is a demigod of editorialship, and I worship her red pen. I have a shrine and everything.

Ditto to Jim McCarthy, who continues to go above and beyond anything I ever hoped for in an agent. Plus the man knows his reality TV shows, so that's just a total bonus.

I'd like to thank my readers so very, very much. Do you know that the book you're holding in your hands would never have come about if it weren't for you? When *Bitten & Smitten* came out, I received a ton of e-mail that essentially said, "We love Quinn!" and "Quinn needs to get the girl!" And I thought . . . *Yeah, he does*! So I asked Quinn if he wanted to be the hero of a book, and he said something along the lines of "Hell, yeah," so there you go. Quinn thanks you. I thank you. And we both sincerely hope that you enjoy his story!

Lady & the Vamp

Chapter 1

It was none of his business, but that never stopped him before.

Quinn watched from the shadows as two hunters moved stealthily through the dark parking lot of the roadside restaurant until they had their prey cornered. He wanted to ignore what he was seeing, turn away and head back to the car, but that wasn't going to happen.

He silently approached from behind.

"Need any help?" he asked.

The two hunters spun around to face him. One was large, with thick forearms and a scruff of beard that looked to be there more from laziness than fashion sense. The other was younger, thinner, with round glasses that magnified his eyes to twice their size. At first glance, a rather unlikely dynamic duo.

"Get lost," the large one said.

Quinn shrugged. "I can take a hint. No problem."

He turned.

Just walk away, he told himself. *You've got more important things to deal with.*

But then he glanced at the pair of vampires who'd been trapped in the Burger King parking lot near the garbage Dumpster—a male and female who could have been anywhere from twenty to two hundred years old, in his opinion. You just couldn't tell about that sort of thing.

"Please, help us," the female pleaded.

She was cute. Small and blond. Looked like a college student out on a date with her dark-haired, wide-eyed boyfriend, who was attempting to shield her from the hunters with his own body. Almost couldn't see his fangs unless you were looking for them.

Quinn laughed. "Help a vampire? Why would I want to do a crazy thing like that?"

"Hey—" the younger hunter moved the wooden stake to his other hand. "I think I know you. Don't I? You're Roger Quinn's kid, Michael. Yeah, we met a couple years ago. Toasted a nest of vamps up in St. Louis."

Quinn tried to see the face behind those large glasses. He didn't look familiar. Then again, he'd drunk a lot when he was in St. Louis. Bad month and a half. Beer had helped. "Sure. Good to see you again."

"Yeah, you, too, man." He absently scratched at his leg with the stake. The vampires eyed the sharp weapon with fear. The hunter turned to his friend. "Quinn here's one of the best hunters I've ever seen. Got a nose for vamps. Can smell them in any corner they try to hide."

Quinn waved his hand. "Aw, you're just saying that."

"I'm Joe, remember? This here's my buddy Stuart. Listen, you can totally help us out. These are our first two tonight. I figure they were lying in wait for victims coming out of the restaurant." He poked the male vampire in the chest as his magnified eyes narrowed. "That what you're doing? Looking for a little snack, you bloodsucking freak?"

"Go to hell." The vampire set his jaw and tried to look brave. It wasn't working very well.

"Well, you know vamps." Quinn eyed the restaurant as a car exited the drive-thru. "Evil to the core."

"You live around here?"

He shook his head. "Just passing through town. Stopped for a bite."

"Hey," the larger hunter spoke up. He was frowning. "You're Michael *Quinn?*"

"That's right."

"Please," the female said. "We're not evil. We just wanted some dinner."

"Yeah," Stuart snarled. "From unassuming victims. Their blood."

"No, I had some fries."

The other licked his lips nervously. "Just leave us alone."

"Bloodsucking freak," Stuart snapped. "Vampires don't eat solid food."

"Some of us do." The female's voice shook.

"Shut up." Then he turned back to Quinn. "I feel like I've heard something about you recently. I'm just trying to figure out what it was."

Quinn crossed his arms and tried to ignore the pleading look the female vampire was giving him. "Oh, yeah? Something important?"

"I think so. But what was it?" He scratched his chin.

"Well," Quinn began. "You may have heard that I've recently retired from hunting vampires."

Stuart nodded. "Yeah, that sounds right. But there was something else." His brow furrowed, and then his gaze shot up. "Wait a minute. I remember. You . . . you're a—"

Quinn punched him in the face. "Bloodsucking freak?"

The hunter howled and covered his nose as it started to gush blood.

Joe tensed and raised his stake. Quinn swiveled and kicked him in the stomach. He staggered backward and banged his head on the Dumpster, which immediately knocked him out. The stake clattered to the ground.

Stuart looked up, holding his nose.

Quinn flashed fangs at him. "I've also lost a lot of friends recently. For some reason they're not speaking to me anymore."

The vampires huddled together, frozen in place.

Stuart rushed Quinn. Quinn grabbed the stake out of his hand and then flipped the hunter over his hip.

Quinn crouched down to press the stake against Stuart's neck. "Like I said, I'm just passing through town. I strongly suggest you do the same."

The hunter gurgled.

"Doesn't feel so good, does it? I've had a change of heart recently about killing vampires. Why don't I let you guess why that is?"

"Don't kill me!" he begged.

Quinn pulled the stake away. "The next time you're out hunting, just remember one of the bloodsucking freaks let you live. Got it?"

The hunter nodded, holding a shaky hand to his neck, fear naked in his eyes.

"Now take your little buddy and get the hell out of here."

Joe was beginning to gain consciousness. Stuart grabbed his shirt, and the two of them staggered away. Quickly.

Very quickly.

Quinn watched them run.

Amateurs. Could spot them from a mile away.

"Holy shit, Quinn," a voice said from his right. "I thought you were going to wait in the car."

He looked over. Matthew Barkley had emerged from the restaurant carrying a large bag filled with fast food. Quinn breathed in and with his newly heightened vampire senses could immediately tell it was two Whoppers with cheese and an order of fries. The smell of solid food made him feel a little queasy. Some vamps, like the two he'd saved, could still eat solid food. Unfortunately, he wasn't one of them.

"I needed to stretch my legs," he said.

"Were those hunters?"

"They were trying to be."

"You kicked their asses?"

Quinn shrugged.

"*Nice.*" Barkley nodded. "Good to see you're not a big fan of your old buddies. I guess that makes total sense."

The vampires approached.

"Thank you so much for saving us!" the female said. "We didn't know what to do. How can we ever thank you?"

Quinn didn't look at them. "You can start by staying the hell away from me."

"But we—"

"Go away," Quinn snarled.

They glanced at each other and then turned and ran in the opposite direction from the hunters.

Barkley had started to eat one of his Whoppers. He chewed thoughtfully and swallowed before speaking. "And you don't like vamps, either. That actually *doesn't* make sense. You're okay with werewolves, though, right?"

"Don't worry, I'm not going to run you off, too."

"Good to know. You ready to leave, or what? We need to put in a couple hundred more miles before we can grab some sleep."

Quinn's heart was beating hard in his chest. He felt a little ill, actually. Cold and clammy. "I need a minute. I'll be right back."

"I'll be in the car. Eating a great deal of food."

Quinn made his way to the public washroom in the restaurant to splash some cold water on his face. He clutched the side of the sink until his knuckles whitened.

Keep it together, he told himself.

Christ. Two months as a vampire and it wasn't getting any easier. When was it going to get easier?

Soon. Very soon.

He touched his pocket to feel the reassuring outline of the letter and immediately felt his heartbeat come back down to the normal rate for a thirty-year-old freshly made vamp. *The letter.* The only thing from his father's many possessions that he'd cared about after the old man died.

The letter was going to lead him directly to his answer. Solve all of his problems.

He had to be patient. Just a little while longer.

As far as he was aware, nobody alive knew about it. Not one soul. His father had spent a good part of his adult life—the part that wasn't concerned with hunting down and killing vampires—in his search for the *Eye.* Quinn thought he knew why his father had never been able to find it. The timing was all wrong.

But now it was right. And the Eye would be Quinn's.

Then none of this would matter anymore. He could fix this mess he'd gotten himself into, once and for all.

He looked up into the mirror, which reflected nothing but the washroom behind him. When he bared his teeth, he couldn't even see the fangs he knew were there.

With one smash of his fist, he shattered the mirror.

The door opened. A young kid in a Burger King uniform poked his head in. "Everything okay in here, mister?"

Quinn growled at him.

The kid gave an uneasy smile as he assessed the damage. "Never mind." The door closed.

Quinn took a deep breath and closed his tired eyes.

Not much longer and he wouldn't have to be a monster anymore.

Janie Parker was going to die.

Accepting it, she thought, *really is half the battle.*

Also, drinking four vodka martinis before it's going to happen helps. A bit.

"He'll see you now," a voice announced.

She nodded. Okay. Showtime.

She stood up from the sofa in the waiting area and walked the long hallway to her boss's office. The walls were lined with photos of other employees. On the left side of the hallway were the stars—the people who'd never failed at a job. For them, the sky was the limit. They could have anything they wanted: money, power, influence.

Well, anything they wanted except for the opportunity to quit. *Ever.*

Along the right side were the employees who had messed up a job. Failed on an assignment.

They hadn't needed to quit.

They would have had an appointment with the Boss exactly like the one she was about to have. Then their photo would be moved from one side of the hallway to the other as an example to others.

She always knew a place that listed "burial options" on the job application form had a few potential human-resource issues.

Janie had had two meetings with the Boss prior to this one. The first had been when her very ex-boyfriend had tricked her into taking his place at the Company (which was what the organization was generically known as to those unfortunate enough to know it even existed). He'd been able to trick her because she'd imagined herself in love with the good-looking creep. He'd been so convincing and charming that she'd signed the dotted line happily. A little less happily when she realized she had to sign in blood, but still. He promised that they would work there together. The jerk lied. He took off late one night when she was fast asleep and she never saw him again. He'd managed to beat the system.

Now she *was* the system.

The second time she'd had a meeting with her boss had been slightly over a year ago when her previous partner screwed up a job and tried to blame it on Janie. They'd both been dragged in on the carpet, and the Boss had been very calm in listening to their explanations before cleanly and efficiently decapitating her partner right in front of her.

Janie swallowed hard. She'd liked her old partner. Trusted her like she hadn't trusted anyone in years. It just showed how people change when having to own up to their failures. Not to mention having their heads chopped off.

She didn't trust anybody anymore.

Since that unfortunate incident, she'd been an exemplary employee. Doing everything she was told. Whenever she was told. Wherever she was told. Gritting her teeth over any unpleasant assignment—and since most of the assignments she had were unpleasant, her teeth were likely to be ground down to nothing but stubs very soon. But the image of her last partner's untimely death haunted her. The Boss was nobody to mess with. Nobody to let down.

And she'd done just that.

She'd very recently let a job slip through her fingers. A regular retrieval of a magical piece of jewelry up in Toronto. A necklace. She didn't know what it was or what it did, only that the Boss wanted her to pick it up and bring it back to him.

She'd failed. Accidentally, on purpose. She knew there was only one way out of this job, and that was the route she was taking.

But now that the moment had arrived, she was shaking in her brand-new Prada pumps.

Sure, she could run. Or try to, anyhow. But it would be no use. The Boss had seers on his payroll who could psychically pinpoint any employee's location no matter where they tried to hide. Running would only delay the inevitable.

She wanted it over with.

"Get in here," the Boss growled from behind the slightly ajar door.

Janie entered the room. Two helper drones stood on either side of the door. They were the Boss's personal assistants—they looked like regular guys but weren't. They were under some sort of spell to make them his slaves, unable to resist his authority. However, they did get a really great Christmas bonus, so she supposed it all worked out in the end.

She painted on her best fake smile. "Hey there, boss man. Good to see you. You look fantastic."

He didn't, but Janie was a very good liar. He was actually a tiny little shrew of a man. Skinny and frail-looking, with hollow cheekbones. He reminded her of a live-action Mr. Burns from *The Simpsons*. Only meaner. And older. And much less yellow.

"Save the compliments for your next life, Parker."

"Listen, Boss, I can explain everything."

He waved his bony hand. "You can save that, too. Come closer."

Janie swallowed and then commanded her feet to start moving. She wanted this. It would hurt only for a second, she hoped. After she was dead, she'd be free from this lonely, disappointing, horrific life once and for all. It was the best decision. Suicide by proxy.

She'd miss her new shoes, but that was about it.

It seemed as though it took about two hours for her to finally reach his desk.

"I'm sorry," she heard herself squeak and then mentally kicked herself.

Shut up.

He stared at her with watery, pale gray eyes. His bony

hand slipped down into the drawer on the right-hand side of his black-as-pitch monster of a desk.

What was he reaching for? A gun? A knife? A vial of acid? A bowl of piranhas?

She squeezed her eyes shut and braced herself for impact.

Nothing happened.

"Take a look at this," the Boss said.

She tentatively pried one eye open, and then the other, and looked down. On the surface of the desk was an intricate color drawing of a small crystal sphere almost completely enclosed by a spider web–like filigree of silver at the top of a golden wand set with a single large ruby.

She forced the smile back to her face. "Is somebody thinking about going out as Harry Potter next Halloween? It's only February, but I always say it's good to plan ahead. You will look adorable, I think."

He tapped the drawing. "I want this. And I want you to get it for me."

"You want me—" She paused. "But I thought I was here for—"

He shook his wrinkled head. "You're a failure, Parker. A disgusting waste of space. But I'm willing to give you one more chance. Retrieve the Eye for me and all is forgiven."

"With that kind of a buildup, how can I possibly refuse?" She snatched the drawing off the desk and looked at it closer. "Why's it called the Eye?"

A cold grin twisted on his face. "You don't have to know anything more than what I will tell you to retrieve it. There is one who has the means to find its location. It was foreseen by a seer this morning. A vampire who wishes to use the Eye's power for his own gain. Follow the vampire and you will find the Eye. Acquire it by any means necessary and bring it to me. This is all I ask."

"Sounds simple enough. And if the vamp gives me any problems?"

"Kill him."

Janie took a deep breath and let it out slowly. "Is he evil?"

"Does it matter?"

She hesitated. *Don't mess this up, dumbass.* "Of course not."

"Then there is no problem." He leaned back in his huge black leather chair, his gaze still uncomfortably fixed on Janie. "The vampire drives with an acquaintance, a werewolf, en route to Arizona." He pushed a piece of paper toward her. "The seers inform me they will be at this location tomorrow at noon sharp."

She picked it up, glanced at the address, and then tucked it and the drawing into her pocket. "Then I guess I'll be on my way." She turned her back.

"Parker."

She froze, then twisted around to face the man who had the starring role in most of her nightmares. "Yes, sir?"

"In case you were thinking about failing again, know that to do so would displease me greatly."

"I understand."

"Do you?" His right hand slipped down into the drawer again, and he pulled out a photo, then placed it on the top of his desk. "Your own life may mean little to you, but should you disappoint me again, there are other punishments I can think of."

She drew closer to the desk and looked down at the surveillance photo of a pretty redhead, and her heart nearly stopped. It was her younger sister, Angela, who had disappeared five years ago, just after her eighteenth birthday. Janie had searched nonstop for over a year but found no clues as to where she'd gone. After that, she'd convinced herself Angela was dead, just like the rest of her family.

Her eyes flicked up to meet the evil ones of her boss from hell.

"Where is she?" Her voice was barely a gasp.

He spread his hands. "Bring me the Eye and we will discuss the matter further. Fail me and she will take your punishment. And I promise you, I will not be merciful. Do you understand?"

Janie fought back the stinging tears that threatened to escape. Shit. She hadn't cried in years, and she wasn't going to start now. Her lips thinned, and she nodded at the bastard with one jerk of her head. "I understand."

"By Friday at midnight, or you will watch your sister die."

She grabbed the photo and jammed it into her pocket, then stormed past the expressionless drones and out of the office, slamming the door behind her. She turned and braced herself against the wall and tried to remain calm. She grabbed her necklace and twisted it. She might try to act all tough, but she wore a memento of what she'd lost at all times. She and Angela had bought matching necklaces—a knotted, natural fiber chain that bore a large oval turquoise—years ago on vacation in Mexico when their entire family had been together and happy. The necklace wasn't fancy, and it didn't exactly go with most of her wardrobe, but she wouldn't trade it for diamonds and gold. She never took it off.

Her little sister was alive. The idea thrilled her and filled her with so much dread she couldn't contain it. Her parents had died when she was a teenager. Her brother had abandoned her to become a vampire hunter, until he'd gotten himself killed a couple months ago. She'd thought she was all alone in the world. Sure as hell had felt like it. Maybe that's why she'd latched on to the loser who'd roped her into working for the Company to begin with—some misplaced need to belong somewhere.

The penalty for failure was huge. But the payoff was even bigger if she was successful. And how couldn't she be? It was just a regular retrieval. She was one of the best at that. She'd grab her current partner, Lenny, and the two of them would leave immediately for Arizona.

She'd kill a hundred nasty vampires for the chance to find out where her sister was.

One little vampire wouldn't be any problem at all.

Chapter 2

As Quinn drove along the seemingly endless historic Route 66, he went over the plan in his mind. It wouldn't be simple, but it would work.

But first he had to take care of something.

He glanced at Barkley, who had rolled down the window all the way and was letting the wind whip through his shaggy black hair. His eyes were closed, and he had a look of complete bliss on his face.

First he'd unload the werewolf. Barkley would only slow him down.

Barkley thought Quinn's motives for agreeing to drive him across the country to rejoin his pack were completely altruistic. Barkley didn't have a driver's license. He was also deathly afraid of airplanes. He'd assumed that Quinn needed a change of scenery—to clear his head and get used to his new status as a reluctant vampire. And what better way than to take part in a road trip across the country?

Right.

But driving Barkley home was only part of the reason for his trip to Arizona. The letter in his pocket was the other reason.

The letter had been sent by his father's best friend and hunting buddy, Malcolm Price, eight years ago, and it arrived only days after Malcolm had been murdered. It contained information that pinpointed the location where the Eye was buried, right there in Arizona in a place called Goodlaw.

The Eye was a magical artifact. Legend told that it once belonged to a powerful demon who was vanquished a thousand years ago; the Eye itself was hidden away by those whose worship of the demon had turned to fear for their tribe's safety. Should the Eye be found, the legend continued, it would grant one wish to whoever possessed it. Roger Quinn had searched obsessively for the relic and met with only failure, and he had quit his search in frustration after many long years.

Malcolm, when alive, had surmised that the timing was off. That the Eye would reveal itself only after a thousand years. Before that time had transpired, it would be a waste of time to even attempt to find it.

But according to Malcolm's eight-year-old letter, it was the right time *now*.

"Almost there," he said, turning down the radio that was set to a seventies rock-and-roll station—Led Zeppelin leading into early Van Halen.

Barkley pulled in the half of his body currently outside of the Ford rental and rolled up the window.

"Great." He didn't sound terribly enthusiastic.

Quinn eyed him. "What's wrong?"

"Wrong? Nothing's wrong. It's all good." He let out a sigh that sounded very shuddery.

"I thought you wanted to go back to your pack."

"I do. Really. I do. Of course I do. Why wouldn't I? It's my duty."

"Right. Duty."

Barkley nodded. "I'm going to be Alpha."

"Yeah, so you were saying before. That's the leader, right?"

"Alpha wolf. Right. The leader."

"You know, I don't know all that much about werewolves." Quinn flicked his right turn signal on and exited the highway. "My specialty was vamps, of course. But I thought that you didn't simply become Alpha—you had to fight your way to the top."

Barkley unrolled his window a few inches again. He was breathing unsteadily. "Yup, that's right."

"So you have to fight somebody?"

He nodded and cleared his throat. "To the death. A guy named Brutus. He's really big."

"You don't have to."

"Yeah, I do. In fact, I was set to fight him when I took off, turned wolf, and ran like hell."

"And you got stuck that way."

"Two long years." He scratched behind his ear. "Man, I think I still have a flea. Damn bloodsuckers. No offense."

"None taken." Quinn frowned. "I always thought turning into a werewolf had to do with the moon's cycle."

"Dude, I'm not a chick. I'm not on a monthly cycle. Weres normally can shift any time we want to, only it's true that during the full moon it becomes a little harder to resist. I don't know why I got stuck, but the moon didn't make any difference at all to me. Now, hopefully, I'm all back to my normal shifty self."

Quinn decided not to mention he used to hang out with a few guys who hunted werewolves. And they were very good at it. Weres could be an even bigger challenge than vamps. They ran faster, for one thing. Also, they had a whole mouth of sharp teeth rather than just two fangs.

"When the fight's over," Barkley said, "and if I'm still breathing, I'm supposed to get hitched to the Alpha bitch."

Quinn raised an eyebrow. "Alpha bitch?"

"A real ballbuster. Name's Rosalyn." Another shudder went through him. "Gorgeous, but a real piece of work."

"And you're going back to the pack *because?*"

"There comes a time in every man's life when he has to face his destiny." Barkley let out a long breath. "This is my time."

"Well, that's good to hear."

"Why's that?"

"Because we're here."

He could have sworn he heard a whimper.

It was a very small town named, perhaps not coincidentally, Wolfington. Surrounded by desert, with a few cactuses scattered here and there, it looked like a modern version of an Old West town. Quinn watched and waited for a tumbleweed to roll past the car and was a little disappointed when there was nothing.

Barkley cleared his throat. "Home sweet home. I guess you can drop me off up by that hardware store. My father owned that."

"Was he Alpha, too?"

There was a long pause. "He tried. It didn't go too well."

Quinn cringed at that. "Why were you chosen to be next in line?"

"It was predicted. There are these old, hairy women whose job it is to predict things. I predicted it, too, in a dream."

"The psychic thing." Quinn said blandly.

Barkley was convinced that he was a werewolf who possessed second sight. Quinn, while he'd seen many unusual things in his thirty years, did not fully believe in psychics. It wasn't tangible enough for him. For something unusual, he had to see it with his own two eyes. And Barkley hadn't done anything yet to convince him otherwise.

"Yeah." Barkley turned to Quinn and frowned. "You know, I was never able to get a read on you. Vampires are kind of like a psychic blank slate."

"Thanks."

"Trust me, it can come in handy."

"I'll remember that."

"You know, it's funny. I've been having this dream the past couple of days. I never even thought it might be precognitive."

"About me?"

"Not unless you're a gorgeous redhead in her early twenties who looks great in a black cocktail dress."

Quinn eyed him sideways. "No, that probably wouldn't be me."

"Didn't think so." He glanced out of the window. "Where are you off to now?"

Quinn shrugged and tried to appear at ease when he

felt anything but. "I have an old friend around this area. I think I might look him up while I'm here."

It wasn't *too* much of a lie. It was an old friend of his father's, currently deceased, and Quinn would follow the directions he'd written in the letter, because that's where the Eye allegedly could be found.

"Good luck to you." Barkley held out his hand, and Quinn shook it.

"You, too. You know, you don't have to fight. There are other options."

"Facing my destiny, man."

"I hope you find it."

Barkley got out of the car and grabbed his duffel bag from the back seat. Since he'd been stuck in werewolf form for so long, he didn't have many possessions. Some clothes he'd borrowed. A new toothbrush. A brand-new forged passport. But that was about it.

"Matthew Barkley? Is that really you?" a voice called from down the block.

Quinn nodded at Barkley and pulled away from the curb. He actually felt a lump in his throat, for some strange reason. They'd been traveling together for three days, and he had to admit that he actually enjoyed the guy's company. Somebody to talk to who was able to make him laugh, and who he was fairly assured wouldn't try to put a wooden stake through his chest at the earliest convenience.

No, Barkley belonged there. It was his home. His, as he'd said, *destiny.* Now Quinn had to go find his own.

He took a last glance in the rearview mirror to see a group of four men approaching Barkley. The Wolfington welcoming committee.

Barkley took a step forward and—Quinn frowned—he

threw his duffel bag at the men. Then he turned and began running very fast after Quinn's car.

What the hell?

Quinn turned to look over his shoulder. Yes, Barkley was running after him and wildly flailing his arms with a distinctly panicked expression on his face. Two of the men who'd come out to greet him began to pursue the fleeing werewolf, and they didn't look friendly.

Some welcoming committee.

He applied pressure to the brakes and pressed the button to roll down the passenger window. Barkley thundered up beside the car after a moment, breathing hard.

"Problem?" Quinn asked.

Barkley looked behind him, yelped, and then yanked open the door so he could throw himself inside the car. "Drive!" he yelled. "Just drive!"

Quinn slammed his foot down on the accelerator and drove. After a minute, the large men running after them became no more than pissed-off specks in the distance.

Quinn turned to Barkley and raised his eyebrow. "Facing your destiny not all it's cracked up to be?"

"They were going to kill me," Barkley panted. "Right there. They weren't even going to let me fight Brutus."

"Why?"

"I don't know. I . . . I think they thought I was dead already. Maybe I should have called first and let them know I was coming back."

"But that doesn't explain why they want you dead."

He shook his head. "Dude, all I saw were silver knives and I ran. Those guys were Brutus's men. I'm not going back there." He let out a long breath. "I guess you're stuck with me for a while longer."

Quinn kept his eyes on the road. "So now what?"

Barkley leaned back in the seat until his breathing slowed down to normal. "Now I guess I'll come with you to see your friend. You don't mind my company for a bit longer, do you?"

"Uh. I don't think that's a very good idea."

"Sure it is. Listen, let's stop for something to eat first. Running for my life works up an appetite. If I remember correctly, there's a roadside diner about ten minutes west of here that serves the best hamburger in the state. You hungry?"

"I don't eat."

"Oh, yeah." He frowned. "You know, I haven't seen you drink any blood lately, either. Do you do it in private? Like a secret Twinkie obsession? You can drink in front of me if you want to. It doesn't gross me out."

Quinn glanced at him sideways. "I haven't . . . drunk anything for a few days. The thought of drinking blood makes me sick."

"I did think you were starting to look a little gaunt. So, what are you? Like, a vampire anorexic, or something?"

"I will drink when I have to, but not before."

"Okay, okay. You do what you have to do. But can we stop for lunch so I can eat something?"

Quinn clenched his jaw and stared at the road ahead. Fine. They'd stop at the diner, and as soon as he was sure that Barkley was safe from his old friends, he'd take off. He'd leave some money so the werewolf could get a lift with somebody else.

He felt a twist of guilt in his gut but knew he couldn't back down now. It had to be done, and the sooner the better.

The Stardust Diner, as the sign read when they arrived, would be the last stop on the Quinn and Barkley phase of his quest for the Eye.

"The Stardust Diner? You're sure this is the right place?"

Janie showed her partner, Lenny, the piece of paper the Boss had given her for, like, the eightieth time that day as they pulled up alongside the restaurant.

"Stardust," Lenny said it again. "Like the Frank Sinatra song. I love that song."

Lenny was six-foot-five and built like a linebacker. His hair was cut so short his scalp could be seen through the dark stubble, and he had a crooked nose that had been broken multiple times in his life. He wore a black leather jacket and Doc Marten boots, and he could scare little children with one look.

He also had the soul of a poet. A bad poet.

And unfortunately, he had a massive crush (unrequited) on Janie and wrote a great deal of that bad poetry about her.

They'd been working together for almost a year. She'd recently requested a change in partners, but the Company took its own sweet time when it came to things like that.

She turned around in the black Mustang convertible to check the back seat.

Five wooden stakes. Check.

Two silver daggers. Check.

Stun gun. Check.

Gun with garlic darts that worked as a tranquilizer to temporarily knock out any unsuspecting vamps. Check.

Her favorite gun—a sturdy and reliable Firestar with silver bullets for the werewolf companion. Check.

She decided to carry the gun with silver bullets. The bullets would work on vamp or werewolf. She turned around to grab it and put it in the shoulder holster under her new navy blue Anne Klein jacket and added two wooden stakes and the stun gun to her designer handbag arsenal, just in case. As a last thought, she added the gun with tranq darts. It would weigh her down a bit, but a girl could never be well armed enough when it came to fighting monsters.

"How will we know who they are?" Lenny asked, scanning the area of the diner.

It was a good question. The Stardust Diner was a busy location, right next to the heavily traveled highway. A good place to grab lunch or take a bathroom break while on the way to one's final destination. Vamps and weres could easily blend in with regular humans, and the Boss hadn't given her a heads-up on their appearance.

It was noon. She knew that sunlight didn't bother vamps, contrary to the popular myth. Most could go out at any time of the day or night. Usually they were a little weaker during daylight hours and also quite sun sensitive, so they could typically be spotted wearing sunglasses even on an overcast day. But today the sun was blazing bright in the sky and everyone in the area wore sunglasses. No help there.

Vampires definitely didn't have reflections. That might be a clue. The diner was surrounded by windows that reflected the surroundings.

She twisted her turquoise necklace until her fingers felt numb. "Just watch for anything out of the ordinary."

"So when we find them, you want me to beat any information out of them?"

She shook her head. "Too many witnesses. Let me handle it, and you be there for backup. The note said they'd be here by now, so keep your eyes peeled."

"While we're waiting, you want to hear my latest?" Lenny flipped through his ever-present notebook.

"Not particularly."

"Oh, come on."

She sighed. It's not as if he ever took no for an answer. Why did she even bother trying to resist?

He cleared his throat. "It's called 'Janie's Got a Gun':

Janie's got a gun
She's got the bad guys on the run
If you're a Were . . .
Beware
If you're a vampire
I ain't no liar
'Cause Janie's got a gun."

That, surprisingly enough, was one of the better ones she'd heard lately.

Janie nodded. "Great."

Lenny beamed. "Thanks."

A car pulled up across from them. A blue Ford Escort. The doors opened up, and two men got out.

Janie gasped and sank down in her seat. "Oh, shit."

Lenny turned to her. "What's wrong?"

She grabbed his arm to make him sink down below window level. "Shhh."

Then she raised herself up just enough to peer over the dashboard. Her stomach began to churn.

Well, there was her sign.

One vampire and one werewolf, right on schedule.

The vampire was broad shouldered. His clothes, a simple dark green T-shirt and faded blue jeans, fit his lean but muscular frame perfectly. His dark blond hair was shorter than she remembered it. She could see only half of his handsome face and square jaw which was speckled with stubble, and those lips—she'd dreamed of those lips many times before—beneath a straight nose. Dark sunglasses that covered eyes she knew were a dark ocean blue turned her way as he scanned the area before entering the diner.

The werewolf was a little taller, about the same build, with black hair. He was smiling. The vamp wasn't.

Lenny elbowed her. "Hey, don't you know that guy?"

Janie didn't answer. What were the odds? The Boss must have known. This had to be another test to make sure she was loyal to the Company.

A dozen years ago, Michael Quinn had been her brother's friend and Janie's childhood crush. She'd seen him recently and had the chance to kill him once she'd realized he'd become a vampire. But she couldn't do it. Instead she knocked him out with garlic darts, since he was blocking her way to what she was after at the time.

But her sister's life wasn't at risk then. It was now.

She didn't give a damn about any vampire, no matter who he used to be.

She'd do what it took to save Angela. *Whatever* it took.

Chapter 3

*H*amburger, fries, Coke." Barkley finished scanning the menu and glanced up at the waitress, giving her a charming smile. "Do you still have that fantastic apple pie here?"

"Sure do, hon."

"Gimme two pieces of that. With ice cream. Please."

The waitress turned to Quinn. "And for you?"

"Coffee. Black."

"You should eat more than that. You look a little thin. And pale."

Quinn frowned. "Coffee. Black."

She raised an eyebrow disapprovingly, closed her order pad, and gave them the back of her ample frame as she went toward the kitchen.

"You do know how to charm the ladies." Barkley played with the salt shaker and glanced absently out the window at the parking lot.

"It's a gift."

Quinn tossed the car keys on the table and leaned back into his side of the booth, letting out a long sigh. He already felt guilty about abandoning Barkley at the diner, and he hadn't even done it yet. It felt like he was throwing a puppy out of the car and driving away without him. But Barkley wasn't a puppy. He could take care of himself.

Besides, he'd noticed that there was a bus stop right outside the diner. When he left, Barkley would hop on a bus, headed to wherever he wanted to go. Everybody would get what they want. No problem.

What would he do once he found the Eye and made his wish to be human again? It's not like he could go back to his regular life, was it? He'd learned the hard way that hunting vampires was wrong. He was one of the very few who'd had a chance to see both sides of the coin.

He'd been a hunter for ten years. In training before that, but he was twenty when he made his first kill.

He shuddered at the thought. His father had brainwashed him since he was a kid that all vamps were evil. Different from humans. Killers who needed to be stopped by any means necessary, no matter how human or innocent they appeared. What he didn't fully realize was that his father was a zealot who relished the chance to wipe out anything different from himself from the face of the earth. Who had used the fears of others to strengthen his case against vampires. He'd convinced Quinn that it was a vamp who'd killed his mother when he was only six years old. But it wasn't. His mother had fallen in love with a vampire, and become a vampire herself, and when his father learned of this, he'd ended them both without a moment of mercy.

Quinn's whole life since that day had been a lie.

He'd killed a lot of vamps in his time. He knew without a shadow of a doubt that some of them were truly evil. When the thirst came upon vampires they lost their minds, and become black-eyed monsters who didn't care who they hurt to get to their next meal. Some vamps were plain evil, just as some humans were. Serial killers existed in all walks of life. But most vamps weren't evil. Just different.

He'd killed them all, figuring that their begging and pleading had been a ruse—that if he'd turned his back on them they would have ripped out his throat.

He touched his neck. The marks from the attack that turned him into a vampire two months ago were long gone. That vamp had wanted Quinn dead because he believed Quinn was responsible for slaying his wife.

Revenge was sometimes justified.

But the attack hadn't killed him. It had only changed him into the very thing he'd hunted for over a decade.

"Penny for your thoughts," Barkley said.

Quinn took in a shuddery breath. "Nothing. Just daydreaming."

"You're not very forthcoming with your emotions, you know that?"

"Sorry, I didn't realize we were doing male bonding here."

Barkley shrugged, then reached over the table to grab the car keys. "I haven't tried this in a while—"

"Tried what?"

He closed his eyes and Quinn looked at him oddly, as did the waitress as she dropped off their orders.

"I'm trying to get a read. Can't get it off you personally, but maybe something you've touched."

Quinn rolled his eyes and swirled the coffee around in his cup. "Don't pop a blood vessel trying."

Barkley's eyes shot open. "I know the real reason you're here."

Quinn froze.

"You've always wanted to see the Grand Canyon." Then he laughed and pushed the keys back across the table. "Nah. I figured I couldn't get a read, but it was worth a try."

Quinn's lips twitched into a forced smile. "Listen, you eat your feast there, and I'm going to get some directions."

"Go to it."

Quinn stood up and went over to the long counter. Another waitress, a younger one with brown hair and a big smile, came closer.

"Hi there," she said.

"Hi." He smiled back. Charm. What was that again? It used to come easily to him, but now he could probably fake it if he tried hard enough. "Listen, I'm wondering if you can help me."

She put a hand on her hip. "Sure thing. What do you need?"

She rubbed her lips together and tucked her hair back behind her left ear. She was cute and seemed to be trying to look appealing in her pink smock waitress outfit. He found it slightly endearing.

His gaze moved along the edge of her top and along her collarbone to her throat.

She'd probably bare her neck willingly to me. All I'd have to do is ask.

He shook his head, trying to cast out such thoughts. He hadn't bitten anybody yet, and he wasn't going to start now. There were establishments where the average vamp could find blood on tap next to draft beer and cocktails, and that was the only way he was going to get his next meal when he needed it. Even then it made him feel wrong. He'd gone almost three full days without blood. In the beginning he'd needed it several times a day, but now he could go longer. He wasn't sure how long, but he wanted to find out.

He reached into his pocket and pulled out the piece of paper that held his destiny. "Do you know the quickest route to Goodlaw? It's not on this map I bought."

She nodded. "Sure. It's more of a district than an actual town, really." She lifted her arm and pointed out the window. "Take the highway there west toward Phoenix. In two hours, give or take, you'll come to Goodlaw. Don't blink or you'll miss it."

He nodded. "Great. Thanks a lot for your help."

"Any time."

He turned away, but she touched his arm, making him turn back to look at her. "And I mean *any* time."

He could see her pulse through the pale skin on her neck. His mouth began to water.

He swallowed hard and shrugged off her hand. Then with a meager smile, practiced so as not to show off his fangs, he turned back to rejoin Barkley, who was already half done with his meal.

"Your coffee's getting cold," he said with his mouth full.

Quinn looked out the window. He could see the Ford and beyond that the bus stop. He reached across the table to reclaim the keys and slid them into his pocket. Time to part ways with Barkley. The werewolf shouldn't have to spend any more time with a fledgling vampire. Way too dangerous. For both of them.

Yeah, justify abandoning a friend any way you can, his conscience scolded.

He gritted his teeth at the thought.

"I'm going to the washroom." Quinn stood up, half expecting Barkley to automatically know what he was about to do.

He didn't even look up and instead just nodded and kept eating. "Have fun."

Good-bye, Barkley, he thought.

And then he turned away to find that someone was blocking him.

"Do you think you can hold it?" the someone said. "Because we need to have a chat."

He was so surprised that he dropped back down into the booth. "What the hell—?"

Janie sat down in the booth next to Barkley. Her huge lug of a partner squeezed in beside Quinn.

"Good to see you, too," Janie said. "Don't worry. This shouldn't take long."

Quinn frowned. "Janelle—"

"I prefer to be called Janie. Be careful or I'll start calling you Michael. Or Mike. Doesn't really suit you anymore, does it?"

Quinn was in shock. The last time he'd seen Janie Parker had been a little over a week ago, when she'd shot him in the chest with a garlic dart before she'd attempted to kill a woman named Sarah, a good friend of his. Before that he hadn't seen her since she was a kid and he used to hang out with her brother.

He absolutely hated the bitch.

But damn, even he had to admit that she'd grown up really nice.

She was blond, with long hair done in that way women paid a lot of money for. Three or four different shades of blond from honey to platinum. She had high cheekbones, cool blue eyes lined in smoky black, and full red lips.

At first glance, she was a total babe. But that didn't make him like her any more. Well, parts of him did, maybe. But the rest of him still couldn't stand the sight of her.

"What the hell do you want?" he growled.

"We want the Eye," she replied.

Quinn's entire body tensed. "I don't know what you're talking about."

He tried not to let anything show on his face, but panic twisted his gut. How did she know? Who told her?

The waitress approached. "What can I get you two?"

Janie didn't take her eyes off Quinn. "Nothing."

"Y'all can't just take up space here. You have to order something. It's the rules."

Lenny, who seemed to Quinn about the size of a cube van sitting next to him in the small booth, reached over and flipped through the menu. "I am a little hungry."

Janie sighed. "Fine. I'll have a coffee."

"Anything else?"

"No."

The waitress rolled her eyes, then looked at Lenny.

Lenny glanced at Barkley. "How was the burger?"

Barkley blinked. "Greasy but worth it."

"I'll have the same as him."

The waitress retreated.

Quinn cocked his head to one side and forced a smile to his lips. "You didn't ask for separate bills."

"You're not going to be a gentleman and pick up the tab for an old friend?"

He snorted and leaned back in his seat, trying to look relaxed when he felt anything but. "We were never friends, Janie."

"No, that's right. You were friends with my brother. The one you watched die."

Janie's brother Peter was a vampire hunter who enjoyed his work a little too much. Instead of feeling it was his job, it became fun to him. One night he got on the wrong side of a gun held by a vamp, and he'd lost. Quinn wanted to feel bad about it, but he didn't. Peter had changed. He wasn't the same guy Quinn had sparred with as a teenager while their fathers discussed hunter politics.

Barkley shifted in his seat, clearly uncomfortable. "Quinn, are you going to introduce me?"

Quinn was busy staring at Janie, wondering how the hell he was going to get out of this. He knew she was a trained Merc—a mercenary—who sold her skills to anyone with the biggest dollar.

"Who are you working for?"

She ignored him and instead turned to Barkley, giving him a sly smile. "I'm Janie. Janie Parker."

He raised an eyebrow in an obvious sign of approval of the pretty blonde seated next to him. "Matthew Barkley."

"I assume you're the werewolf."

He frowned. "Uh."

"Don't tell her anything," Quinn advised. "Janie, why don't the two of you leave. You're not wanted here."

"Quinn, I don't think you're taking very good care of yourself. You look kind of pale. Being a vamp getting to you? Not getting your three squares of hemoglobin a day?"

He narrowed his eyes. "So kind of you to be concerned, considering the last time I saw you you shot me in the chest."

"With a tranq dart. Big deal. And you totally deserved it."

The waitress returned with Janie's coffee. She grabbed for the creamer and sugar and put in an ample amount of both. "Now, let's get back on topic. The Eye. Give it to me right now and we'll leave."

"Like I said before, I don't know what you're talking about."

She took a deep breath in and let it out slowly. Lenny simply sat, quiet as a large boulder, watching the proceedings. Then she looked at a confused Barkley.

He raised his eyebrows. "I don't know what you're talking about, either."

Her left cheek twitched. She was acting very cool, calm, and collected, but could she be nervous?

Quinn frowned at her. "Don't you believe us?"

"Oh, I believe wolf-boy here. You? Not so much."

"Then I don't know what to say."

"How about this—" The unmistakable sound of a gun safety clicked off. "I have a gun loaded with silver bullets pointed at your travel buddy. You hand over the Eye and I won't send him to doggy heaven."

Barkley looked down. "She's got a gun, Quinn. What the hell is going on here?"

She glanced at Quinn. "Your move, handsome."

Chapter 4

Not good. Not good at all.

She hadn't wanted to resort to Rambo measures quite so soon. She didn't want anybody to get hurt, but maybe she was more desperate than she'd thought. It seemed so easy just marching into the diner and acting tough, but when she saw Quinn face to face, it definitely knocked her confidence off balance. And when she was off balance, she tended toward extreme measures.

Was she going to shoot the werewolf? No. He'd never done anything to her, and it would be a frosty day in hell before she killed for no good reason. It was obvious that he didn't know where the Eye was, let alone *what* it was. But she hoped that Quinn would think she was capable of such a coldhearted act.

Whatever she'd have to do to save her sister, she'd do it. Hopefully that wouldn't have to include murder.

Quinn was very cool about the whole situation. So much so that she thought for a moment he was going to let her pull the trigger. That would be very uncomfortable when she *didn't*.

"Well?" she prompted after what seemed like a very long moment ticked by.

He studied her, his gaze glancing briefly against the line of her throat, those dark blue eyes watching every move she made, like a snake. Like a really good-looking vampire snake that continued to make her feel like an awkward twelve-year-old when she thought the seventeen-year-old Quinn was the hottest guy she'd ever seen.

"I don't have it yet," he finally said.

She almost let out a long sigh of relief. Then she realized what he said.

"You don't have it *yet?*"

"That's right."

"Where is it?"

"Nearby."

"Nearby *where?*"

The waitress returned with Lenny's hamburger. No one spoke or looked up at her.

She let out a small annoyed sigh before walking away.

"You're going to take me to it," Janie said. "Right now."

Quinn just stared at her, steady and calm. "You're going to regret coming here."

"Is that a threat? Not the right situation for that kind of macho talk, in case you haven't noticed."

"What happened to you, Janie? You were such a cute kid."

She snorted. "I guess cute kids grow up and learn how to use concealed weapons. Now, back on topic, handsome. The Eye? You have until Lenny's finished lunch to tell me where it is, or I'm going to make werewolf stew over here."

Quinn glanced at Lenny, who was already halfway through his burger.

Barkley now had sweat beading on his forehead, but his eyes had narrowed, his brow wrinkled as if he was concentrating hard. And he was staring directly at her chest.

"Thirty-four C if you're wondering," she said. "Can I take a picture for you? It'll last longer."

He shook his head. "I'm not . . . well, okay, maybe I was a little bit. You've got a body like a Hooters waitress. But actually, I'm looking at your necklace."

Automatically, she reached to her throat to touch the cool stone and then looked at Lenny, who raised an eyebrow at her. He, however, didn't stop eating. "What about it?"

He brought his fingers to his temple and rubbed as if he was fighting off a bad headache. "Nothing. Probably nothing. I've just been having this dream the past two nights, and that necklace was in it. A redhead was wearing it. Also with nice hoot—" He looked up and cleared his throat. "Never mind. Maybe I saw the same necklace for sale somewhere on the trip and it wedged its way into my subconscious."

Janie's throat felt tight. Her necklace was handmade by an old woman she'd met on the beach in Mexico. There were probably only two like it in the world—she had one, and the other belonged to her sister. Her sister who just happened to have red hair.

Who the hell was this guy?

"Tell me more about the dream," she said.

"Who cares about the stupid dream?" Quinn growled.

She gave him a sharp look, then turned back to Barkley and poked him in the ribs with the gun. "Tell me."

"Okay, okay. Uh . . . the redhead was wearing this black dress. Really expensive, I think. There were a lot of people around her. Somewhere inside. No windows. She played with the necklace, touching it like a good-luck charm."

"Where?"

"I don't know. It was a dream."

"Oh, come on Barkley," Quinn said. "It may have been a prophetic one, what with the whole psychic werewolf deal you have going on."

It sounded as if he was being sarcastic.

"You're psychic?" Janie repeated.

He blinked. "Sometimes."

She clicked the safety back on the gun and put it into the shoulder holster under her jacket. Her palms were sweating. She'd visited countless psychics over the past five years. Not one of them had gotten a read on her sister. It had been so frustrating. Maybe she'd just gone to the wrong people, hadn't paid enough money, or asked the wrong questions. Professional psychics were notoriously temperamental.

"I'm all done," Lenny announced, wiping his mouth with a napkin.

"Just a minute." Janie held up a finger and then reached around to undo her necklace. It slipped off her neck and pooled into her hand. She thrust it toward Barkley. "Touch the necklace. Can you see anything?"

Barkley and Quinn exchanged a look. Then Barkley

tentatively reached out and took the necklace from her. He closed his eyes and rubbed his thumb over the turquoise.

She watched him warily.

His forehead creased. "I'm not getting anything about the dream, but I am getting something about . . ." His eyes opened slowly. ". . . about *you*. You're worried about somebody."

"Forget it."

"You're *really* worried. That's why you're doing this. Is the person you're worried about the redhead? Is that why you're here? Man, talk about destiny." He cupped his hand over the necklace again and closed his eyes for a moment. "And you weren't going to shoot me. You're not a bad person, Janie. You're not. You just need a chance to prove that to yourself."

"If I shoot you right now, will that prove something?"

Barkley's expression softened. "You know, if you really need somebody to help you, then me and Quinn can . . . *oh, shit!*"

She frowned. "What?"

"Oh, *shit!*" Barkley repeated. "How the hell did they find us?"

Quinn followed Barkley's gaze out of the diner's window. Four huge men had pulled up in the parking lot in a big black pickup truck. They got out simultaneously and moved toward Barkley and Quinn's rental car.

"Who are they?" Lenny asked.

Quinn sighed heavily. "They just happen to also be Barkley's destiny."

"They're wrecking your car."

He nodded. "Yes. Yes, they are."

The men had baseball bats, and they were going to town on the Ford, bashing in the sides and breaking the windows. One whipped out a knife and slashed the tires. After only a minute had gone by, the car was definitely not roadworthy anymore. And the men hadn't even broken a sweat.

Janie looked at the rampage blankly. Looked like a good way to let some frustrations out.

She grabbed her beloved necklace from the table where Barkley had dropped it, and she put it back on.

There was a very subtle trace of amusement in Quinn's expression. "I'm so not getting my security deposit back."

Barkley slunk down in his seat. "They're going to kill me."

"Who *exactly* are they?" Janie eyed the men, assessing if they were her problem and deciding that they weren't. At least not yet.

"Pack. They hate me. Want to kill me. Why didn't we go farther than ten miles?"

Quinn stared through the window. "You wanted the best hamburger in the state, remember?"

"I take it that you don't want them to find you in here," Janie said.

Barkley shuddered. "You take it correctly."

A plan was quickly formulating in her mind. Not a good one by any stretch of the imagination, but it would have to do. As soon as those men strolled in the diner, that would be the end of her negotiation, or whatever this had turned into. A bust, most likely. But at least Lenny was fed.

Why was nothing ever easy?

"Lenny . . . take the keys." She tossed them to him.

He caught them in his left hand and frowned. "What?"

"Take wolf-boy out the back so his friends don't find him."

Barkley turned to her with a tentative smile. "You'd help me? Thank you so much."

She held up a hand. "Not so fast. Here's how this is going to work. Are you listening, Quinn?"

He glowered at her. "I'm listening."

"Lenny will take Barkley and keep him safe. For now. He will wait for my call. In the meantime, you will take me to the Eye."

"I don't think that's a very good idea."

"I disagree." She leaned across the table so they were eye to eye. "I may be a bit squeamish about shooting somebody in cold blood, it's true, but Lenny doesn't have a problem with it. So I strongly suggest you don't give me any problems today. Do you understand?"

Barkley and Quinn exchanged glances.

A small crowd had gathered near the front door as people watched the men finish destroying Quinn's rental car. Janie slipped out of the booth, but Barkley didn't make a move.

"Don't have all day here," Janie prompted after another moment. "They're going to be coming in here any minute. Then again, if you two think you can take those boys, then have at it."

"Quinn—" Barkley whimpered.

Quinn's eyes narrowed, and he looked at Lenny as if assessing the brute power behind the bodybuilder's physique, then returned his gaze to Janie's to give her a truly withering look. "Fine. We'll do it your way."

His words were so cold that they managed to freeze

her just around the edges. She returned his look with a frosty one of her own. "That's good to hear."

Barkley finally got up from the booth. Lenny stood up, twisting the key chain around his finger. He stared at Janie as if he was waiting for something.

She raised her eyebrows. "Yes?"

"Be careful."

She nodded. "Of course."

"I worry."

She glanced at Quinn, whose blank expression held.

"Would you two like to be alone?" he asked.

"Go," Janie told Lenny. "I'll call."

With a last longing look, Lenny turned away, grabbed Barkley by his elbow, and steered him toward the back entrance of the diner.

Barkley looked over his shoulder. "I'll try to remember more of my dream."

Before she could say anything in reply, they were gone. She quickly composed herself and sat back down in the booth across from Quinn.

She glanced at him. "Now you're going to take me to the Eye."

He nodded slowly. "And if I don't, you're going to get on the phone and tell that human Rottweiler to kill Barkley."

She shrugged.

His expression darkened. "What makes you think I give a damn what happens to him?"

"Are you saying that you two aren't friends?"

"I don't have any friends."

"Oh come on, now. You were very popular back in the day."

"Things have changed."

"Yeah, I noticed." She glanced out of the window to where Barkley and Lenny were skulking toward the Mustang.

Quinn eyed her with anything but friendliness. "And I thought my day was a disaster to start with."

"We'll give the boys a few minutes to make their getaway."

"Whatever you say."

She felt a chill go down her spine at his cold expression and struggled to keep her composure.

What did she think she was doing, anyhow? Baiting a vampire like this? A lot of vamps were completely harmless, that was true. But some of them . . . some of them were as dangerous as anything she'd ever faced. She still had the marks on her neck to prove that little theory. Two weeks ago, a master vampire named Nicolai nearly ripped out her throat. She'd trusted the bastard—even worked for him part-time—right up until she learned he was a serial killer.

Had he fed on her any longer, she would have either been permanently dead or picking up her vampire membership card. She was in a business where it was easy to get jaded and unfazed by life-threatening situations, but that vampire had taken her by surprise, and she'd never been particularly fond of surprises—especially the kind that left scars behind.

She studied the man in front of her for a moment as he looked away. She knew that Quinn was dangerous to start with. When he'd been a hunter, there were rumors that he would rise in the ranks and become a real leader. That's what his father had always groomed him for. From what she'd heard through the grapevine, Quinn was good at the job. Real good. But there was something missing. A lack of passion for it. He took no joy in slaying vamps.

Now he was a man with nothing to lose. A wild tiger waiting to hunt his next meal. And she was sticking her hands in the cage and trying to take his catnip away.

She frowned at the thought. *Or something like that.*

The werewolves entered the diner. Janie didn't even have to turn around to see, she could feel it. Werewolves, especially in the company of other pack members, gave off a preternatural vibe—a pulse of energy that raised the hair on the back of a human's neck.

Three years ago, on her very first assignment with the Company, she'd killed a werewolf. He was a bad guy, a lone wolf, and he had taken hostage the wife and three children of a U.S. congressman from Mississippi. The Company had sent Janie in on a rescue mission. Janie received her first of many scars, on her upper thigh, from that experience, but she'd lived.

She'd managed to stare death in the eye. It had been terrifying and also rather . . . *furry.* Before she pulled the trigger to send the silver bullet into the beast's heart, she vaguely recalled making a Little Red Riding Hood joke. Damned if she could remember what it was now. She did remember the fear that filled her and almost made her run away. But the thought of the woman and those innocent kids, and imagining what that monster planned to do to them, was enough to keep her moving.

Yeah, she was such a hero.

Sure.

With that memory firmly fixed in her head, she turned to look. The werewolves had cornered the manager of the restaurant, who had his hands up and was talking to them with a panicked expression on his face. Panicked, but not surprised. Maybe the fur patrol were regulars at the Stardust Diner.

The main werewolf grabbed the guy by his grease-stained apron and shoved him up against the cash register. The others stood back with their arms crossed in front of them. The manager was shaking now, and he turned and looked in Janie and Quinn's direction.

Then he pointed.

The werewolf dropped him and immediately came over to stand in front of Janie and Quinn's booth, followed by his friends.

She pushed back the memory of the wolf's teeth in her leg and the sudden urge she got to run.

"Where is he?" Werewolf number one growled.

Janie's gaze shot to Quinn, who looked surprisingly calm.

"Who?" he asked.

"That damned coward Matthew Barkley. Where is he?"

"I still don't know what you're talking about."

Out of the corner of Janie's eye she noticed that the manager was approaching the werewolves with a tray.

"I have t-two coffees, a c-c-cappuccino, and a d-decaf here," he said with a distinct tremble to his words.

The main werewolf turned and grabbed one of the mugs without a thank-you, then turned back to Quinn.

"Look, I'm in a shitty mood today. Wife's got me on decaf, and I love my coffee. Something to do with it causing my migraines."

"Sorry to hear that."

He took a sip and grimaced. "Disgusting." He smashed the mug against the floor.

"I'll g-go and make a f-fresh pot." The manager skulked away as the beast shot him a scowl.

Quinn and Janie exchanged a look.

"That your car?" The cranky, decaffeinated werewolf gestured out of the window toward the decimated car.

Quinn shrugged. "If it was, I'd be pretty pissed about what you did to it, wouldn't I?"

"'Cause that's the car that Barkley was in." His eyes narrowed. "And you were driving it."

Janie let out a long, exasperated sigh. She didn't have time for this garbage. She stood up from the booth and looked up—way up—at the werewolf.

"Why don't you go away now? Obviously the guy you're looking for isn't here."

"Who asked you, bitch?"

"How did you know my pet name?"

The werewolf eyed Quinn. "This your girlfriend?"

Quinn snorted at that. "Not by a long shot."

The werewolf moved to face Janie completely and then backhanded her across her right cheek. She fell back into the booth and hit the wall, the back of her head smacking the window.

Her eyes bugged. Why she hadn't expected that, she wasn't sure. Her cheek burned almost as much as her sudden surge of hot anger.

But before she could get back up and cram her own mug of caffeine down wolf-dick's throat, Quinn sprang up to his feet.

"That how you treat women around here?" There was a definite edge to his voice now.

"Women who get in my way."

Quinn glanced at the other men, who had placed their mugs down on top of an adjacent table.

They sized each other up, and Quinn's upper lip curled back from his fangs in a dangerous smile.

The werewolf raised an eyebrow. "What are you going to do about it, *vampire?*"

"Nothing. I was just asking." He sat back down. "You okay, Janie?"

"Just fine," she said calmly.

The werewolf snorted and then turned back to look at Janie, who now had her gun out. This time *she* smiled. The werewolf's face fell.

The familiar weight of the Firestar immediately calmed her. "In case you were wondering . . . yes, it is filled with silver bullets. And yes, I have killed a were-wolf before. Sometimes I even get paid for it, and those aren't even the ones who lay a finger on me first. So you and your coffee-drinking friends should probably leave now, because oddly enough, I'm not in a very good mood anymore."

He didn't flinch. "I've never met a woman who didn't back down when confronted with a big strong man."

His eyes changed to wolf gold, and his lips curled back from rapidly sharpening teeth.

She lowered the gun and shot him in the upper thigh.

He howled in pain and staggered backward. The diner went completely silent.

She held out her left hand, palm up. "Give me the keys to your truck."

The other men eyed her and the gun warily.

"*Now,*" she added.

A set of keys flew through the air, and she caught them with one hand. She tossed them at Quinn.

"Oh, and in case you've never been shot before," she said to the whimpering werewolf, "a wound from a silver bullet will take nearly one year to fully heal."

He glared at her, pain in his eyes. "I'm going to kill you."

"Honey, if I had a nickel for every time I've heard that." She glanced at Quinn. "Let's go, handsome."

He eyed her as he tossed a twenty on the table. "Yes, ma'am."

They weren't followed to the parking lot. Quinn grabbed a duffel bag from the back of the decimated rental car, and they got into the Ford Ranger. The tires squealed as Quinn peeled out of the parking lot. Janie watched the Stardust Diner grow smaller and smaller in the rearview mirror and waited for her heart to stop pounding like a jackhammer.

Chapter 5

Quinn wasn't exactly sure if he should be pissed off or impressed. He wanted to be the former but was feeling more of the latter than was probably healthy.

Which left him with a sick feeling in the pit of his stomach. He was hoping for a chance to escape from Little Miss Merc as soon as possible, but the way Janie handled that gun, the way she handled those werewolves . . .

She was a professional. A cold, calculating professional, and she wanted the Eye. He had no idea how she knew about it. It was a secret, or at least he thought it was. He wasn't giving it up without a fight, but now that he'd seen a small bit of what she could do, he knew it was going to be a slightly more difficult one.

However, Quinn was no pushover himself.

She hadn't said anything since they'd left the diner and basically stolen the werewolves' truck. Not that he felt guilty about it. He wasn't going to take a baseball bat to it like they'd done with his rental. Then again, maybe he could let out a little stress when he was finished with it. It's not like it was a new model or anything.

He gripped the steering wheel tightly when he thought about Barkley. Had he left him at the diner earlier as he'd planned, the werewolves would have gotten him. Now, instead, he was with Lenny. He wasn't sure what was worse.

Three months ago he wouldn't have given a shit about the fate of a werewolf. But now things were different. Very different.

Damn, he thought. *Why does everything have to be so complicated?*

Quinn glanced at Janie again and racked his brain. How could he deal with this crazy chick? After going through a dozen scenarios, he decided there were only two courses of action that would potentially work.

Kill her.

That was the worst-case scenario. Was he willing to kill somebody to get to the Eye? How much did he want it? A lot. But enough to kill for it?

He wasn't ready to answer that question. Not yet.

His second option was something that caused him even more apprehension.

It was no secret that when Janie had been a kid she'd had a crush on him. All he remembered was a little blond girl with freckles who used to play with her dolls. She also took care of her adorable younger sister, Angela, quite a bit and tried to keep her from watching what he and Peter were up to. Playing Hunter and Vampire like some kids played Cowboys and Indians. She'd protected her sister from seeing that, but he remembered catching her watching from around a corner.

So she'd liked him back then. If he went with this plan,

he was banking on her *still* liking him. At least enough so that he could charm her into helping him. Or just going away. Either would be good.

He almost laughed. Sure. He was a full-fledged, blood-drinking vampire. He'd been involved in her brother's death. He looked like hell and felt even worse.

A total catch.

But it was worth a shot.

"So," Quinn began, a tight smile fixed on his face. "Have you been to Arizona before?"

She eyed him warily. "Seriously?"

"What?"

"I'm not really much for small talk."

"That's not small talk. It's an attempt at conversation, since we've got a bit of a drive ahead. Now, if you'd rather play a car game to pass the time, I'm always up for 'I Spy with My Little Eye.'" He grinned.

She didn't. "Just drive."

What a bitch.

Maybe he could just knock her out. If she left him with no other choice . . .

No. The whole hitting-a-girl thing had never gone over with him very well. Even if the girl could kick his ass.

"We're headed to Goodlaw," he told her after another minute.

"That's where the Eye is?"

"That's what I think."

She frowned. "You mean you don't know?"

"Not for sure. No."

She let out another sigh; this time it was shaky.

"Who sent you for it?" he asked.

She crossed her arms over her white tank top. The

edge of her shoulder holster peeked out past her blue jacket. "That doesn't matter."

"You don't look very happy, Janie. Is everything okay?"

She actually laughed a little at that, but it didn't sound friendly. "Yeah, life's a dream. Every day's a gift. Keep your eyes on the road, cowboy."

Quinn clutched the steering wheel so tightly his hands began to go numb. He couldn't help but cast a dark look at her, which earned him another humorless laugh as she looked back at him.

"That's more like it. I wasn't buying the whole chatty thing you had going on." She eyed him slowly, from his worn jeans up to his dark sunglasses. "So, how's being a creature of darkness suiting you, anyhow? Should I have my wooden stake at the ready?"

"For anyone else, it wouldn't be necessary. But for you, Janie? I think it's a reasonable precaution."

"Bitten any interesting necks lately?"

"I don't do that."

"Sure you don't."

He glanced at her again and noticed she was playing with the side of her neck. Her long blond hair swept away enough that he noticed the fading red marks there.

"Who bit you?" he asked, feeling tension creeping up his shoulders.

"A vampire."

"Obviously. Are you okay?"

She brushed her hair over her neck to cover it. "Never better."

Quinn forced away the concern that came immediately to him. She wasn't the cute, harmless kid he used to know. She was a twenty-five-year-old Merc who was standing in the way of the only thing in the universe he wanted and who'd already proven with the tranq dart last time they went face to face that she didn't mind pulling the trigger if he was at the receiving end of it. "Well, you probably deserved it."

Her eyes narrowed. "And he deserved the stake I put through his heart. See? Everybody's happy."

He sighed. So much for the "Charm Janie" plan. Looked like her crush was long dead. Not that he blamed her.

"You were a cute kid back in the day," he said.

"Thanks so much," she replied, dryly.

"I remember all those dolls you and your sister had. You used to dress them up and put them around the table. Make up stories about them. I always thought you'd grow up to be a writer or something."

"Writer," she said. "Paid assassin. Not much of a difference, is there?"

"And what did you like to be called? Was it the Lady of the Manor?"

She rolled her eyes. "I read a lot back then. I was a stupid kid."

"No, you weren't. You had a great imagination."

"Peter didn't think so. He always made fun of me."

"Peter was your older brother. It was his solemn duty to make fun of you."

She leaned back in the seat. "That was a long time ago. Things were different."

"True." His mind drifted for a second back to a much simpler time. "I just remembered something."

"Stop the presses."

He shot her a look and then shook it off to give her a

forced grin instead. "You were the only one who ever got my jokes. Remember the one about the penguins in the bathtub?"

"Not even remotely."

He couldn't stop now. "Two penguins are sitting in a bathtub. One penguin looks at the other and says, 'Can you pass me the soap?' The second penguin says, 'What do I look like, a penguin?'"

She fixed him with a blank look. "That's the stupidest joke I've ever heard. It doesn't even make any sense."

"That's what's so funny about it. I remember you laughed so hard, milk shot out of your nose."

Frankly, he'd thought it was gross at the time, but now he could see the humor. Didn't even seem like the same person. Could somebody change that drastically, from laughing at stupid penguin jokes to being a trained killer?

Well, *he* could.

He watched her warily. She didn't say anything, but suddenly her eyes got a faraway look as if she was remembering what it was like back in those days. She looked at him and then . . . then she did something he really wished she hadn't done.

"Stupid joke," she said again.

And then she smiled.

A true, genuine, thousand-watt smile that lit up her gorgeous face and did something strange to his insides.

He suddenly wondered what he could feel pounding at the back of his eyeballs and then realized it was his heartbeat, which had increased to double speed.

"Yeah." She continued to smile and shook her head. "Those were some good days."

He swallowed. His mouth felt very dry all of a sudden.

Then he cleared his tightening throat and shifted positions in the seat. It was damn hot in the truck, and he pulled at the constrictive T-shirt material around his throat.

What the hell was wrong with him?

Her smile slowly disappeared, and she turned to look at the road. She licked her lips, and he found himself unable to look away from her mouth.

"Hey, watch it," she snapped.

He turned his attention back on the road and swerved out of the oncoming traffic lane.

Focus, Quinn, he told himself. *Snap out of it.*

Janie Parker wasn't some beautiful girl he was thinking about taking out for dinner and a movie. She was the enemy, and if he forgot that, then he was going to be in big trouble.

This was not good. Not good. Being in such close quarters with Quinn was making her feel very uncomfortable.

She could drive with Lenny for hours. Days even, and she didn't feel like this. Other than his cologne being a little on the overpowering side, the big guy was a decent travel companion. He made conversation about innocuous things like TV shows or the weather. Even when he recited his poems, she didn't feel as awkward as she did driving with Quinn.

She just wanted this over with. Get the Eye. Take it to the Boss. Save her sister. And then turn her back on Quinn and never see him again.

Ever.

It was somewhat ironic that she'd started dating the

guy who'd tricked her into working for the Company because of his slight resemblence to Quinn. With that dark blond hair and broad shoulders, and . . . she glanced over at Quinn to see his biceps flex as he turned the wheel. She shook her head.

She'd dreamed about every inch of him. Well, every inch that she'd seen. For the rest she'd just used her imagination.

She had a really great imagination.

It was obvious that he hated her. She could see the disgust in his eyes for what she'd become. The thought filled her with anger, but she repressed it. She was doing what she had to do. She didn't care what anybody thought.

Quinn pulled off to the side of the road and got out of the car without saying anything. The area wasn't exactly well populated. It was desert for miles in every direction. She could see the peaks of the Superstition Mountains in the distance. The sky was blue and bright, and she knew it made his eyes water, because she watched him reach under his dark sunglasses to rub them. Blazing Arizona midafternoon. Not a good place for your average vamp.

She opened the passenger side door. "So where's the Eye?"

He shot her a look, as if she were an annoying child who asked the same question over and over again.

"Tell me what you want it for," he said.

"I don't know or care what this thing is, but it's a pain in the ass so far. Let's just find it and get it over with."

He frowned. "You don't even know what it is?"

She shook her head.

"So you're working for somebody."

"You should be a detective. A vampire detective. Is that a little cliché?"

"The Eye is a very powerful thing. Whoever has you after it is up to no good."

She rolled her eyes. "I don't really care."

"You don't care that if you get it and hand it over you might be doing the wrong thing?"

"The wrong thing? Since when are you such an expert on what's right and wrong? You're a damn vampire now."

He ran the tip of his tongue along the edge of his fangs and gave her a look that made her think he wanted to bite her.

"The Eye will grant one wish, once every thousand years."

"I already told you I don't care what it is or what it does. But I want it now."

"Tell me why."

"Because—" She pressed her lips together and glared at him. She didn't want to tell him about her sister. It was none of his damn business and would only complicate matters.

Her cell phone rang.

She smiled at him and held up a finger. "Hold that thought, handsome." She moved a little away and pulled her phone out of her pocket, flipped it open, and held it to her ear.

"Parker here."

"Parker." The Boss's voice slid across the line, sending a chill down her neck that made her cringe.

"Hey there, Boss." She moved farther away from Quinn and walked a few more yards off the side of the road. "What's up?"

"What is your status? Have you the Eye in your possession yet?"

"Don't you already know? I thought you used your seers to keep tabs on us."

"Of the two seers I have under contract, one is on vacation and the other . . . passed away just this morning."

"Passed away?"

"I killed her. She displeased me by producing very uninteresting visions."

She hated the seers. Strange little women in black clothes who sat in dark rooms predicting the future or seeing the present. The Boss used to love his seers, but he'd been getting even more specific about what he wanted from his employees. Nobody was safe at the Company anymore.

When she didn't say anything for a moment, he continued. "Is there a problem?"

She licked her suddenly dry lips. "No, no problems. I have the vampire leading me to it right now."

"You haven't killed him yet?"

Was that his answer for everything?

"Well, if I killed him, how could he lead me to the Eye? Then I'd have to raise his corpse, and he'd go all vampire zombie on me, and as you know, that never turns out very well."

He sighed, a dry, hoarse little sound that would have made her feel worried for the overall health of anyone else.

"Have I entrusted this mission to the wrong person, Parker? Are you going to make me follow through with my threat toward your beloved sister?"

His tone made her feel more angry than scared. "No. Everything is fine. It won't be long now."

"I will be in Las Vegas tomorrow and will contact you when I arrive. You will meet me there and bring the Eye. Don't fail me, Parker."

"I won't."

The phone went dead. Janie had the urge to hurl it at the nearest cactus, but destroying electronic gadgetry never solved anything. It felt really good, but it wasn't the answer.

She turned back to Quinn, who now had his back to her. She marched up beside him.

"Let's go." There was no more friendliness in her voice. Not that there had been before. In fact, if she'd been remotely friendly before this, lame penguin joke or not, then it was a mistake.

Taken by surprise, he shoved something back into his pocket. A piece of paper.

She frowned. "What's that?"

"Nothing."

"Show me."

He turned to look directly at her. Standing next to her, he was about four inches taller than Janie. She was five-six, and she was wearing low-heeled boots. The hot sun reflected in his black sunglasses.

He didn't make a move to show her the paper.

"Don't try me, Quinn." Eyeing him, she flipped open her cell phone and pressed a number, then held it to her ear.

Quinn's eyes narrowed and his expression grew colder, but his Adam's apple worked as he swallowed hard. No sweat, though. She didn't have him sweating yet. Vampires weren't affected by the heat. They maintained their body temperature in extreme heat or cold, but they would sweat if nervous or scared . . . or turned on.

She'd made a few vamps sweat. And it wasn't because of her bedroom eyes.

After a couple of rings, she was greeted with a "Yello?"

"Lenny, it's me."

"Do you have it yet?"

"No, not yet."

"Uh. There's a little problem with the wolf." Lenny sounded nervous.

She cleared her throat and kept her face neutral. "What is it?"

"He . . . uh . . . sort of shifted."

"Shifted?"

"He turned into a big black dog. Wolf. Whatever. Anyhow, he said he felt sick, so I pulled the car off the highway. He ran to the side of the road, puked, and then shifted."

"Great. Just great. What's happening now?"

Quinn frowned at her.

"He's curled up in the back seat. I can hear him snoring. He reminds me of a dog I had when I was a kid. Big Newfoundland. Like the ones you see on the ski hills that have the whiskey in a little barrel around their necks? Except those are Saint Bernards. Like in that movie *Beethoven*. They made a ton of sequels for that movie."

She looked directly at Quinn to make sure he was paying attention. "Lenny, Quinn isn't cooperating with me. I think you should cut off one of the werewolf's fingers."

She was lying. They didn't do torture, nor did she want to start now. But Quinn didn't have to know that.

Besides, in wolf form he wouldn't really have fingers.

"But he's a big cute wolf dog." Lenny sounded a little distressed by the suggestion. "I can't hurt a dog."

"Janie—" Quinn's voice sounded strained. "Just hang up."

She put her hand over the receiver. "Sorry, what?"

"Hang up the phone."

She held out her hand. "Show me the paper."

His jaw clenched, and he gave her a look that would send lesser women running away. She didn't even back up a step but felt the blood throbbing in her head.

Stress. She definitely didn't need this. Why couldn't everyone just cooperate? It would make life so much easier.

He didn't say another word but instead thrust his hand into his jeans pocket and pulled out the ratty piece of paper. She snatched it away from him.

"Thank you," she said. And then in the phone, "Never mind, Lenny. You two just . . . I don't know . . . go on a long walk or something. Buy a Frisbee. That should keep you busy for hours."

He let out a long breath. "Oh, good. Thanks, Janie."

She turned away from Quinn and whispered into the receiver. "Lenny, do not get soft on me."

"I'm not. I'm . . ." He let out another long breath. "He's so cute! You should see him."

She hung up.

Her partner was a doofus. With an affinity for the canine population. Call the SPCA and give the man a medal.

She looked down at the piece of paper.

It was a letter dated eight years ago from somebody named Malcolm Price and addressed to Quinn's father. It rambled on for a couple of paragraphs about hunter business. The last paragraph had every fifth word highlighted, including the word "Eye," some numbers, and the words "garden" and "cross."

She raised an eyebrow at Quinn. "You know, sudoku is a fun game to play, too."

"It's not a game."

"Then what is it?"

"Directions."

"To the Eye?"

"Janie, you're blond, but you aren't dumb. What do you think?"

"I think I'm going to stake you and leave your body for the coyotes to have for dinner. But that's plan B."

"They're coordinates. To Goodlaw. Where we're standing right now. And the words . . . it's a game Malcolm and me used to play. He was like an uncle to me. He'd send me letters when he was on tour with the other hunters. My father read all of my mail, and Malcolm wanted to see if we could get anything past him."

"Did it work?"

"Yes. Sometimes I think that my father never even read my mail and just opened it to remind me of who was in charge. I think Malcolm sent this letter to my father knowing that I'd see it and decode it. It's a message for me."

"Where's this Malcolm guy now?"

"He's dead."

She nodded, trying to push away the distracting moment of empathy she was having for Quinn. Then she looked around at emptiness for miles around. "I see. What great clues he's given you, too. Definitely narrows down the search. Why don't I start looking over by that big anthill over there, and you get to work on that lovely thatch of cacti?"

He crossed his arms. "You know, I was thinking Peter was the bad apple in your family, but I think I was wrong. The words *cross* and *garden* are less help than I'd hoped. I thought there might be a—"

"Cross or a garden?" she finished. "Aren't you afraid of crosses? The whole undead animated corpse thing never goes over with the religious sect very well."

"I'm not undead."

"If you say so."

"Let's go into town and ask around. Maybe somebody can help us."

She stared at him blankly for a moment. Nothing was easy. Officially.

"Fine."

She could have sworn the temperature in the truck had gone down ten degrees when they drove the short distance to the center of Goodlaw—such as it was—and it wasn't because the air conditioner was turned up. It didn't even work.

Chapter 6

Janie was going to do it, Quinn thought. She was going to tell Lenny to hurt Barkley. Just like that. Just to get her hands on something that she knew nothing about.

Why was he surprised? He'd met his share of Mercs in his career as a hunter. They weren't driven by trying to do the right thing and make the world a better place— which actually *was* Quinn's philosophy back when he hunted vampires. As deluded as it was, he thought he was being the good guy. And sometimes he was. Usually he wasn't.

Mercs didn't have that same work ethic. Greedy and deceptive and lacking a caring soul, they were driven by one thing and one thing only: money.

Why it bothered him to know that Janie had turned out that way he wasn't sure. Why he wanted to believe that she was different than the rest he didn't know, either. Was it because she was attractive? He'd met his share of beautiful women in his day. A respectable number of them had even been interested in him. So it took more than a pretty face and a nice body to turn his head.

Besides, he didn't want to get involved with any women anytime soon. He'd been burned lately. He'd thought he was in love with a fledgling vampire named Sarah Dearly. When he first met her a couple months ago in Toronto, he'd been traveling with his father and a group of other hunters. Despite his attraction to her, the moment he found out that Sarah was a vampire, he'd tried to kill her. A couple of times. Luckily he'd failed. When he'd been turned into a vamp and left for dead, she'd helped him when everyone else turned their backs on him. Sarah was cute, sweet, caring, and all-around wonderful.

But she didn't love him. She was in love with a jack-ass six-hundred-year-old master vamp named Thierry who liked to wear black and sulk around in the shadows. Nursing a broken heart and a bruised ego, Quinn had left Toronto at the first opportunity he had—driving Barkley back to Arizona.

Only now could he look at the situation objectively and see that she wasn't the right girl for him. His feelings had grown out of gratitude for her help when he was in a bad place. It was all an illusion. At least that's what he had been trying to convince himself of.

After that, he'd sworn no more women. They were a distraction and gave unneeded angst to his already angst-filled life. He'd felt very confident with his decision.

That hadn't even been two weeks ago.

Janie might be cute, but she wasn't sweet or caring like Sarah. One out of three didn't cut it for him. Not any-more.

He'd find the Eye. Then he'd knock her out.

There was no other choice in the matter.

The truck rolled into town, which appeared to consist of only one gas station. He drove up to a pump and cranked down his window.

An old woman with coarse gray hair sticking out from under her Arizona Sun Devils baseball cap slowly approached. She didn't say anything and instead just started to fill up the tank. Then she started back for the station.

Quinn looked at Janie.

"Go get her, big boy," she said.

He snatched Malcolm's letter out of her hand and got out of the car without another word.

He caught up to the woman outside the door of the small station. "Excuse me," he said. "Can you help me?"

"That depends." She looked him up and down. "What needs helping?"

This is going to sound really stupid. "Do the words *garden* or *cross* mean anything to you?"

"You doing a crossword puzzle?"

He glanced back at the truck. "We're actually looking for something."

She noticed the paper he held. "There were some people earlier who were doing some scavenger hunt party thing. You a part of that?"

"Yeah. A scavenger hunt. I need to find something here in Goodlaw, and all I have to go by is the clues garden and cross." He grinned at her hopefully.

She grinned back, showing sparkling white dentures in the middle of her leathery, creased face. "I do love scavenger hunts. Used to do them when I was a girl. Lived in Phoenix then. Big sprawling metropolis compared to this good-for-nothing desert." She nodded at the surroundings. "God's abandoned all of us here. Only a bunch of no-good stragglers come to Goodlaw."

He worked hard to keep the friendly grin on his face. "Well, if you don't like it here, why don't you move back to Phoenix?"

"I killed a man in Phoenix. Son-of-a-bitch husband. They never found the body, and they never will. Bad luck to go back. Bad luck." She crossed herself and then spat to the side of him.

Okay. "So—" He held on to that grin with all his strength. "Garden or cross? Anything come to you?"

She rubbed her wrinkled face and creased her already lined forehead. "No, can't say as it does."

"Dammit," he swore under his breath. "Malcolm must have been wrong. Or maybe this wasn't a code, after all. Back to square one."

"Malcolm?" she repeated. "You ain't looking for Malcolm Price, are you?"

His gaze shot up. "What did you say?"

"Malcolm Price. Comes here once a month to pick up his supplies. Got a shack up on Garden Ridge. Now that I think about it, that might be your garden clue for the scavenger hunt."

"Malcolm," he said again, not believing his own ears. "You've actually seen him?"

"Well, yes, of course. I've got twenty-twenty vision even after all this time."

He'd told Janie that Malcolm was dead, but he didn't tell her how he'd died. The letter arrived eight years ago, shortly after he'd been killed by a clan of vampires who'd been kept in a basement by hunters so long that the hunger had turned them savage.

It had been a closed casket.

He was alive? How was that possible? He felt stunned and suddenly uncertain what to do next.

"Where's Garden Ridge?" he asked hoarsely.

She told him. He left.

When he got back into the car and shifted into drive, Janie eyed him curiously.

"Everything okay?"

He nodded stiffly. "Just fine."

He pulled out of the gas station without realizing that he'd neglected to pay and the gas nozzle was still attached to the truck. Hearing that Malcolm might still be alive—which made no damn sense at all—shocked the hell out of him.

Five miles south, the desert turned greener. The browns of the arid landscape gave way to a patch of lusher foliage. Garden Ridge was a valley area shadowed by two medium-sized hills. The winding gravel road led them to a "road closed" sign.

"Dead end," Janie said. "What did that woman tell you?"

He ignored her and pressed down on the gas to maneuver around the sign and onto the rough path beyond. After a while they came to a very small house shielded by vegetation. It looked run-down, overgrown, and as if no one had lived there for a hundred years.

Where are you, Malcolm? Quinn thought and felt a churning in his empty stomach. *And why have you been in hiding all these years?*

Just as he'd told Janie, the man had been like an uncle to him. Nice and understanding when his father was cold and rigid. He sent the letter. That meant if Malcolm was still alive, he would also be after the Eye—that is, if he didn't already have it. If he'd found it and made the wish already, then all of this would be for nothing.

It was worth checking out, anyhow. Besides, he had to keep Janie occupied until he had a chance to . . . *incapacitate* her.

She scanned the area with a look of distaste. "This place is probably crawling with bugs."

"Shhh."

"What? Isn't it abandoned?"

"Just be quiet."

She got out her gun.

Quinn held up his hand. "That won't be necessary."

She hesitated and then reholstered the gun. That thing made him nervous. Very nervous. He'd never liked guns. Way too unpredictable. Not the guns themselves, but the people holding them.

He walked through the overgrown landscape and behind the house. A grime-covered window looked out on the back. Quinn walked cautiously over to it and peered inside, but it was too dirty to see through. The place felt abandoned.

The woman at the gas station must have been wrong. Simple as that.

Then he laughed. Just a small sound of disappointment, and he shook his head. What did he expect? Malcolm to suddenly appear and give him a fatherly hug? Tell him that everything was going to be okay?

What was he doing, anyhow? Coming all this way to find some stupid artifact that was only rumors and speculation. Talk about grasping at straws. And what if he did find it? What if he did make the wish to become human again? What was that going to solve?

It wouldn't change what he'd done. What he was. It didn't change the fact that he was a nobody now, and neither vampire nor human wanted a damn thing to do with him.

He frowned. Maybe he should wish for a full-time therapist. Yeah, that might be something to consider.

"Hey!" Janie called. "Take a look at this."

He turned to give her a dirty look. Hadn't he told her to be quiet? Honestly, the woman was annoying to the sum of a thousand.

She was pointing at the ground.

He sighed and came closer. Beneath the overgrowth and weeds was a two-foot-tall stone cross.

She grinned. "Well, what are you waiting for?"

He looked at her blankly.

She put her hands on her hips. "Start digging."

"With what?"

"You have extra vampire strength. Use your hands."

He eyed the cross. It did fit the clues. There were at Malcolm's alleged home in Garden Ridge at the correct coordinates. There was a cross right in front of him.

He started to dig.

After ten minutes he'd gone down about two feet. He looked up at Janie. "There's nothing down there."

"Keep digging." Then she frowned and pointed down. "Wait. What's that?"

He looked. It was something small that glinted in the sunlight. He reached down and brushed it off and then reached farther down into the dirt to uncover it.

"Is it the Eye?" Janie said breathlessly. "Let me see."

It was a shiny red rock, two inches in diameter. Looked like a ruby, but coated on one side in gold and engraved with a symbol. A circle surrounding a smaller circle.

It was something, but he was certain it wasn't the Eye.

"Dammit. That's not it." Janie crossed her arms. "Well, keep digging."

"That won't do you any good," a voice said from behind them. "The stone is the only thing that's buried there. I know that because I buried it myself hoping that you'd come to find it."

Quinn turned around slowly. He recognized that voice. Even after all of these years.

It was Malcolm. Standing there in the overgrown back yard. Not quite the Malcolm Price he knew before—a well-dressed, well-spoken, well-groomed man with dark hair gray at the temples. No, this version had a long white beard and hair to match, pulled back into a ponytail. Deep creases under his eyes. He wore a dark blue shirt and tan cargo pants.

But his eyes were the same. Those pale green eyes that had never looked at Quinn with cruelty or disappointment. They crinkled as he smiled widely. "I've waited for you a long time, my boy."

So many conflicting emotions ran through Quinn he didn't know where to start. Confusion, happiness, relief, mistrust. Complete and total shock and disbelief, even though he was now looking directly at the man he thought was dead for eight years. Just a small sampling.

He shook his head. "I can't believe this."

"Who are you?" Janie demanded as she backed away a few steps.

Quinn glanced at her. "That's Malcolm."

"I thought you said he was dead."

"That was the impression I wished to give to anyone who might be looking for me." Malcolm looked at her.

"This is a trap." Suspicion edged every word Janie spoke.

She had her gun in her hand again and with the other hand reached for her cell phone.

"Put the phone down, Janie. I told you Malcolm's an old friend of the family." Quinn regarded Malcolm. "What the hell is going on? You're *supposed* to be dead."

He smiled, and deep wrinkles spread out from the corners of his eyes. "I am, aren't I?"

Quinn found that he couldn't help the smile suddenly on his face. He swallowed past the lump of emotion that had formed in his thoat and approached Malcolm cautiously, taking in the sight of him. They clasped hands. "It's so good to see you. You look like hell, old man."

"But I feel wonderful." Malcolm's smile widened. "Please bring the red stone and come inside."

They followed him into the house, which wasn't as run-down on the inside as it was on the outside. Clean floors and counters, modern appliances. The open shelving in the kitchen confirmed that Malcolm had enough canned food and bottled water to feed a small army.

"How long have you been here?" Quinn asked as he tried very hard to push past the lingering sense of disbelief he was having.

Malcolm tensed. "Since . . . since the accident. Or shortly after."

"What accident?" Janie's words were clipped, and she eyed the men with mild curiosity. She kept her hand under her jacket, close to her shoulder holster.

"I had a little run-in of the fanged variety. They definitely got me back for what I'd done to them all those years."

Quinn cringed at the memory. He'd mourned the old man for a very long time. Helped to hunt down the vamps who did it. And now to find out it had all been a mistake?

"What happened?" he asked. "Why didn't you contact us? Contact *me?*"

Malcolm approached him and patted his cheek with a gnarled hand. "I'm sorry I caused you grief. There are reasons for everything I do, my boy. I hope you can still trust me."

Quinn pressed his lips together, a lump forming in his throat. He swallowed past it. "So you live here now? All of the time?"

"I have Mildred at the gas station to keep me company."

"She's the one who told me where to find you."

The right side of his mouth quirked. "Ah, I doubt that you were looking for me. You were searching for the Eye, weren't you?"

He nodded. It was on the tip of his tongue to tell Malcolm everything. Just spit out all of his troubles and woes in a tirade of words. But he stopped himself, glancing briefly at Janie, who was silent as the two of them had their reunion.

"It's been some time since I sent that letter," Malcolm continued.

"Eight years. It's been eight years that you've been gone. My father thought you were dead. You have a burial plot. I thought your body was inside."

"All was essential to my plan." He sighed heavily. "How is Roger, anyhow?"

"He . . . he's dead."

Malcolm's brow furrowed. "How did it happen?"

Quinn's father had been shot when he'd tried to kill Quinn. But not by him. The man had no mercy, no second thoughts about ending his own son's life when he found out he'd been turned into a vampire. It hadn't been a good end.

"He . . . he was shot."

Malcolm nodded gravely. "Was that before or after he found out about your little problem?"

Janie sat back and watched them with cool appraisal.

"What's my little problem?" he asked carefully.

"Your slight case of vampirism."

Quinn had personally witnessed Malcolm slay scores of vamps over the years. He'd learned a lot from the old man. He may have been kind to Quinn growing up—a mentor, a friend, a sounding board—but he showed no mercy when it came to the business of hunting. Quinn immediately felt his adrenaline kick in and hoped this confrontation wouldn't lead to a fight. Not with Malcolm. Any hunter but him.

"How did you know?" he asked.

Malcolm smiled. Wide enough to show off his own set of shiny white fangs.

Quinn stifled a gasp. "What the hell—?"

Malcolm slowly walked to the corner of the kitchen and grabbed a walking cane that rested against the wall right next to a new-model computer. "Internet is expensive here, but I have it. I have managed to stay informed of everything going on in the hunter world. Yes, I knew Roger was dead and how he died. For his sake, I hope he isn't burning in hell for how he treated those close to him in life. I also know of your recent predicament. I'm sorry I couldn't have been there to help you. It is a difficult time, believe me, I know."

Quinn couldn't believe his own eyes. "You're a vampire."

Malcolm smiled as if this wasn't information that had just shaken Quinn's entire world. Malcolm was a hunter who'd been turned into a vampire. Just like him. "Yes. We have a great deal in common. When I was attacked, the vampires gave me a choice: I could live or I could die. But by living I would become one of them. I am not proud to say that I made my decision based on fear of the unknown. Fear of death. After it was done, I hid. I knew what my peers would do to me if they found out."

"You could have told me."

He gave Quinn a weary smile. "I fear that you would not have been as understanding of my situation as you are now. Can you honestly say that you wouldn't have hunted me?"

Quinn couldn't answer that, and Malcolm didn't wait for him to. "I had been researching the Eye, with your father, for years and had finally come upon some leads. When I left the world I once knew, I came here in search of it alone. The search led me to the red stone you have in your hand. And it led me to much more than that. I would be honored to share this information with you."

Quinn glanced at Janie, who watched them like a predator. She absently played with her turquoise necklace, twisting it, and his vision closed to the small pulse he could see in her throat. He tore his eyes away from her, breathing heavily. "I think I need to sit down."

Malcolm frowned. "Are you well, boy? You look as if you haven't slept in weeks."

"I'm fine." The backs of his legs found the edge of a chair at the kitchen table, and he sat down hard. He placed the red stone on the tabletop in front of him.

"No, you're not. You aren't sustaining your strength. Are you refusing to drink blood?"

Quinn grimaced. "Whenever I can."

Malcolm shook his head. "As distasteful as the thought might be for you, it is a necessary evil. It took me years to understand that simply because I ingested something my body required to survive, it didn't make me a lesser being. It didn't make me a monster."

"I feel like a monster." He felt Janie's silent and appraising gaze from the other side of the table.

"You're not." Malcolm patted his back. "You . . . and I . . . are a new breed. We are two of the few who have seen the world from both sides. As hunter and vampire. And we can use that knowledge to now find the Eye together."

"I just wish you could have contacted me. To tell me you were all right."

"And what if I had?" he asked. "What if I had called you one night to tell you I was in town? That I was alive, only now a vampire. What would you have done then?"

Quinn closed his eyes and shook his head.

"You would have killed me," Malcolm said bluntly. "Or you would have told people who would have done it for you. I had no choice. I had to leave and put as much distance between myself and my past as was possible. And I've done exactly that. I've had the past eight years to think and to plan." He held out his hand. "Give me the stone."

Janie reached over to grab it before Quinn could. He looked at her. "Janie—"

"I've had just about enough with this little Transylvanian family reunion," she snapped. "I want the Eye."

Malcolm raised an eyebrow and smiled patiently at her. "Whatever for?"

She stared at him. "Because it'll really go with my outfit."

His frowned and then glanced at Quinn before turning his attention fully on Janie. "You're a mercenary. I don't know why I didn't spot it before." He shook his head. "A beautiful woman such as yourself should not have chosen such a dangerous path. Whoever may have hired you will have to do without the Eye."

"We'll see about that, vampire." She smiled coldly at him.

"Indeed, we will. However, without the stone in your hand, I won't be able to find it for anyone." He held out his hand, palm side up.

She studied him for a long moment before finally, grudgingly, giving him the stone.

Malcolm held his other hand out to Quinn. "Now the letter, if you please."

Without hesitation, Quinn dug into his pocket and gave him the worn piece of paper.

Malcolm laid the paper flat on the table with the printed side down, smoothing it out. Then he went over to a cupboard and opened it up, reaching in to draw out another, matching piece of paper.

"What's that?" Quinn asked.

"Just another piece of the puzzle." He laid it next to the other piece.

"What do you mean?"

Malcolm smiled. "The true location of the Eye has

been cloaked until now to any who would search for it—who wish to use its magic for their own gain. It requires two immortal beings—such as you and me—using this stone to reveal its true location. The Eye is out there, Quinn, in plain sight for those who don't wish to harness its powers but invisible to those who do. It's waiting for us."

Quinn watched, fascinated, as Malcolm took the stone, symbol side down, and rubbed it in along the seam of the two pieces of paper. As the rock glided over the surface, the two fused into one single piece as if they had always been joined.

"I have waited to do this for a very long time," he said with a sparkle in his blue eyes. He turned the larger piece of paper over to the printed side and began to rub the rock over it. The writing began to disappear, instead being replaced with lines and shapes that appeared as if out of nowhere.

"What are you doing?"

"Revealing the true location of the Eye. My original search for the Eye led me to this stone wrapped with this paper. It's a map. It wasn't until later that I discovered that it would be revealed only with two immortals present, at the right time, during this ritual." He shook his head and looked down at the old paper, his eyes glistening with emotion.

Quinn couldn't believe his eyes. It was a full-fledged treasure map. And it had appeared magically when Malcolm ran the stone over it, as if it had been written in magical invisible ink. He shook his head and looked at Malcolm, his heart swelling. This was turning out to be the best day of his life. Finding the Eye and finding

Malcolm after all this time. He wasn't sure which was better.

Malcolm beamed at him. "You see? Now the Eye will belong to both of us. I see great things for our future."

Quinn glanced at Janie. Her eyes had widened at what had just happened, and she stared at the map on the table. Malcolm went to cover it up and pull it away, but she grabbed the corner of it.

"I'm going to need this," she said.

Quinn stood up from the table. "Take your hands off that, Janie. I'm warning you."

She glared at him but didn't let go of the map. "Is that right? You're *warning* me?"

Suddenly Malcolm grimaced and let go of the paper. With a sharp gasp of pain, he clutched his chest.

Janie's face fell. "What's wrong with you?"

"I get pain sometimes," he explained through clenched teeth. "So much pain."

"But you're a vampire, aren't you?" She frowned, and her determined expression softened slightly.

Quinn made a move to go to Malcolm's side, but the old man held up his hand to stop him.

"No, I'll be fine in a moment," Malcolm said. He looked at Janie. "But . . . could you be so kind as to pour me a glass of water, dear? If you wouldn't mind."

She hesitated, frowning, but then moved toward the cupboard, the map still clutched in her hand. Her shoulders were tense as she reached up to grab a bottle of water and unscrewed the cap.

While she did this, Malcolm straightened up his posture, closed the small distance between them, and with one smooth motion swung his cane at the back of Janie's head.

The sound of her body falling heavily to the ground covered Quinn's gasp.

Malcolm turned to him. "It had to be done, I'm afraid."

He struggled to keep his face expressionless. He blinked rapidly, not quite registering what he'd just witnessed.

Malcolm looked down at Janie's unconscious form. "Even as a mercenary, she was a minor inconvenience until she saw the map."

He licked his dry lips. "Of course you're right."

Malcolm clutched Quinn's shoulder and squeezed it hard. "You and I will follow the map to the Eye. Together. Then we will change the world."

"Change the world?" He glanced down at Janie out of the corner of his eye. She wasn't moving. He couldn't tell if she was breathing. Had he killed her? His jaw clenched at the thought.

"Vampires are evil," Malcolm said simply. "I feel the darkness inside me. Don't you? But I have been blessed with my intelligence. I can take what I've learned and use it to save others."

Quinn swallowed hard. "I think the hunters have that under control. Don't you think they're the ones who are evil? Has that ever occurred to you?"

Malcolm put a hand on Quinn's shoulder. "Yes, of course. Hunters can be just as bad as vampires. With the Eye in our possession, we can change things. Make things better. Don't you see?"

Use the Eye to help others. Not only himself.

It was a thought.

He finally forced a nod. "What's our first move?"

"First you must regain your strength." He nodded down at Janie. "Take her. Drain her. If she isn't dead, kill her. It must be done."

His stomach lurched. "So you're saying you don't get pizza delivery out here?"

Feeling like throwing up sometimes worked to kick in Quinn's defense mechanisms—in this case, his sense of humor. His *morbid* sense of humor.

Malcolm nodded gravely. "In the beginning, I, too, fought it until I was weak and at the point of starvation. It is a losing battle. I will tell you one thing, the more I drink, the better I feel. I need the strength to keep fighting." He looked down at Janie. "Now, eat her."

"But it's only our first date." He forced a smile that masked the storm going on inside him. A joke—yes, a joke to lighten the mood and give him a second to think things through.

He glanced down at the prone Janie, her throat naked and exposed to the air.

His fangs ached.

He glanced at Malcolm. "I don't feel right doing this with an audience."

"I knew the moment I saw her that despite her beauty she was one of the evildoers. I would be willing to bet that her selfish deeds have hurt and killed many over the years. Don't feel any guilt for what you are about to do."

Quinn stared at Malcolm for a moment and then nodded without saying anything.

The old man grabbed a piece of paper and a pen and jotted something down. "Take these directions to a place in downtown Phoenix. Meet me there at nine p.m. tonight and we will discuss what our next step will be."

Quinn took the paper and looked at it briefly before shoving it into his pocket.

Malcolm's kindly eyes crinkled. "Everything will be fine now, Quinn. Now that we have each other."

He snatched the map from the floor next to Janie, rolled it up, and tucked it inside his shirt. Then, with a final nod, he turned away and left the small house. Quinn watched him through the window as he walked down the pathway out front and disappeared into the distance.

Then he sank to his knees beside Janie.

"Hey"—he brushed the hair off her forehead—"are you okay?"

Her utter silence gave him his answer.

He pressed two fingers against her jugular and was relieved to feel a pulse.

The woman was willing to kill him and Barkley—not to mention Malcolm—at the drop of a hat, and he was concerned for her well-being. He shook his head at his own lack of self-preservation, but it didn't change anything. He wasn't just going to let her die if he could do something about it.

The back of her head was bleeding from where Malcolm had hit her with the cane. His concern was then mixed with a hot line of hunger that wrenched his stomach. There was blood on his fingers. Her blood.

"Christ," he swore. Then he stood up so quickly he felt dizzy.

Drain her, Malcolm had said.

He ran the tip of his tongue along his bottom lip. He'd

gone too long without blood. Just the sight of it was making him feel crazy.

Malcolm had always been the one who gave him advice. Great advice. When he was a teen about to go out on his first date. After his first time. After his first kill. Malcolm had never, not once, steered him wrong. Never let him down in a lifetime of being lied to.

Malcolm took what he wanted, and he obviously felt no remorse about it.

Janie's blood. The sight and the smell of it was making him feel more than hunger. It was more . . . sensual than that.

He got down on his knees again next to her and rubbed his face along the line of her neck, smelling her.

She smelled so good. So very, very good. Sweet . . . like apple pie and ice cream. He licked along the pulse in her throat because he couldn't help himself.

Dammit. He clenched his jaw. *Keep it together.*

He pulled way from her, swearing loudly.

The woman was injured, and all he could think about was how good she'd taste.

Then a thought poked through the heavy layer of bloodlust he was fighting.

She'd been nothing but trouble and a huge pain in his ass ever since she'd bungee jumped into his life earlier that afternoon. This was his chance to end his misery once and for all.

He'd planned to knock her out himself, anyway. Malcolm had saved him the bother.

He looked at her again, all sprawled out unconscious on the tiled floor of Malcolm's kitchen. She looked so innocent. So attractive.

So delicious.

So what if he drank from her? It's not like she was an innocent. Just lean in. Like a kiss. Nuzzle into the warmth of her neck. Feel the firmness of her skin a moment before it gave way to his fangs.

The world began to narrow in on him until there was only him and her.

No one would ever know.

Malcolm wouldn't tell anybody. Maybe he knew how it really was. He'd never steered him wrong before.

He felt his small fangs begin to elongate. It felt really good—as if they should always be that way.

The line in the road he'd drawn for himself between right and wrong began to blur as the world darkened and he ran his tongue along the pulse of her neck again.

Yes. This is the way it should be. Just like this.

But a moment after his teeth grazed the surface of her skin, he drew back, horrified by what he'd almost done. He pushed back from her and away, scrambling to his feet. He ran outside and threw up next to a five-foot cactus whose pink flowers seemed to be mocking him.

Chapter 7

The last thing she remembered was opening a bottle of cheap, generic water. But then she'd thought—what difference did it make what the packaging looked like? It was all just water. Like what you can already get out of a tap.

Then she'd obviously died and gone to hell.

The blazing pain in her head rivaled any migraine she'd ever had. The only thing similar was that time she'd been knocked unconscious by that pissed-off banshee on an assignment last year. What a bitch she'd been. Wouldn't stop with the screaming.

She opened her eyes slowly. Everything was blurry. Her vision slowly came into focus until she realized she was still in Malcolm's house.

"Whhaaa...?" Her mouth felt dry. A little of that generic water might be nice right now.

"You're awake. Finally."

A voice. She knew that voice. She liked that voice. Too

bad it was currently beating into her head like a bolt of lightning.

"Not so . . . not so loud . . ."

Janie felt a cool, wet cloth press gently against the back of her head. It made her realize that she was sitting up. In a chair. A straight-backed chair that wasn't padded.

"You've stopped bleeding. Trust me, that's a very good thing for both of us."

"Bleeding?"

"Malcolm knocked you out cold. You're lucky you're not dead."

Being dead would solve so many problems, she thought absently.

"No, it wouldn't," Quinn said.

Shit. Did she say that out loud?

Wake up, she commanded herself. *No time for napping on the job.*

"He knocked me out?" she managed. "That old man? He seemed so frail and nice."

"Vampires aren't frail. But some of them are nice."

"Are you one of them?"

"Definitely not." He shifted position. "How many fingers am I holding up?"

She frowned and concentrated. "One."

"That's right. Which one?"

"Your middle one. Very funny. Ow."

She went to hold her aching head in her hands but then realized she couldn't move. That was strange. It didn't make sense for a moment through her still-woozy consciousness.

The world around her became clearer with every passing moment.

She glared up at him. "You tied me up?"

Quinn shrugged and didn't look the least bit sorry. "Trust me, you got off easy."

Her hands were tied firmly behind her back. Her ankles were bound to the chair legs.

She pulled at the binding until her wrists hurt. "Untie me."

"Not just yet."

"I'm critically injured. I might have a concussion."

"I'm sure you do. He hit you really hard. Thank God you're blessed with an incredibly thick skull."

"Save the compliments and untie me."

"You need to call Lenny and tell him to let Barkley go."

She shook her head, more from confusion than denial, and it hurt like a son of a bitch. "Ow. Untie me and we'll talk about it."

"I'll hold the phone to your ear."

Janie eyed the room. "Where's Malcolm now? Is he going to come out here and taunt me with his glass of water?"

"He's gone."

"Where did he go?"

Quinn hesitated. "I don't know."

"You're a shitty liar."

"I'm a very good liar."

"Liar." She grimaced against the throbbing pain. A nap would be nice. Three or four days might do the trick.

"What's Lenny's number?"

Her eyes snapped back open. "You're serious."

He nodded.

"I'm not telling you."

"Then this is going to be a long wait. Just to remind you, I am immortal now. I will definitely win."

She strained against the bindings to no avail and looked around the room again—her level of anxiety growing with every passing second. "Where's the map?"

"Malcolm took it."

Her stomach dropped. "He *what?*"

"He took it with him."

"How could you let him do that?"

"Trust me, it wasn't an easy choice."

A thought occurred to her. "You stayed to take care of me?"

Quinn cocked his head to one side and studied her. "Malcolm wanted me to feed off you and then break your neck. He didn't specify the breaking of the neck, but it would have been my choice if I'd decided to take him up on his suggestion. Very quick death. You wouldn't have felt a thing."

A chill ran down her spine at his words. He could have killed her, and she wouldn't have been able to do anything to save herself. She hated feeling like a victim.

But he hadn't killed her.

She focused on her neck. Could she feel anything?

"Did you bite me?" she finally asked.

"No."

"You said I'm bleeding. Did you . . . oh, my God . . ." She shifted uncomfortably in the chair. "Did you lick my head?"

He snorted. "Sweetheart, I have a million comebacks for that one, but since you've probably got a brain injury, I'm going to let it pass. No, I didn't. I held a cold cloth to it. That's all."

Why didn't he bite her? She was completely incapacitated, and he was a very hungry vampire. It was completely irrational, but she almost felt insulted.

Yeah. It was irrational.

Brain injury. Definitely.

Then she remembered what he'd said a minute ago. Way more important than any discussion of potential licking.

"Malcolm's gone to get the Eye, hasn't he?"

"That is his master plan."

"And you just let him go without trying to stop him."

"Did I press rewind on the TiVo? Yeah. And now you're going to call Lenny."

"The Eye," she said weakly.

"You never told me why you had such a mercenary hard-on to get it in the first place."

"I need it."

"Why?"

He was so frustrating she was ready to scream. "Because. Just because. If I don't get it soon . . ."

"What?"

"Bad things will happen."

"That's a little vague." He crossed his arms. "Bad things will happen to *you?*"

She averted her gaze. "I just need it. There are no other options."

"Janie, be straight with me. If you're in trouble, maybe I can help you."

She laughed, and it made her head nearly explode. "Trouble. That is my middle name."

"Janie."

She looked up at him. Damned if he didn't look concerned for her. Maybe he was a good liar and she was too gullible. At least where Michael Quinn was concerned.

"The man I work for wants it."

He nodded. "Who do you work for?"

"I don't know his real name, so I just call him the Boss. It's an agency of sorts. Think Charlie's Angels crossed with the CIA crossed with the Mafia. And throw in some black magic and a really lousy car allowance. That's us."

"Did he tell you why he wants the Eye?"

"He didn't tell me anything except who knew where it was."

"Me."

"Well, he wasn't specific, but yeah." She took a deep breath and let it out slowly. "Got to say, though, it's been a bit of a disappointment. Thought I could grab it at the diner and be back by dinnertime. I'm going to ask for overtime pay on this one."

"How did he know I'd have the means to find it?"

"He has seers. They saw."

He scowled down at her. "You like working for this asshole?"

"It pays the bills."

"How can you be so flippant? You work for the bad guys."

"Bad guys. Good guys. Who says who's who anymore? Corruption is the new black, and it's everywhere. And no offense, but look who's talking?"

"What?" he snapped.

"Um . . . ex-hunter? Not exactly the most noble profession in the world, is it? You've seen both sides of the coin now. Must be great to catch up with somebody like Malcolm. Somebody just like you."

"Actually, it is."

"Whatever. Anyhow, these ropes are getting a little itchy."

"So your boss threatened to kill you if you don't bring him the Eye."

"Among other things."

"Such as?"

She stared at him for so long she felt sure he'd look away. He didn't.

"He has something on you, doesn't he?" Quinn asked. "Something he's blackmailing you with? Making you do his dirty work?"

"I prefer my work to be dirty."

He shook his head. "I don't think you do."

"Oh, and you know me so well, right?"

"What's he got on you, Janie? What's so bad that you're willing to go through all of this and not just run away?"

"I don't run away."

"Just answer the question. Tell me."

She sighed. The man was relentless.

"My sister has been missing for five years. My boss knows where she is. If I bring him the Eye, he'll tell me where to find her."

"That's it?"

She nodded.

"That can't be all it is."

"Isn't that enough?"

The look on his face told her that he didn't believe her. And why should he? She was leaving out a great big chunk of the story—the fact that the Boss would kill Angela if she failed. But telling Quinn wouldn't change anything. They were still on opposite sides of this war, and she'd rather not give him any more ammunition. How was she to know he wouldn't use it to put a bullet in her back?

She decided to try something to help change the subject. She closed her eyes and moaned. "I feel . . . like I'm going to pass out."

He moved closer. "It's your head?"

No shit, Sherlock. "I . . . I'm seeing spots. Everything's getting a bit dim. I think I need help. He must have hit me harder than I . . . than I thought."

He started working on her bindings. "I should get you to a hospital."

"After we find Malcolm."

He stopped untying her and straightened up, giving her a grim look. "Faker."

"I wasn't faking. Untie me."

"I'm not just anybody you can play to get what you want, Janie."

"If you don't untie me, I'm going to start to scream."

"Go ahead." He pulled a cell phone—*her* cell phone—out of his pocket. "Now, let's start again. What's Lenny's number?"

She glared at him, but he just looked back at her expectantly with his finger on the number pad.

"It's on speed dial, Brainiac."

He pressed a few buttons, then took the phone to Janie and held it to her ear.

Lenny answered after three rings.

"Janie? Is that you?"

"Yeah, it's me."

"Everything okay?"

"Best day of my life."

"What's the word?"

She glared up at Quinn. "The word is that you can let Barkley go now."

"Let him go? So you have the Eye?"

"Not yet."

"And you want me to let him go?"

"That's what I said."

"He's been sleeping for an hour. He's just waking up now. Turned back into human form. If you ask me, looks like he can't control his lycanthropy."

"I don't really care. Let him go."

"If you say so."

"I do." She glanced at Quinn, who nodded.

"What about the Eye?"

"Forget it. It's gone." Her voice cracked on the words. "I don't know if it's even retrievable anymore."

"What?" he exclaimed. "The Boss is going to be furious."

"Yeah. I know. I'll take the blame."

"He'll hurt you if you take the blame." He paused and let out a long breath. "There's got to be a solution."

"Where are you?" she asked.

"In Phoenix. There's a motel here called the Sleepytime Inn. I'm in room three."

"I'll meet you there later."

She nodded at Quinn that the call was over. He closed the phone and put it to the side. She shut her eyes and tried to think. The ropes burned, and she was now in an even fouler mood than before. The moment Quinn let her go, she was going to stake him with the nearest piece of sharp wood she could find. She didn't even care if it was imitation. He was so dead.

* * *

Quinn studied Janie. Her eyes were closed, and she didn't look happy. But at least she looked alive. She'd never have any idea how damn close she'd come to being his first official snack as a vampire.

He felt a twinge of pain in the pit of his stomach, and it took him back to the day he was changed two months ago. He'd been bled nearly dry and contaminated with the venom in a vampire's fangs that will change one from human to vampire. The shorter the bite, the less venom is passed. The longer the bite, the more blood that's drained—well, it made a sick, twisted kind of sense. He'd been infected with vampirism. Typically the vampire "sire" would then give the fledgling some of his or her own blood to counterbalance the venom. Live through that and *whammo,* welcome to Vampire City. Don't get enough blood or get none at all, as was his case, and you will die a slow and painful death.

The stomach cramps were the first sign. Then the pain crawled through the rest of your body until you could barely function. Your only thought then is to drink blood. From anywhere or anybody. And it didn't really matter how you got it.

At the time he'd gone in search of his hunter friends. He'd wanted to die, because becoming the thing he'd always hunted, the thing he'd always assumed was evil, was worse to him than being dead. But then he'd run into Sarah, the same woman he'd tried to kill twice, and she wouldn't let him die. She'd dragged him, literally, to see her boyfriend whose blood was strong enough to get him through to the next day and beyond. It had been so strong that he'd gotten a fast-forward on many vampire traits. He'd lost his reflection quicker than normal. He needed less blood on a daily basis than a fledgling who would have ingested normal strength blood. His fangs grew almost immediately. He also knew he had the master vampire to thank for his increased strength. All these things could take months, if not years, for the regular, run-of-the-mill vamp to experience.

Yeah, he was so lucky. Right.

The ache in his stomach left as soon as it had arrived, and he decided to ignore it for a while longer. He didn't feel so hot, though. He hated to admit it, but he'd have to seek out a vampire bar soon. He couldn't go much longer without some of the red stuff.

Just the thought of it made his mouth water. How could he be so disgusted and so hungered by the same thing?

The screwed-up dichotomy of his life.

Ever since being turned, he'd felt like a freak of nature. Those hunters back at the Burger King the other night had thought him just another bloodsucking freak.

He had to agree with them on that point.

And that's what he saw when he looked into Janie's eyes. She hated what he was. And he didn't blame her in the least.

He'd thought Janie was just a bitch. A bitch with a wicked body and a mouth he wanted to explore intimately. He'd thought she was cold as ice and willing to kill at the drop of a hat for whoever paid her the biggest dollar.

But there was something else. He hated thinking that Janie's younger sister was missing, but his gut told him there was more to the story. After all, couldn't she simply hire a private investigator to locate a missing person without having to jump through hoops on a dangerous assignment?

He remembered Angela being a sweet little kid who was always smiling. Janie wouldn't lie about her sister. She couldn't fake the concern in her eyes.

She didn't want to tell him what threat this boss of hers had made if she didn't return with the Eye. He was willing to bet it was severe—that Janie's life was in jeopardy.

He shook the thoughts away and looked at her again. Then he began to work on the knots he'd tied.

"Thanks," he said softly.

She frowned. "For what?"

"For letting Barkley go." He swallowed hard. "He's a good guy. Got his own problems. It would be par for the course if I'd gotten him killed. I always screw up everything."

"Always?"

"Always. You should have asked my father. He thought I was a waste of skin. A total disappointment to him, right to the end."

"I only remember meeting him once, but my first impression was that he was a jerk."

"Didn't make him wrong. Malcolm was the only one who ever was nice to me back then. I owe that guy big-time."

"The guy who knocked me out and told you to drain me."

His mouth quirked. "Yeah, that one."

Her frown deepened, and she searched his face. She rubbed her wrists after the rope fell away. "I need to find that map. You can either help me or you can stand in my way."

He studied her for a moment. "Angela's really been missing for so long?"

She cringed and nodded. "I thought for a second that your werewolf friend might be serious about being psychic."

"The redhead from his dreams? You think that Angela's the one he was talking about?"

"Probably just wishful thinking." The expression on her pretty face hardened. "So you're saying that your long-lost best bud Malcolm didn't even tell you where he was going? Why would he leave you behind like that?"

He didn't reply.

She tensed. "He *did.* He *did* tell you where he was going, didn't he? He must have. You have to tell me, Quinn, where he—" She stood up in one fast movement, then swayed on her feet and brought her hands to her head. "Oh, my God."

"Take it easy, Janie." He caught her before she hit the ground.

He eased her gently down to the dusty floor and stroked the hair off her forehead, tracing his thumb over smooth, pale skin.

"Brain hurts," she said, keeping her eyes closed.

"Yeah. I guess your head isn't as hard as I thought it was. Who knew?" He moved back a little. "We should get you to the hospital."

"No, don't stop. That feels good." She grabbed his hand and brought it back to her forehead.

Who was he to argue? He continued to stroke her forehead, pushing errant strands of blond hair from her beautiful face. She sighed.

He stilled for a moment. "I do charge sixty bucks an hour, I'll have you know."

"Money well spent."

She looked so innocent lying there. Not helpless like she'd looked before when she was unconscious and he'd almost devoured her. This was different.

At that moment all he wanted to do was to make her smile again, like she had on the drive over there. The smile that was bright enough to light something up inside him that had been dark for a long time.

She opened her eyes and reached up to take his hand, holding it against her cheek and with her other hand, reached up to run her fingers through his hair, just staring up at him without saying anything. Her hand felt warm against his.

The cell phone rang and he jumped.

Moment over.

She reached for her phone and brought it up to her ear. "Yes?" she said wearily. She closed her eyes and pressed her eyelids together. "Fine. Hang on."

She pulled the phone away and looked up at Quinn. "The werewolf wants to talk to you."

He nodded. He probably wanted to say good-bye. Nice guy, that Barkley.

"Barkley," he said. "You okay?"

"I don't know if I'd say that exactly. I'm finding it hard to hold one form. One minute I'm a werewolf, and the next I'm human again. Is there some sort of lunar eclipse scheduled that I don't know about?"

"Not that I know of."

"Anyhow, I'm calling because I realized something. When I'm asleep in wolf form, I can totally channel my dreams into visions. I can basically ask to see something and then I see it."

"Like *Monday Night Football*?"

"No. Although that would be really cool. But I'm talking about that dream that had to do with Janie. Her necklace, remember?"

"Yeah." He glanced over at Janie, who hadn't gotten up from the floor yet. She lay there with her eyes closed again. His gaze moved down to the necklace in question. "What about it?"

"I realized why the necklace set off my powers. It was made by somebody from my pack. She and her pups moved down to Mexico years ago, but she always stayed in touch. The woman weaves actual werewolf hair into the pieces of jewelry she makes. She called them were-looms."

"And?"

"The redhead," he paused. "I get the weird feeling that she's related to Janie. By blood. That's why they wear the same necklace, maybe. When I was dreaming a minute ago, everything became a whole lot clearer."

"What did you see?"

"She's in Vegas. The redhead's in Vegas. Damn, she's gorgeous. The odd thing is, there's a sort of blank on her soul."

"You can actually see that?"

"Not see it. Feel it, man. I'm psychic."

"So you keep telling me."

"Despite this blank aspect, I'm seeing that she got serious psychic abilities, too, and add in the werewolf hair necklace, and bang . . . I've got a connection. I'm thinking me and her are soul mates and her soul is calling out to mine. I always thought I'd hook up with another lycanthrope, but I'm willing to experiment extensively to find the right woman as my lifelong mate."

"Focus, Barkley. Please."

"She's in Vegas, and she's using her psychic ability to win at the tables. A woman with questionable morals. I'm falling in love more by the minute."

"Vegas," Quinn repeated, and Janie's eyes snapped open.

"Yeah. Listen, me and Lenny are heading out for dinner, and then we're going to hit a strip club. Except for the fact that he was willing to kill me at Janie's order, the guy is actually really cool. He's read me some of his poetry. It's . . . it's interesting. He's got a serious thing for Janie, though, just to let you know."

"Why would I care about that?"

"Oh, no reason. Just the fact that she's blond, gorgeous, and previously gaga for your sorry ass."

"*Previously* is the important word in that sentence. And besides, how do you even know that?"

"Haven't you been listening to anything I've said? I'm *psychic.*"

Quinn rolled his eyes. "So now what?"

"We can hook up tomorrow."

"And do what?"

"And go find the hot redhead in Vegas, of course. Duh. Anyhow, see you tomorrow."

He hung up.

Quinn let out a long breath.

"Why did you say Vegas?" Janie asked.

"It's not too far away, and Wayne Newton puts on a great show."

"That's where the Boss told me to meet him to hand over the Eye."

Quinn nodded. That would make sense. Obviously this rat bastard knew where Angela was and was keeping that information away from her until she came through with the goods. He wanted to come right out and tell her what he knew—such as it was. But something stopped him.

No, not yet.

"He can't have it," he said evenly.

She stared at him. "Anyone ever call you a heartless bastard?"

"Many times."

"Why the hell do you want it? What was Malcolm saying about it granting a wish? What would your wish be?"

He licked his lips. "To be human again."

She blinked. "That's it?"

He nodded.

"You could wish for anything—money, power, a bevy of Playboy bunnies. And all you want is to be human again?"

"Hold on. Can you be more specific about the Playboy bunnies? Maybe I haven't given this enough thought."

She shook her head. "You really hate being a vampire that much?"

"More."

"See, to me, vamps have it pretty good, all things considered. The fact that you'll stay young and handsome forever isn't a total bonus for you?"

He raised an eyebrow. "You think I'm handsome?"

She rolled her eyes. "Sorry, that's enough ego stroking for one day."

"I used to be sort of cute, I think. But I've got the whole lack-of-reflection deal going on. A guy can forget. Handsome. Hmm."

"I should keep my mouth shut."

"Never had a problem with the ladies."

"Oh, lord. Kill me now. Okay, so we both want to find the Eye. The question is, how do either of us get it if we don't know where Malcolm is?"

He hesitated. "I know where he is. Or at least, where he's going to be."

"How do you know?"

"He told me."

She got slowly to her feet while bracing herself against the wall. "Fine. Let's go."

"Together?"

"You may have the keys, but I have the gun." She checked her holster to make sure.

Damn. He should have taken more than just her cell phone away. Opportunity knocked, but nobody was home.

She didn't look so good.

"Are you feeling all right?" he asked, trying to mask the concern in his voice but failing. "We can stop at a hospital if you like."

She shook her head. "No. No hospitals. I'm fine."

"I can carry you to the car if you like."

"Not necessary." She reached around and pressed her hand to the back of her head and winced. "Yeah, that's going to leave a mark. Ouch."

When she pulled her hand away, it had blood on it. She looked down at it, then looked up at Quinn with a smirk. "Still hungry?"

"I'll be in the car."

He left the house before she could witness his fangs lengthen painfully in his mouth again.

Chapter 8

The odds of letting Quinn out of her sight before she had her hands on the Eye were slim to none. She'd tested the waters with him a bit. It seemed as if a little sugar helped the medicine go down. If she wanted something from him, she had to be nice or, at the very least, not a total bitch. The Boss said he'd be in Vegas tomorrow. Time was precious. She could feel the grains of sand slipping through the hourglass already. There was no room for mistakes.

Quinn had been keeping quiet on the drive. She tried to make conversation with him a couple of times to try out her sugar/medicine theory during the two-hour drive to Phoenix, but he answered in monotone one-word answers, which was fun only for a little while.

"Are we almost there?" she asked.

"Yes."

"What did Barkley want to tell you about Vegas?"

"Nothing."

"Is he still in werewolf form?"

"No."

Like that.

So, instead, she checked for text messages on her cell phone. Zero. Her voice mail. Zero. Oddly enough, that was the sum total of her friends at the moment, since she rarely stayed in one place long enough to make any.

After that, she looked out the window as the bright Arizona afternoon turned to dusk and the stolen truck sped closer to their next destination.

She turned to face Quinn, resting her throbbing head against the headrest of the car seat, and pretended to be asleep. Every now and then she'd open her eyes wide enough to peer at him through her dark lashes.

She'd called him handsome by mistake. She covered it up pretty well, though. Luckily, he'd laughed it off. When he'd brought her down to the ground after she'd nearly passed out, he did it so gently. And feeling his hand against her forehead was so soothing. All she'd wanted to do at that moment had been to grab him and pull him down on top of her and kiss him.

Luckily for everyone involved, the massive head injury had prevented that.

Talk about embarrassing.

Maybe it was the fact that he was so completely different from her. Maybe that was the reason she had this major thing for him. Still. After all these years. She hated the fact that she still wanted him. It made her furious with herself. But she couldn't deny that she was hopelessly attracted to him.

She needed this job over with ASAP.

Even the fact that he was a vampire didn't bother her

as much as she would have thought. She'd met her share of vamps. Everyone from the dark and dangerous types to the meek and nerdy ones. Gorgeous European vampires with long dark hair and pitch-black eyes, and the blond ones with freckles and bad breath.

They'd been so romanticized in media—television, movies, books—but she'd never been uncontrollably attracted to one before. After all, the whole drinking-blood thing was a little outside of her comfort zone, especially with the memory of her last vampiric run-in with Nicolai. That bite had hurt like hell. There was absolutely nothing sexy or romantic about it. It was just another way to kill somebody—a vicious, animalistic way.

Quinn said he'd never bitten anybody. Did she believe him?

She studied his handsome but slightly gaunt face. He'd look better with a little color. Maybe a few more pounds. He was starving himself because he hated what he was and what that meant. If he'd accept it, he might be happy. He could cover up his self-hatred all he wanted with jokes and quips, but she could see through it. Why else would he want to make a wish to be human?

That wouldn't change anything. It wouldn't change his past. It wouldn't make him any happier. Why couldn't he see that?

They entered Phoenix in silence a little after eight p.m. and found the Sleepytime Inn. Quinn parked the stolen truck and went into the office to get two rooms.

Lenny said he was in room three which was just to the right of the office. She got out of the car and walked to it, keeping an eye on Quinn in the windowed office.

She knocked but there was no answer.

She eased her cell phone out of her pocket and speed dialed Lenny's number. It rang.

And then went immediately to voicemail.

"Lenny, I'm at the motel. Where the hell are you?" She hung up.

Just terrific.

Quinn emerged from the office with two keys and saw her to her motel room.

He eyed her with concern. "Are you sure you're going to be okay?"

"I will be. Eventually. I think I'll have a shower."

He frowned, nodded, and then turned away from her. "I'll be back in a half hour to check on you."

"Wait a minute—"

He stopped and glanced over his shoulder. "Don't worry, I'm just going to my own room for a bit. Why, don't you trust me?"

"Not even remotely."

His serious expression turned amused. "Well, I can stay and help you with the shower, if you'd like."

She'd roll her eyes if she didn't expect it to hurt. "A half an hour. I swear I will hunt your ass down if you take off on me."

That earned a full on grin. "It's a deal."

He walked to his own room a few doors down and closed the door behind him.

Great. So much for staying in control of the situation.

Her head hurt too much to worry about it more than she already did. Maybe she should have gone to the hospital after all.

She closed the door of her motel room slowly and then her eyes widened. She didn't need a hospital. She had everything she needed right in her own purse. She hefted it onto the bed and dug down to the bottom of it, pulling out a small tube of healing balm which she'd completely forgotten she had on hand or she would have used it much earlier.

She squeezed out a dab of the ointment and reached around to apply it to her wound. Immediately her head began to feel better and she felt the familiar tingle as the balm worked its magic. After her last run-in with the vampire who nearly tore out her throat she'd forgotten that she'd replenished her supply and placed it in her purse for just such an occasion.

Good for cuts and scrapes.

Or stabbings or bullet wounds.

Then Janie fished back into her purse, pulled out a vial of Tylenol, and took four of the pills with a few handfuls of water from the bathroom sink.

Getting the blood out of her hair was her next priority. She stripped, then took a quick shower. The two-in-one motel-supplied shampoo did the trick.

She toweled off her hair and went to sit on the side of her bed and tried to pull her racing thoughts together now that her head didn't feel like it was about to split down the middle.

She lay back on the bed and closed her eyes and tried not to think of anything but healing thoughts for the five minutes it would take for the ointment to kick in.

When she opened her eyes, she was dismayed to see that she must have fallen asleep despite her tension—the half hour had long since passed, and Quinn hadn't come back to check on her as he said he would.

Damn liar. Why was she surprised by this?

She forced herself to get up and get dressed and went outside to look for Quinn. She spotted him immediately as he exited the main office. When he emerged, she cut him off.

"I thought you said you'd check on me. I could have been dead in there."

"I was asking for directions." He studied her for a moment. "You look better."

"Were you asking for directions to where Malcolm told you he'll be?"

He hesitated. "I'm going alone."

She took that as a yes. "Like hell you are."

"If Malcolm sees you, he'll know I didn't kill you."

"He won't see me. I'm not letting you get the map without me."

"You don't trust me?"

She snorted at that. "Not as far as I can throw you."

"You look strong enough. I have a strange feeling you could throw me pretty far."

"I'm coming."

He let out a long, exasperated sigh. "We can debate this all night, Janie. Just try to see reason. It's better if I go alone. I'll be back later."

The man was almost as stubborn as she was. She was used to people going along with what she wanted after she badgered them a bit. Quinn wasn't going to let her have her way. But there were ways around that.

"Fine."

"Fine?" He raised an eyebrow. "So you'll stay here? Just like that?"

She shrugged. "I'll stay here. If you say you'll be back with the map, then I believe you."

He nodded. "Well, good. I need to go. I'll be back in a couple of hours."

"Good luck."

He walked away and then looked back at her again as if he didn't believe she was going to let him go so easily. She smiled and waved, and he turned and went toward the truck.

As he was starting it up, she was busy hotwiring a cute little white Corvette parked nearby so she could follow him. She wasn't stealing it. She was borrowing. She limited herself to stealing one car a week. After all, a girl's got to have boundaries.

The Electric Cactus, the place Malcolm had written on the piece of paper he'd given Quinn earlier, was a very crowded country-and-western bar, complete with sawdust on the floor and a mechanical bull. A Garth Brooks tune permeated the air through the sound system. Thunder was definitely rolling by the volume of the music.

A couple of pretty girls with red lips, Daisy Dukes, platinum blond hair, and artificially enhanced cleavage approached him as he scanned the club for Malcolm.

"Hey there," one said. "Buy us a drink?"

"Both of you?"

They smiled at him. One approached close enough to run her acrylic fingernails down the front of his T-shirt. "We'll make it worth your while to spend a little time with us, sweetie. Promise."

"Oh, I have no doubt about that." He couldn't help but smile inwardly. A year ago this would have been the beginning of a great night. Two hot girls who wanted him to . . . *spend time* with them? Bring it on.

He'd changed since then. He had, right? He frowned.

Yes. Yes, he had. Definitely. More important things to think about at the moment. ➤

"Sorry, ladies. I'm meeting somebody here."

They didn't seem deterred. "If you change your mind, we'll be around."

"Noted."

He turned away and wasn't sure exactly which of them brushed his jean-clad rear as he walked away. He froze in place.

No. He'd changed.

More important things to think about. Et cetera.

Okay.

That damned Janie had gotten him all warmed up. Other women had to work at being sexy, but that girl was drop-dead gorgeous without even lifting a finger.

Dead being the operative word there. As in what she'd probably end up being if he gave this annoying infatuation with her more than a passing notice. He hated how she managed to affect him.

Focus, Quinn, he told himself.

He spotted Malcolm over in a corner booth. The old man waved at him. Quinn nodded in acknowledgement and closed the distance between them, ignoring the crowd that made him feel claustrophobic. He didn't like being around humans in large numbers anymore. This was most definitely not a vampire bar. Humans had a distinctive scent to them, especially in large crowds.

They smelled a lot like food.

Not a good start to the evening.

"Quinn, my boy." Malcolm grabbed his hand and squeezed it hard as he sat down across the table. "I'm pleased you could make it."

"Wouldn't miss it for the world."

He hated what the old man had done to Janie but tried to see it from Malcolm's point of view. He'd thought Janie was a mercenary—which she was. And he thought she wanted to take the map away from him—which she did. Janie was definitely no innocent bystander.

It felt right, Malcolm still being alive. Even aside from the Eye, there were so many things Quinn wanted to know about Malcolm's plans. Just knowing there was another person he could rely on, who had gone through the same experience he'd been through, made him feel a little less alone.

"You haven't gone and got the Eye without me, have you?" Quinn asked.

Malcolm laughed and raked his fingers through his long white beard. "No. That part of my plan can wait until tomorrow. I ordered you a beer."

"Much appreciated." He leaned back in the booth and shook his head. "I can't tell you how good it is to see you again, Malcolm. I didn't realize how much I'd missed you."

Malcolm glanced around the surroundings. Someone got on the bull and stayed on for all of two seconds before they were thrown down to the padded floor. A drunken cheer went through the crowd. The music shifted to Keith Urban.

"What do you think of this place?" he asked.

Quinn gazed around. "Seems okay. Never really into country music that much."

"So many people all out to have a good time." Malcolm smiled. "When I grow hungry, I come here and watch them to see who's being the most careless. Who is drinking the most and wanders off."

Quinn watched him, suddenly wary.

"Have you ever fed from a drunk human?" Malcolm asked.

He wondered what the best way to answer that would be and decided for the truth. "Can't say as I have."

"The blood acts to enhance the inebriant. Like a fine aged scotch. After experiencing it, you'll never want to go back to regular blood again. It just doesn't have that same . . . *kick*."

"I know I can't get drunk on any alcohol unless there's blood involved, so that makes sense." Quinn tried to keep his voice neutral. "Gives a new meaning to a Bloody Mary, doesn't it?"

"Indeed, it does."

"So you're here a lot?"

"Once or twice a month. Any more and people might start wondering about the missing more than they already do."

Quinn felt cold then. "So you don't just drink from them. You kill them?"

"If I didn't, I'd have a police report out about some crazy man who bites necks."

His heart began to pound harder. God, he didn't want to know these things about Malcolm. "I . . . I wanted to ask you a question. From earlier."

Malcolm waved his hand. "Of course."

"Back at your house, you said that you sent me the letter years ago in the hopes that I'd follow the clues to find you. And the red stone."

"That is correct."

"But then you said that it takes two immortal beings— two vampires—to reveal the map."

A smile played at the corners of Malcolm's mouth. "Also correct."

Quinn frowned. "But when you sent me the letter, I was human. I didn't become a vampire until recently. How would I have been any use to you if I'd come here as a human?"

The smile spread. "I intended on siring you when you arrived. I actually was slightly disappointed when I learned that it wouldn't be necessary."

Quinn's mouth felt dry. "You . . . you were going to make me into a vampire?"

"It is the only way for this plan to work."

Quinn was silent for a very long time, just taking this information in. Processing it. Trying to get it to make some sort of damn sense.

Malcolm gazed again at the swelling crowd at the bar. "How is it possible that humans still have no idea that vampires exist?" he mused aloud.

Quinn swallowed past the thick lump in his throat. He felt numb, suddenly. "They don't want to know."

"That's true. For to know of such a darkness lying so close to their everyday lives would change the entire world for them, wouldn't it? The number of times that a vampire has shown its true face in the midst of a crowd . . ." He sighed. "And afterward, the humans just speak about the odd event and go back to their normal lives as if nothing had happened. Fangs are not enough to convince anyone anymore. Teenagers have their teeth filed sharp to dress up as something they want to be but don't truly believe in. They wear dark clothes and white makeup and even try to drink blood as if that makes them a vampire. It's pathetic. Humans are an utterly pathetic species."

Quinn frowned deeply. "So you hate vampires, even though you are one. You hate hunters even though you were one. And now you hate the entire human race? Is there anyone or anything that you do like?"

Malcolm was quiet for a moment, but then the old man's lips parted into a smile.

"I like us," he said.

"Which means what?"

"We are better than all who have come before us. We have the origin as humans. We have the knowledge of hunters, and now we have the strength and immortality of vampires. We are better than all three put together." He reached into his pocket and pulled out a piece of paper. "You see this list of names?"

Quinn looked at the precise, neat handwriting. "Who are these people?"

"A few are hunters. Smart men with vision for the future. That one is a writer—a Nobel Prize winner. That one is a child genius who was written up in *Time* magazine last year. The rest I have chosen based on nearly a decade of study and research of who are already superior beings."

"And?"

The expression on Malcolm's face was pure determination. "We will turn them into what we are. It will be an army of greater immortal beings who will change the course of history and mold the future to our will."

Quinn felt ill. "I think I need another beer."

Malcolm flagged down the waitress to order two more bottles of Heineken. He eyed her as she walked away. "Perhaps we can turn some others, too. Like Clarisse, there. She would be a fine companion."

Quinn's head was spinning. The man had made a list? A list of people he wanted to make into vampires—including Quinn himself had he not already been changed. He came to this club frequently to pick out his next murder victim. He had a preference for imported beer.

Only on the last point could he agree with the old man.

"And you want to use the Eye to help us do this?" Quinn managed.

"Of course. I believe by harnessing the power of the Eye we can become truly powerful. It was owned by a demon and is part of that demon's power. It has sat untouched for a thousand years. It is our fate that we shall possess it and make our wish for power. After all, when we create our army, we need to have strength over them, or there could be an uprising."

"Wouldn't want that."

"So what I've told you hasn't shocked you?"

Quinn drained the last of his first bottle of beer before he felt that he could answer that. "Only shocked by how much sense it all makes."

Malcolm arched a white eyebrow. "I am pleased that you feel that way. While you were an excellent hunter, you perhaps felt too much empathy toward the creatures you ended."

Right. Empathy. Quinn thought he was so much more moral than Malcolm's errant food choices. But what had he done for ten years? Killed indiscriminately. As long as they had fangs and a thirst for blood, they deserved his stake. At least that's what he tried to convince himself of. How could he ever make up for all he'd done?

Malcolm didn't wait for Quinn to reply. "Perhaps I am the one who understands you better than anyone, Quinn.

The guilt you feel for what you did all those years. I felt it, too, when I was first turned. After all, how could I have murdered all of those vampires? What made me better than them? But with time and research and patience, I now know that I was turned for a very specific reason. I was chosen, Quinn, just as you have been."

"Chosen? By who?"

"By God." His face lit up as he said it. "He wants us to act as the plague that will kill off all that is unclean and start again."

With every word Malcolm spoke since he'd first entered the bar, Quinn felt deep disappointment and repulsion growing within him.

Quinn couldn't do anything to stop what had happened before, but at least he could try to prevent a little of Malcolm's planned massacre.

He leaned across the table and tried to keep his voice steady. "I'm sure that God would want us to have the Eye. It's fate."

"I agree."

"Do you have the map on you right now?"

"I do, indeed. I wouldn't leave it anywhere else. Much too risky." Malcolm hesitated. "I also have the red stone we used to reveal the map's true face."

"Will you need it again for something?"

Malcolm eyed him for a moment. "I don't believe so. But one can never be too careful."

A dull ache began in Quinn's stomach. He knew that pain all too well and what it meant. He needed to eat. And if he didn't do it soon, there would be severe consequences.

"Tell me"—Quinn leaned over the table and tried to keep his voice steady—"are there any vampire bars close by?"

"Why?"

"Just in case I get thirsty and I don't feel like going to any additional work."

"You should be completely satiated after that lovely meal I left you this afternoon."

Janie. Right. He was supposed to have drained and killed her. "Oh, I am. She was . . . delicious. Just call it morbid curiosity."

"There's a bar around the corner behind a red door. There's a neon sign in the window that claims it is a palm reader named Madame Rosa, but beyond that is a bar that could contain up to a hundred vampires."

Quinn nodded and tried to ignore the ache in his gut. Just a little while longer. Get the map, get away, and then visit Madame Rosa's to fill a necessary evil.

"So tell me, what are we going to do?" he asked.

"Tomorrow we follow the map and find the Eye. As long as I know that you understand my plans and agree with them wholeheartedly."

"I'm with you, Malcolm. Whatever you say."

"I'm very pleased to hear that."

For a moment when Malcolm first revealed that he was alive because he was now a vampire, hope sparked inside Quinn. Hope that there was somebody exactly like him—a hunter who'd been turned into a vampire who had survived and thrived and come out the other side in one piece. Evidence that his current situation wasn't as dire as he had believed. He'd hoped that Malcolm might be a mentor to him again. Someone to confide in and who could advise him, and make this transition better than the lonely, scary journey it had been so far.

But he'd gotten something much different.

A glimpse into his future if he didn't get the Eye and wish to be human again.

He knew that he'd eventually turn into somebody like Malcolm. Confused and irrational and more than a little crazy.

Well, more than he already was, anyhow.

Now all he could do was focus on getting the map away from the old man before it was too late.

Malcolm smiled at Quinn and glanced off toward the mechanical bull again as he sipped from his glass of Heineken.

"The woman today," he said. "The mercenary. Did you know her well?"

Quinn kept his face neutral, striving for bored despite all the upsetting information he was dealing with. "No. The bitch was willing to kill me to get her hands on that map. You did me a favor."

"Did she wake while you fed from her?"

He shook his head. "No."

"And she's dead now."

"Very. Didn't want to risk siring her."

"Siring a vampire is a serious business. You must be there with them at all times. You will develop a bond that sometimes allows you to sense where they are, how they're feeling. It is best that you didn't sire this one. She was pretty, but obviously a very stubborn, driven woman who would do nothing but cause problems."

Quinn shrugged. "I've never been a huge fan of blondes, so it was a no-brainer to just kill her. Why are you asking me questions about her? She's dead. So's this topic. Let's talk about the map."

Malcolm turned his gaze away from the mechanical

bull, and his expression was now cold. "I'm asking you about her because she's here right now. Over by the bar."

Quinn's aching stomach dropped. "That's impossible."

Malcolm's eyes wrinkled as he smiled—a very cold expression. "I'm disappointed in you, boy. I had such high hopes for our future. But I see now that you're a liar."

"You must be seeing things. I drained her. She's dead."

Or at least she will be when I get through with her, he thought, restraining the impulse to turn his head and look.

She followed him to the bar? After he asked her to wait at the motel?

Unbelievable.

Malcolm stared icily at him. "I never understood why your father was so disappointed in you. He was never satisfied, wished that you had a deeper resolve to the kill, to strive for better, to follow in his footsteps. To me you seemed the perfect son. Obedient, strong, willing to learn and grow. But I think I see now that you're all that Roger said you were. You're a complete disappointment."

He stood up from the table.

Quinn's cheeks twitched and he forced a nervous laugh. "Come on, Malcolm. Sit down and let's talk about this. The map—"

The cold expression disappeared, replaced by one of fury. "You'll never lay one finger on that map." He brought his cane up to his chest with both hands, clutching it like a weapon.

Quinn eyed it and allowed the false friendliness to slide from his own expression. "What are you going to do? Try to knock me out, too?"

"No, that only works best with humans." He removed

the silver tip from the end of the cane. "For vampires I have other methods."

Just as Quinn noticed that the silver covered a sharp wooden point, he shot up from the table and turned away. He was fast enough that the weapon missed his heart, but not fast enough to prevent it from thrusting into his body under the right side of his rib cage with a searing, white-hot pain.

He grabbed the long stake on either side, stunned speechless as he watched Malcolm quickly walk away from the table.

Chapter 9

Quinn tore his pained gaze away from the departing Malcolm and stared down at the stake. He braced himself against the side of the table and slowly eased the sharp wood out of his flesh.

The stake hurt more coming out than it had going in and he stumbled, dropping back down into the booth. It left a dark mark on his T-shirt. He hadn't eaten in so long that his own blood had changed consistency. Instead of red and flowing, it was dark and thick.

He gagged.

On the bright side, it meant he didn't bleed very much.

The country music blared in his ears and, since he hadn't made a single sound, the crowd that surrounded him seemed to have no idea of what just happened.

He staggered to his feet with only one thought. He couldn't let Malcolm get away. If he did, he'd never see the map again. He couldn't let Malcolm keep it. His plans were too extreme, too specific. He couldn't have the Eye if it was the last thing Quinn did.

And based on how the night was going, it just might be.

He scanned the bar for Janie but didn't see her anywhere. If she really had been there, she was gone now.

Holding his hand against his wounded stomach and trying to ignore the pain, he began to make his way through the crowded club, being jostled on every side. As he passed the long bar, the blondes eyed him again like hot-bodied vultures.

"We knew you'd be back," one said.

"Got to leave," he managed.

"Come on, one drink. We promise we won't bite."

If he'd been feeling half himself he might have laughed at that. Instead, he roughly pushed past them as they attempted to block his escape route.

One made an annoyed sound. "Probably gay, aren't you?"

Quinn gritted his teeth. "Never been happier, thanks for asking."

He got to the front doors, pushed them open, and was greeted by the surprisingly cool breeze from the dark night. The bouncers eyed him as they would any obviously inebriated, staggering patron, and gave him a wide berth.

Out of the corner of his eye, he saw a flash of white hair as Malcolm disappeared behind a corner.

He followed.

Dammit. Where had Janie gone? He could actually use her at the moment.

A couple more inches and Malcolm would have got my

heart, he thought. *Why did I have to move? This could all be over.*

Thoughts like those weren't exactly helping matters.

He staggered down the street toward the alleyway, feeling weaker by the minute. It felt as though the only thing keeping everything from spilling out of his gut was his hand on top of the wound. Past the pain of the stab wound, he felt the vampire hunger gnaw angrily inside of him. It had been denied for too many days. It wasn't just going to go away now like a dull toothache. This time it was here to stay. And the more blood he lost—such as it was—the worse it was going to get.

Your own fault, he told himself.

He made it to the corner, worried that he was too slow to stop Malcolm and too weak to get the map.

Instead he was surprised that Malcolm stood there, facing him, as if he'd been waiting.

"Malcolm—" Quinn managed, immediately concerned by how weak and shaky his voice sounded.

Malcolm just stared, his forehead creased with a deep frown.

As Quinn was trying to form his mouth around the words, Malcolm's expression grew blanker and blanker, and then he fell forward at Quinn's feet.

"And you said I shouldn't come."

He looked up to see that Janie was in the shadows of the alley, holding a gun. Looked like the same gun she'd pointed at him a couple weeks ago.

She shook her head and holstered the weapon under her jacket. "If I hadn't followed you here, he would have gotten away. That was quite the lead he had on you, too. Did he take off when you were in the little boys' room or something?"

He blinked at her.

She blinked back. "Anyhow . . ." She crouched down next to Malcolm, efficiently patting him down before she pulled out a folded piece of paper. "One map, recovered." She peered closer at it. "What the hell is *that?* A beer stain? No respect. I should have shot him with more than just a garlic dart."

"Janie . . ." The world was starting to get blurry and even darker than the night was to start with.

"So now we have the map. Tomorrow we get the Eye, and then we take it from there. Hey, what's wrong?"

His knees hit the pavement, and he pulled his hand away from his chest. Janie gasped and closed the distance between them. She put the map down on the ground so she could grab Quinn's T-shirt and push it up and away from the wound.

She looked up to meet his unsteady gaze. "Old friend of the family, huh? Some friend. Did he figure out you were lying to him?"

He licked his dry lips and managed to push her hands away from him. "He . . . he saw you. In there. You're supposed to be dead."

"Shit."

"Exactly what . . . what I thought."

"How could he see me?"

"He has eyes."

She shook her head. "Dammit, I must be really off my game. I'm usually much better at being inconspicuous. So this is my fault."

"One hundred per . . . percent."

She bit her lip. "Well, on the plus side, he didn't get your heart."

"Unfortunately."

"Don't say that. We need to get you back to the motel and bandage you up."

He shook his head and forced himself to stand, when all he felt like doing was curling up in a ball and possibly crying. In the most manly way possible, of course.

She grabbed his arm, and the scent of her flooded his nostrils.

No. That's not all he felt like doing.

He could actually feel the warmth of her neck in the cool night, the blood just underneath the surface calling to him. He restrained himself from pulling her to him.

"Get away from me," he warned.

"I'm trying to help you."

"You can help me by staying as far away from me as possible right now." As he said it, he could feel his fangs elongating and his hunger increasing. "I'm dangerous."

"Yeah, as dangerous as a wounded puppy."

He looked at her, and whatever she saw reflected in his eyes made her visibly flinch. "Quinn—"

"I need to get to a vampire bar. Malcolm told me that there's one nearby. I need to go right now. Don't follow me."

He staggered away from her without waiting for an answer.

Guilt and concern flooded through Janie. This was her fault. She shouldn't have followed him.

No, she *should* have. She just shouldn't have been seen.

Dammit.

She watched Quinn make his way down the street. The

man was in bad shape. If he'd been at full strength before getting staked, or stabbed, or whatever had happened to him inside that bar, then he might just be feeling some pain. Not this . . . obvious agony he was dealing with.

She'd seen her share of starving vampires. Some hunters found it fun to keep a vampire locked away in a room for days or weeks or even months on end, depending on the age and strength of the vampire, and then let them out. Made for a more interesting kill. Perhaps took away that residue of guilt that gnawed away at the corners of a hunter's conscience about what was right and what was wrong when it came to killing another sentient being.

Quinn was definitely sentient. But that look he'd leveled at her had given her the chills. His eyes had turned black, just like those starving vampires. His wound seeped only a small amount of blood. How long had he gone without eating?

He was seriously the most stubborn man she'd ever met.

Not like the seventeen-year-old boy she'd fallen head over heels with. He'd been handsome, charming, funny and, well, *perfect* back then.

The thirty-year-old version was a total mess.

She followed him out of the alley anyhow. She'd stay back and let him do what he had to do, but she wasn't letting him out of her sight. Not this time.

Suddenly she froze in her tracks as a breath caught in her chest. She spun around and ran back to snatch the map off the ground from beside the still-unconscious Malcolm.

She'd been so concerned with Quinn that she'd almost left it behind. God, what was wrong with her? She shoved the map into her pocket and silently chastised herself for allowing herself to lose focus.

Every few steps, Quinn would stumble. He had his arms wrapped around himself. He looked like a drunk, or a vagrant, or somebody most normal people would stay well clear of. Definitely a good idea at the moment.

She touched the fang marks at her neck and flashed back to how it felt when that monster had bitten her. She'd thought she was going to die. One misstep, one big mistake, and that's all it took. If you didn't watch your back at all times, some scary thing was going to sneak up behind you and tear you to pieces.

The scary thing she was currently surveying ducked down another alleyway. She slipped into the shadows and watched as he approached a red metal door lit by a street-lamp. He pounded on it, then waited a moment, bracing one hand against the side. He pounded again. And again.

And then he kicked it. Kind of a pathetic weak kick.

Then he swore and slid down to the ground.

She approached and noticed he was now sweating. His face was ashen.

He looked up at her after a moment. His eyes were still black.

"I think they're closed," he said, and then laughed quietly and hopelessly.

"We're going back to the motel."

"Didn't I tell you not to follow me?"

"I don't think you're quite getting the whole 'I don't listen to you' thing."

"I'm learning."

She offered him a hand. "Come on."

He shook his head and stared at her with black eyes. "Don't touch me."

"I'll have you know I'm a lot stronger than I look. I can carry you if I have to."

He snorted at that. "That's hot."

"Stop being a child, and let's go."

He went very still. "If you come near me, I will bite you. I can't control myself right now. I need blood."

"We'll deal with that."

"You are the most stubborn person I've ever met."

"Right back at you. On your feet."

She wasn't sure for a moment if he would or not. But then, very slowly, he rose to stand. She looked up at him warily.

"I don't feel very good," he admitted.

"It's called death throes. Seriously, Quinn, why are you starving yourself? I thought you'd be smarter than that."

He gave a weak shrug, then grimaced as if it hurt.

His face was so pale, even in the darkness, and coated with a fine sheen of perspiration. His chest moved in and out with labored breathing. And his eyes were fully black—no whites at all.

She shook her head. "Come on."

She hustled down the street back to the bar. She left the car she'd hotwired there. The police would probably pick it up in the morning and return it to whomever she'd borrowed it from. No harm done.

"Keys?" She motioned impatiently to Quinn.

He pulled the keys to the other borrowed vehicle out of his pocket and threw them to her. His hand was shaking.

"Go back to the motel," he said. "I'll meet you there.

Seriously, Janie, it's not a good idea for me to ride with you. Not the way I'm feeling."

"Yeah. Way ahead of you, handsome."

He gave a small snort at her choice of words. "Smart girl. Just leave me here."

"No, that's not what I meant." She eyed the truck. "You're riding in the back. Try to keep your head down, or you'll get bugs caught in your fangs."

Fifteen minutes later, they arrived back at the motel. Janie parked the truck and got out quickly. Not quickly enough, though. Quinn jumped off the back and, without a word, ran to his motel room, slamming and locking the door behind him.

What the hell was she supposed to do with a starving vampire who wouldn't eat anything? This wasn't exactly her area of expertise. She was used to staking trouble-some vamps, not becoming their personal dietician. There wasn't any time for an intervention. No time to head to the hospital and get a bag of blood. No time to get animal blood. And forget about the synthetic variety—at Quinn's stage of the game, he needed the real stuff and he needed it soon.

Or he was going to die.

A small voice in the back of Janie's mind whispered that it didn't matter if he died. After all, the only thing she needed him for in the first place was safely tucked away in her pocket. She was now wasting time looking after somebody who didn't even want her help.

If she walked away now she'd have that much more time to follow the map to the Eye and get to her Boss to-morrow in Vegas. Not much time, but enough.

Keeping an eye on the closed door to Quinn's room, she fished into her handbag to grab her cell phone.

"Lenny," she said when he picked up after the eighth ring. "You better have a good explanation why your phone was on voice mail before."

"Janie?" Lenny replied, having to raise his voice above the loud music in the background of wherever he currently was. "Where are you?"

"That doesn't sound like an explanation to me. I needed you. You said you'd be at the motel and you weren't here. Why didn't you call me back?"

"Uh . . . I'm really sorry. I didn't even realize my phone was off until a minute ago. I was hoping you were doing okay."

"*Hoping?*" She tried not to raise her voice. "Oh, yeah, I'm doing just great."

"Oh, that's good."

She took in a deep breath and let it out slowly. No reason to freak out on Lenny. She was fine. He was fine. Everyone was just fine.

Well, except for Quinn, of course.

"I'm at the motel," she said after another moment. "And where are you?"

"Uh . . . we're around the corner at a place called Tails and Rails. Barkley insisted we stay a bit longer than I wanted to. Sorry."

She blinked. "You're at a strip club?"

He cleared his throat. "Um. It was Barkley's idea."

She exhaled slowly. "I don't want to know."

"I'm leaving right now. I can meet you in five, maybe ten minutes?"

"No, no, forget it. It's okay. Listen, I've got the map.

We'll go get the Eye first thing tomorrow. There's a restaurant attached to the motel here. I'll meet you in the morning at seven-thirty."

"You sound worried. Everything okay?"

"Yeah. Fine. It's just . . . Quinn's not well."

"So?"

She bit her bottom lip. "Right. Yeah. I don't care. I'll see you tomorrow."

"Good night."

She hung up.

He was right. She shouldn't care about the vampire. She *didn't* care. Besides, you could offer advice and help, but if somebody wouldn't take it, well, then they were just stubborn enough to die.

In agony.

Wounded.

All alone.

In a crappy roadside motel.

Thank God she'd lost her compassion years ago working for the Company. A total burden that would be in her line of work. Start to feel sorry for the monsters and what did that get you?

A whole mess of trouble.

Janie already had enough trouble to deal with.

She'd learned that lesson the hard way. One of her first assignments had been to infiltrate a black magic organization run by a dark wizard. The wizard had been handsome, and much more charming than she would have expected. She'd fallen for the guy and knew that he'd cared for her in return. As soon as her cover was blown, all hell broke loose. The wizard had turned on her and tried to kill her, but she'd killed him first, an act that succeeded in shattering her heart into a million pieces. Which, in the end, worked out fine, because her heart had been more of a liability than an asset. She'd prided herself on her cool, calculated decisions ever since that lapse in judgment.

She wasn't going to make a mistake like that again by caring for the wrong person at the wrong time.

A nice solid night of sleep would do her well.

Yes, sleep. Very good.

And that's exactly what she'd get—right after she dealt with Quinn.

Dammit.

She marched up to his door and knocked. "Quinn? Let me in."

No answer.

She knocked again. "Hello?"

"Go away," came the weak answer.

"Do you want to die?"

"Not really having a problem with that outcome. Go away."

"Quinn, let me in right now, or else."

To that she didn't get any answer at all.

She hissed out a long breath. Instead of getting more worried, she was getting pissed. Since when did her empty threats get so completely ignored?

"I'm giving you to the count of five," she warned the locked door.

It didn't answer.

"One, two . . ."

She listened.

"Three."

Well, at least he wasn't laughing.

"Four."

Or maybe he'd already passed out.

"Five."

She braced herself and kicked the door, pleasantly surprised that it swung inward on the first try. Lousy craftsmanship. And for fifty bucks a night? Not great security.

She peered inside.

The room was pitch-black.

She stepped over the threshold. "Quinn?"

"That was a mistake."

"I think you have me confused with some weak floozy who's scared of the dark." She stepped deeper into the interior of the room.

The door slammed shut and she jumped.

No, she wasn't nervous. Not at all. However, it would be nice to have a little light so she could pinpoint exactly where the starving, injured vampire was standing.

"So, what now, Janie?" he asked quietly from the darkness. "Are you offering yourself to me? Are you baring your neck to me so I won't die?"

Her eyebrows raised. Was that what she was doing?

"I'm sure we can think of something to help you—"

A hard-muscled body flew at her, grabbing her wrists and pressing her flat against the wall. She could hear his breathing, loud and irregular, the warmth of his breath against her face. She had a stake tucked into the back of her pants in a special stake holster—a Christmas present from Lenny—but she didn't make a move to try to grab it. Not yet.

Soon, probably. But not yet.

"Do you realize that I already know what you'd taste like?" He breathed against her neck. "Just by how you smell. It's my heightened senses. Usually it's so subtle I hardly notice it, but sometimes, like right now"—his lips grazed against her throat—"it's unbelievably over-powering."

Then she felt the wet heat of his tongue slide along the line of her neck, and something happened to her that she didn't like at all—something that scared her more than anything else that had happened that night.

Her damn knees weakened.

She was crushed up against a wall by a hungry vam-pire, who apparently already knew what her blood would taste like, and it was *turning her on*.

How completely embarrassing.

Even though she knew what it felt like to get bit—and how very close to death (or worse) she'd come last time something like this had happened—all she wanted Quinn to do was sink his fangs into her.

His fangs. Yes. Just his fangs.

He continued to tease her neck. "Got nothing to say?"

"You want to bite me?"

He groaned. "Oh, yes."

"I thought you said you'd never bitten anyone before."

His shoulders stiffened. "I haven't."

"Do it."

"What?"

"Bite me. Just . . . try not to take too much."

His breathing became even more erratic. "What am I doing? What are you saying to me? This isn't right. Go away, Janie. Just go away."

He pulled away from her. Her eyes had become ad-justed enough that she could see the outline of him in the darkness.

And he thought *she* was stubborn?

She wasn't going to let him die out of principle and misplaced morals.

She slipped off her jacket and pulled her tank top off over her head until she was standing there in the dark in her tight black jeans and lacy black bra, her neck and shoulders now completely exposed to the air. She closed the distance between them and grabbed his face, pulling it down to her neck.

"Bite me or I'm going to kick your ass," she hissed.

"You're such a sweet talker, Janie."

For a moment she thought he was going to pull away again, and that would have been it. She would have realized what a crazy, dangerous thing it was she was doing and grabbed her shirt and run away to her own room. Figured out a plan B, as it were.

But that wouldn't be necessary.

The scent of her bare skin was enough to do it. She felt him press against her, aroused now with more than simple blood lust. He slid the bra strap off her left shoulder, then his hands traveled down the bare skin of her back. He pulled her closer against the hard length of his body, flattening her breasts against his chest. Just as she was adjusting to how surprisingly good he felt against her, she felt his fangs pierce her skin.

She started, gasping with the sudden pain but remembering that she'd offered this. This was her idea.

She twisted her hands into his hair and held his mouth to her in case he tried to pull away again before he got enough blood to help him. His hands kneaded the backs of her upper thighs, actually raising her off the ground as he fed from her. She wrapped her legs around his waist.

A small sound escaped from him. A satisfied, aching groan as he ground his body against her.

She knew that it took five minutes until the toxins exuded from a vampire's fangs were enough to offset the balance of human blood and infect that human with vampirism. Janie counted, trying to concentrate, deciding to hold on and let him feed for three full minutes. That should be enough. Then she would make him stop any way she could.

She didn't need to. He stopped at just after two minutes and then ran his tongue over the wound he'd made on her neck. The feel of his mouth was making her writhe against him, only then realizing that they were now horizontal in the dark, on top of the soft motel bed, and her bra had somehow magically disappeared. His mouth moved downward, along her collarbone. He kneaded her breasts in his hands, and her back arched off the bed.

"Janie . . ." he murmured, as he captured her right nipple in his mouth.

She gasped.

Feeding vampires was a good thing, she decided. Especially this one. He was wonderfully grateful.

Besides, she was probably light-headed from the blood donation, and there was no orange juice or Oreos in sight. She should really keep lying down for . . . an hour or two.

Possibly longer.

He moved back up her body and kissed her mouth, thrusting his tongue against hers in a way that made her moan against his mouth. Even the slight coppery taste of her own blood on his lips did nothing but make her body tighten and ache for more of him.

The door crashed inward.

"Janie! Are you in here?" Lenny yelled.

A light came on just before the lamp smashed to the floor. Lenny grabbed Quinn and pulled him off of her. She quickly moved to cover herself.

Not that anyone was looking. Lenny was busy beating the crap out of Quinn.

Barkley stood at the doorway, with eyes wide. He glanced at her.

"Oh, my God," he said, noting with horror the blood on her neck. "What did he do to you? Quinn! What did you do?"

She grabbed for her clothes and put them on so fast she got tangled up and almost tripped. Then she ran over to grab Lenny's arm to stop him from hitting Quinn, who'd gone silent and still in the half darkness.

"Stop it, Lenny," she yelled. "Don't hurt him."

With a fervent glance at Quinn, she pulled Lenny with her out of the room.

Lenny turned around and growled, "Come near her again and you're dead, vampire. You're dead!" He turned to Janie once they left the room. "Thank God I got back. He nearly had you."

"Yes," Janie said. "Yes. That he did."

For some reason, "Thank you" was not the words that came to her mind at the moment.

Chapter 10

Quinn was curled up in the corner of the room, his knees pulled tight to his chest, his hands covering his face. Barkley sat on the edge of the bed waiting for him to say something. Patient, that werewolf was. Very patient. He didn't want to look up to see the expression on his face, though. He knew already what he'd see.

Disgust. Shame. Fear.

All the things that Quinn was feeling himself.

Why hadn't she stopped him?

He was truly lost now. He'd gone over the one line he'd kept for himself. The line that he felt kept him remotely human.

It was his own fault. He shouldn't have gone so long without blood. Why did he think he was special? Any stronger than the rest of them? He'd waited too long, and now he was paying the price.

She acted all tough and strong and as if she was nobody to mess with, but he'd been able to feed from her.

She might have thought it was her idea—what in the hell had she been thinking?—but he was the one who'd taken her like an mindless animal.

Christ. She'd tasted so good. He'd known she would. And it hadn't been just that . . . if that wasn't bad enough. He would have taken her in more ways than just her blood if Lenny hadn't stopped him.

Janie must hate him now even more than she already did.

He screwed his eyes shut tighter.

"Quinn," Barkley's quiet voice finally broke through his wall of self-hatred. "You okay?"

He forced himself to look up. Barkley looked back at him with the strangest expression. Concern? Why the hell did he look concerned?

"I bit her," he said simply, his voice strained.

"Yeah. I managed to figure that out already."

"I drank her blood."

"Well, you *are* a vampire."

He grimaced. "I hurt her."

"She didn't look all that hurt to me. A couple of Band-Aids and a cold shower and I think she'll be fine."

"Don't try to make me feel any better."

"Quinn, I know you're not feeling great right now, but—"

"No, you're wrong. I *do* feel great. I feel fantastic, better than I have in days." He laughed, but it sounded dry and desperate. "I got what I needed."

"Well, then it's all good."

"No, it's not. I need to get that Eye. It's my only hope."

"The Eye. That's the thing that's supposed to grant a wish—the thing that Janie and Lenny are looking for?"

He nodded. "I need to wish to be human again. If I stay

this way . . . I don't know what I'm capable of. Who I might hurt next."

"The past is past. The future is all you got. Whether you're vampire or human doesn't really change a damn thing."

"What are you talking about?"

"You can be a lousy vampire. You can be a lousy human. What you are doesn't mean anything. It's what you do with what you are that counts."

"This coming from a cowardly werewolf. Terrific. Just the advice I was looking for. Thanks a lot."

Barkley's expression soured. "I was trying to help. Why don't I leave you alone now to feel sorry for yourself? Would that work?"

"That would work just fine."

Without another word, Barkley turned his back and left Quinn's room.

He covered his face again with his hands and pressed his lips together. He could still feel Janie's warm body against his own, still taste her on his lips.

She'd tasted and felt better than anything he'd ever experienced before.

Ever.

He reached forward and grabbed the map that he'd pulled out of her pocket without her knowing. It was the only thing that mattered. This scrap of paper was everything to him now. He couldn't hurt it, and it couldn't hurt him.

Janie had effortlessly managed to work her way into his life, into his heart and mind and body in less than a day. The thought of never seeing her again actually hurt. But that's what he'd have to do.

For her own sake.

*   *   *

Lenny was applying some of the healing balm to Janie's neck in her motel room. It would take care of the wound, heal it up by tomorrow so she wouldn't bear the scars like she did of the last vampire bite. She hadn't found the balm in time for that injury.

The proof that Quinn had bitten her would be gone, but the memory remained.

Her cheeks warmed. God, she wanted him. She wanted that messed-up vampire like no man she'd ever known before.

Did that make her crazy?

Yes. Of course it did. But it didn't change her mind.

It was almost eleven o'clock. Lenny insisted that they go to the restaurant, because he heard her stomach start to growl, and then she realized that she hadn't eaten all day. After her recent blood donation, she figured she should get something on her stomach as soon as possible.

Lenny was cranky. She could tell because he ordered only a plate of fries and a Coke. That was like a diet-sized serving of food to Lenny.

"What's wrong?" she asked him after she placed her order for a club sandwich and coffee that the waitress poured immediately.

He shook his head. "I don't know how you can be so calm. He almost killed you."

"I appreciate your concern, but that's not true."

"Janie, I've seen you with other vamps. You've never had a problem with them before. How did you let this asshole get you off guard?"

She rubbed her lips together and took a sip of her coffee before answering. "He didn't catch me off guard."

He stared at her blankly.

"I let him bite me," she said.

"What?" His eyes bugged out of his huge face as if that was the craziest thing he'd ever heard. "Why would you do something like that?"

"He needed blood. He was dying. There were no other choices."

"You should have staked him, then."

"I couldn't do that."

"Why not?"

Dammit. Why did she feel like she owed Lenny the truth? Well, maybe because out of everybody in the world, he was probably the one that cared the most for her. Call it a misplaced crush or just simple loyalty to one's partner, Lenny genuinely was concerned for her safety and well-being. When somebody feels that way toward you, you don't lie to them and blow them off. They deserved a lot more than that.

"I didn't want him to die."

He scrubbed his fingers through his short hair. "Janie, I know you knew this guy when you were a kid, but what difference does that make now? How could you be so sure he wouldn't have drained you?"

"Because I trust him."

He laughed. "You trust him?" He shook his head and brought his notebook out to rest on the tabletop.

She eyed it warily. "Don't do it, Lenny."

"I have to. You've obviously forgotten." He flipped toward the middle of the book to a page filled with scrawled writing. One of Lenny's many poems. This one was titled "Why Vampires Are Bad."

He cleared his throat:

Vampires suck
And not just blood
They are mean and nasty
And definitely no good
When you're drained
And close to death
Vamps will laugh—
To your screams they're deaf
They are not human
Not even close
Get too close to one
And you're going to be toast

He closed the notebook. "See?"

She sighed and took another sip of her coffee.

Happily, the food arrived then. Lenny snatched a bottle of ketchup off a nearby table. Janie bit halfheartedly into her sandwich and swallowed the dry mouthful down.

"I have another," he said.

"Please no."

He ignored her and flipped to another page in his notebook.

I know an amazing woman
Her name is Janie Parker
Pretty face and red lips
Her hair used to be a bit darker
She looks real sweet and innocent
But she's tougher than you think
She's killed a hundred monsters
At slaying she does not stink

He closed the notebook again, leaving his fries untouched. His forehead was furrowed deeply. "See? That's the Janie I know and love—um . . . *respect* deeply. Where did that Janie go?"

"That Janie is still here."

He shook his head. "I just don't get it. I've seen you protect yourself from guys way bigger than him. I don't know how he managed to pin you to that bed and rip your shirt off like that. It's almost as if you—"

He broke off and looked at her.

She blinked. "Almost as if I—?"

"Almost as if you *wanted* it."

"I was helping him. Try to understand that, Lenny. We need him."

"No, we don't. And you weren't simply helping him. You were . . . you were kissing him. After he bit you!"

He said it loud enough that the waitress looked over.

Janie tried to smile at the woman. "Could I get a little extra mayonnaise over here, please?" Then to Lenny, "Keep it down, would you?"

"Are you in love with him?"

"In love? Lenny, you're talking crazy."

"I haven't seen you with any other guy since we've been partners. I know they ask you out all the time, but you don't go out with them. I thought—" He swallowed. "I thought maybe that meant that we could . . . that we . . ." He turned away to study the darkness outside the window.

She reached over and grabbed his hand. "Lenny, please—"

He pulled away from her. "All of my poetry is about you."

"I'm sorry."

He shook his head. "I'm so stupid."

"No, you're not. And I'm not in love with Quinn."

"You're not?"

She shook her head.

Of course she wasn't in love with him. That would be completely ridiculous. After all, she'd only just started to spend time with him that day—a mere twelve hours ago.

Her childhood crush was meaningless now. She was an adult and definitely not swayed by silly romantic fantasies. Lust, sure. But love? Only a weak, pathetic woman would let herself fall in love so quickly with a vampire who didn't even like her in return.

Yeah. Totally pathetic.

The waitress dropped off her extra mayo, and she dunked the sandwich into it before taking another bite, then pushed the plate away.

For some reason, she wasn't hungry anymore.

She looked out of the window at room sixteen. Was Quinn okay? Should she go and check on him again?

Oh, my God, she thought with dismay. *I am pathetic.*

She didn't love him. She *didn't.* She could be pathetic just fine without being in love—especially not with that train wreck of a man.

The door bell jingled as someone entered the restaurant. She looked over and saw it was Barkley, who looked less than friendly. Lenny waved him over.

Barkley nodded at Janie. "You okay?"

"I'm surprised you even give a damn, considering I almost had you killed."

"I'm a very forgiving person. Just in my nature."

"How is . . ." She swallowed hard. "How is Quinn?"

"He's a total asshole. But I'm sure you already know that."

She raised an eyebrow. "I thought you two were friends."

"Yeah, that's what I thought, too. But friends don't call the other friend a coward when they're just trying to be helpful. I'm not a coward."

"Of course you're not."

"Just because I ran away from my pack because I didn't want to get killed doesn't make me a damn coward."

Janie shook her head. "That's just being sensible, I think. So is he feeling better?"

"He says he feels great. You must have fantastic blood."

"Don't get any ideas."

"Don't worry. I prefer my steaks well done." He looked at Lenny. "You're quiet. What's up?"

"Nothing." He poked at his French fries. "Janie's in love with the vampire."

Barkley looked at her. "Really? With Quinn?"

She forced a smile. "I think I'm going back to my room now."

"Good idea. I did tell him that you looked like you needed a cold shower. I would have figured you for black lace lingerie. Since it was on the floor I was able to confirm it." He grinned at her.

Her cheeks flushed even more, which pissed her off, because she couldn't remember the last time someone had made her blush.

"Forget getting Lenny to do it—I think I'm going to kill you myself just out of principle."

She stood up from the table.

A smile curled up the side of the werewolf's mouth at her obvious embarrassment and he motioned toward the waitress that he wanted a coffee. "So, tomorrow what happens? Are you and Quinn going to find the Eye together and Lenny and me'll head to Vegas to look for your sister?"

Janie froze. "What did you just say?"

"The redhead from my visions. It's your sister, right? Didn't Quinn tell you I'd had the dream that pinpointed her location somewhere in Las Vegas?"

She felt the color drain from her face. "It hadn't come up yet."

"Oh." Barkley looked nervous then.

"She's in Las Vegas?" she repeated.

He nodded. "I got a really clear picture this time. Couldn't figure out exactly what casino she was in, but it was definitely Vegas. She's still wearing the same necklace as you." He explained why the necklace was vital to his visions. "You know, other than the hair color, you two look a lot alike. Do you know if she's single? Does she have an aversion to werewolves?"

She moistened her lips. Her mouth had gone suddenly bone dry. "She . . . she always used to love puppies."

"Close enough."

She looked at Lenny and narrowed her eyes. "Did you know about this, too?"

He looked sheepish. "Of course. I thought you did, too, or I would have brought it up earlier. We're going to find her, Janie. Don't worry."

Without thinking about it, she pulled the turquoise necklace from around her neck and handed it to Barkley.

"Take this. If it helps you to find her, then I don't need it right now."

He nodded and took it from her. "It might."

"Good." She nodded back and turned away. "I'll see you in the morning."

She would have felt a sense of relief if she'd let herself. There was a chance she could find her sister and protect her before the Boss got his hands on her? And they weren't even that far away from Vegas. A few hours' drive and she'd be there.

Could she let herself believe that it was true? Barkley was a true psychic who had seen her sister and that she was okay? She felt tears well up in her eyes but fought them down. No time for that. There was never any time for tears. It just made everything blurry.

Angela had always been a real pain in the ass. Typical little sister. Always borrowing Janie's clothes, makeup, magazines. One time even stealing Janie's boyfriend—a distant, meaningless memory now but at the time had been a huge deal. They got along like cats and dogs, but it didn't stop her from loving her little sister and protecting her with all of her might. Then and now.

She glanced at room sixteen as she passed it by. Quinn knew? He'd known for God only knows how long and he hadn't told her?

That son of a bitch. He must have laughed, keeping that information from her. It changed everything.

She realized right then and there that it was true what they said. There was a very thin line between love and hate. And she'd just jumped sides.

Chapter 11

Quinn slept. At least he was pretty sure he did, since he had some bad dreams. When he opened his eyes, he was still on the floor of the motel. It wasn't as clean as he would have liked. He brushed the dust bunnies from his shirt and slowly got to his feet. It was now light outside, from what he could see past the cheap curtains covering the window that looked out on the parking lot. He grabbed his watch from the nightstand to see that it was a quarter after eight.

Good time to make his escape.

He changed clothes silently, pulling a fresh black T-shirt and a pair of khaki trousers out of the duffel bag he retrieved from the truck. He splashed some cold water on his face and ran a hand across his jaw, feeling the roughness of the stubble that he couldn't see in the mirror.

No reflection. He couldn't even see the clothes he wore. It's as if anything that touched him became nothing. Just like him.

Neat trick.

He understood a lot about vampires. Wooden stakes, and the ability to infect others with vampirism through bites. He could even make sense of the blood drinking, but the reflection thing never made sense. Some said it was because vampires lacked souls and silver didn't reflect a soulless being. But mirrors weren't made of silver anymore, so that blew that theory out of the water.

All it proved to him was that he was something different. Something bad. Something touched by evil magic. And something he didn't want to be anymore, reflection or not.

When he was human again, he'd try to make something of his life. Help people. Do things to make up for his past.

He hadn't quite worked out all the finite details yet, but he wasn't simply going to forget everything. Being mortal would help to make everything make sense again. At least he really hoped it would.

If he could have seen his reflection, he knew that how he was feeling on the inside—conflicted, shaky, uncertain—wouldn't be reflected on the outside. The blood he'd drunk the night before had infused him with vitality. He felt healthier, more energetic, like he could take on the world. It almost made him forget what he'd done to get it in the first place.

He rolled his eyes. *Stop feeling sorry for yourself, asshole. It solves nothing.*

He was out of there. No real reason to stay. Barkley hated him now. Add him to the growing list.

Getting out of everyone's life would be good for everyone.

And he wasn't going to think about Janie. It was enough that he'd dreamed about her, in both good ways and bad. Good because he'd dreamed about making love to her on the beach of a tropical island. Bad when he'd lost control, torn her throat out, and watched her bleed onto the sand.

Just a dream? Or a premonition?

Screw it. Barkley's the psychic, not me.

He grabbed a pen and a piece of paper from his duffel bag and sat on the edge of the bed to write a short note that he hoped would help.

Janie . . .

He paused, suddenly blanking on what to write. But he couldn't just take off without saying anything to her.

He took a deep breath and let it out slowly.

I can't hope for your forgiveness, so I won't ask for it. It's better that I leave now. Touching you sends me over the edge of sanity, and I don't want to hurt you like I did last night ever again. Go to Las Vegas with Lenny and Barkley. I have faith that he'll be able to help you find your sister. I hope you find what you're looking for. —Quinn

Dammit. He wanted to rewrite it. It sounded too clinical. Too cold. But what was he supposed to say? That he wanted her with every fiber in his being? That he wished she could forgive him for being a bloodsucking vampire and he wished things could be different?

It should be easy. Knowing what she was. What he was. There was no room in either of their lives for sentiment.

However, leaving that morning was going to be tough.

He knew he'd never see her again, and that was the sacrifice he was going to have to make. She wasn't a cold, calculated Merc killer as he'd originally thought. She did what she had to do with the life she'd been given. She was strong and independent and kind and beautiful, and funny and sweet, and she could easily make him want to tear her clothes off when she was within ten feet of him.

Shit.

He definitely had to get out of there.

She'd think he was a heartless bastard, but then again, she seemed to be a good judge of character. The best thing he could do for her would be to get the hell out of her life while the getting was good.

He folded the letter and left the room, heading for Janie's room. He'd push the letter under the door. He couldn't leave with her thinking that he'd known about her sister the whole time and hadn't said anything to her. Why he hadn't told her immediately, he wasn't sure. He didn't trust her. She sure as hell couldn't possibly trust him. But she had a right to know.

Through the dark morning, bright headlights blinded him for a moment. He squinted and held his hand up to his brow. A black Mustang with Barkley in the passenger seat drove past him and out of the parking lot to the highway beyond.

He felt a little stunned. Well, what do you know? They'd left. The three of them must have left together, getting up early enough that he wouldn't notice.

How rude was that?

It was one thing for him to do it, but three against one was just tacky.

So much for good intentions.

"Going somewhere?" a voice said from behind him.

His shoulders tensed and he slipped the note into his pocket. "Just out for a breath of morning air."

"Yeah, I bet."

He turned around to see Janie leaning against the stolen werewolf truck. She wasn't smiling.

"Your friends just took off," he said, nodding toward the exiting Mustang.

"I know."

"Where are they going?"

"Vegas."

"Yeah, Janie, about that—"

"About what? The fact that my sister might be there?"

He stared at her. She did not sound like she'd had nearly enough caffeine yet.

"I guess Barkley told you? I was going to tell you."

She nodded. "I see. Well, I guess having your fangs stuck in my neck kind of inhibits small talk, doesn't it?"

"About that, too—"

She waved a hand. "Forget it. See?" She turned to the side to show him her throat. "Marks are all gone. It's like it never happened. Besides, I've had bigger vamps bite me." She smirked. "I barely even felt you."

Smartass. But at least she wasn't hurt. Not physically, anyhow.

"Then let's forget it happened," he said.

"I thought I already said that."

He forced a grin. "So I guess we're not friends anymore?"

"*Were* we friends?" She raised an eyebrow. "I don't remember that. I do, however, remember my assignment to follow the expendable vampire to the Eye. Expendable means, of course, that it doesn't really matter in the end if you live or die. Where's the map, Quinn?"

"I thought you had it."

She approached him and shoved him against the driver's side of the truck. "Where is it? You took it from me last night. Thought you were all injured and helpless, but I guess you played me pretty good, didn't you? Got your snack *and* got the map."

He really wished she wouldn't get so close. She wore the same clothes from yesterday, but they still looked fresh. She smelled like motel soap, but somehow made that incredibly intoxicating.

"Give me the map," she said.

"No."

"You heartless jerk."

"You're the Merc, Janie. I don't know what you're doing. You're a strong, independent woman. Who is this boss of yours who has you so wrapped around his little finger? Why does he have so much power over you?"

"That's none of your business." She produced a stake seemingly out of nowhere and held it tightly in her hand as she glared at him.

He raised an eyebrow and took her in from head to feet. "Where did you have that hiding? I'm impressed."

"Give me the map or I'm going to kill you."

His lips curled into an unpleasant smile and he shook his head. "You're going to have to put your money where your mouth is, sweetheart."

"You think I won't do it?" She slammed her forearm against his chest, pressing him up against the truck. There was no humor in her expression. "Because I will. I don't know you, Quinn. I don't know a damn thing about you anymore, other than the fact that you're a vampire. Do you know what I usually do to vamps that get in my way?"

"Talk them to death?"

"No, I do the same thing you did for ten years. I kill them."

"Then do it, Janie."

She blinked.

"Do it," he repeated. "Kill me. If you kill me, you can take the map. I have it on me right now, and I'm not planning on giving it to you. If I don't find the Eye, then I've got nothing. And if I'm stuck as a vampire, then I'd rather be dead. You understand me? So do me a favor—kill me and put me out of my misery."

He swallowed as he felt the needle-sharp end of the stake dig into his flesh. His stomach still stung from Malcolm staking him last night. Having a fresh infusion of blood had helped to heal it up, but it still hurt like a son of a bitch. First time staked. This would be the second time. He wasn't planning on being around for a third.

He held her gaze and thought for a moment that she was actually going to do it. In that moment, he felt a flash of something unexpected go through him. Panic? Fear?

However, instead of killing him, she pulled the stake away and looked at him with a frown.

He let out a small laugh—whether it was from relief or amusement even he wasn't sure. The sound of it made her eyes narrow, and she slapped him hard against the side of his face, just short of a full punch.

He rubbed his stinging cheek. "Ow."

She shoved a finger in his face. "Don't laugh at me."

"I wasn't."

Then, before he could stop her she was on him, patting him down as though she was a cop and he was under arrest. Suddenly, she slid a hand into the front pocket of his pants, which took him by surprise in more ways than one.

"Hey!" he managed. "A little too early for that sort of thing."

"Don't flatter yourself." She pulled out folded paper.

The map.

Just goes to show, a gorgeous woman grabs his pants and he forgets his own name, let alone how to stop her. Guess he wasn't as changed as he thought he was.

The note he wrote earlier fell to the ground, and before he could bend over to pick it up, she beat him to it. She unfolded it, holding the map in her other hand, and read it.

Her eyes moved over the few lines he'd written and her forehead creased. She looked up at him.

"You were going to tell me about my sister?"

"Of course I was."

She studied him for a moment. "And you were going to leave this and disappear. Is that it?"

"That was the original plan."

She shoved the note into her pocket. "Plans change."

"Don't I know it."

She unfolded the map and looked at it briefly, and then her blue eyes flicked up to meet his again. "Get in the truck."

"Why? Are you going to set it on fire?"

"Maybe later. But right now you're going to drive it."

"Where?"

"To find the Eye."

"You and me?"

"That's right. I'm no damn good at following maps. We're going to find it together."

"And then?"

"And then all bets are off. But we'll deal with that when the time comes."

He swallowed hard again. "Are you sure you want to be alone with me, after . . . after what happened last night?"

She rolled her eyes. "Obviously you're putting way too much meaning into that. How many times do I have to tell you it was nothing? It's over. Let's move the hell on. I've got places I need to be."

He grabbed the truck door. "Fine."

"Good." She walked around to the other side and got in.

So she didn't hate him, he thought. She was indifferent. That made things much, much easier.

What are you doing? Janie's conscience scolded her. *Are you a stupid bimbo? Are you? B-I-M-B-O. That is your new name. Why did you let the jerk vampire come along for the ride? You can't read a map? WHAT THE HELL ARE YOU SMOKING?*

She cleared her throat and stared out the window.

Okay, so she lied. She could read a map just fine. Especially this one. It looked like a frigging treasure map from *Pirates of the Caribbean.* X even marked the damned spot.

Damn. Damn. Damn.

She'd been fine and dandy until she read that stupid note.

The part where it said: *Touching you sends me over the*

edge of sanity, and I don't want to hurt you like I did last night ever again.

And that was on top of the look he gave her when he thought she was going to kill him. If every vampire had given her that look, then she would have been completely screwed. Literally and figuratively. He just looked so achingly hopeless and despondent that she wanted to slap him or kiss all of his pain away.

The slap would have to do for now.

She'd convinced herself, while tossing and turning on her hard motel mattress last night, that she hated him. She'd *convinced* herself. And now the damn note had to change that again.

She'd felt like the Grinch when his tiny little shriveled-up heart swelled to three times its size. Which was painful and rather inconvenient. She'd never driven anyone over the "edge of sanity" before—at least not that she was aware of.

But maybe he literally meant she drove him insane. Like the drooling, straitjacket kind of insane. That wouldn't be good.

"Looks like we need to follow the map from the beginning to the end," Quinn said. "It's not to any sort of scale I've ever seen before. Looks like a kid drew it."

He was right about that much, and she took a moment to study the map for the first time with all her attention. There were scrawling, hump-like marks to the left side of the page that she was fairly confident represented mountains—probably the Superstition Mountains, which were close by. Four main symbols, very roughly drawn, decorated the page. A squiggle that looked like a child's drawing of a ghost. From there, a dotted line connected to a tree-like shape that was marked in barely discernible writing: *Asesino del Monstro.* Then a picture of a bird of some kind took up the right side of the page. Past the bird, the last symbol was a square shape marked "desert ridge," which was rather obviously, she decided, the ridge of some desert. A small X was marked on the upper right-hand corner of the square.

Who'd drawn this thing? The fact that it led to something so important was truly ridiculous. Maybe Malcolm had put one over on them. Why did she trust what he'd said? Well, mostly because she didn't have any other choice, that's why.

She held the map up so Quinn could see it and pointed at the mountains. "I figure those represent the Superstition Mountains?"

"Looks like just lines to me."

"That's not very helpful. I think it's the mountains. And we're looking for . . . what do you think that's supposed to be?"

He took his eyes off the road for a moment to squint down. "Definitely a ghost."

"Our first stop is the ghost."

"That's as clear as mud."

She glanced out of the window and to the side of the road. "There's a tourism office. Pull off here."

"We can figure it out."

"Pull off the road. Geez, you men are all the same. Let's ask for directions."

She got out of the car just as her cell phone rang. Quinn went in the office ahead of her.

She glanced at the call display and cringed, but then held the phone to her ear. "Yes?"

"Do you have it?" the Boss snapped.

"I . . . I . . ."

"It's a simple question, Parker. *Do you have the Eye?*"

"I'm so close I can taste it."

There was silence that made Janie's arms break out in goose bumps, and a trickle of sweat slid down her spine. Out of the corner of her eye, she watched a small, light brown scorpion creep under the truck.

"I want it. I'm about to leave for Vegas right now."

"I know."

"*Do you* know how much I want the Eye? How could you possibly? Obviously you don't, or you would already have it. Tell me, Parker, what is the problem?"

The question was, what wasn't the problem?

"There's no problem. There's simply a delay. As we speak I'm on my way to get it."

"So you still feel confident that you will not fail me and face my consequences."

Confident? Not so much.

"Absolutely. I won't fail, Boss. I swear it."

"And the vampire. Are you still with him?"

She eyed the tourism office. Through the large glass doors she could see Quinn lean over the counter to talk to a middle-aged woman with beer bottle glasses who handed him a brochure or booklet.

"Yes, I'm still with him."

"He must be part of the problem, Parker. My new seer tells me that there is a conflict of interest for you that centers around the vampire."

"Your seer is wrong."

"I've changed the protocol of this mission. Not only do I want the Eye brought to me in Vegas by this evening, but I want you to kill the vampire."

Janie's throat tightened. "I don't think that will be necessary—"

"Kill him," the Boss snapped. "And bring me the proof that you did it. A picture, his head, a sample of his remains, it matters not. Kill him, or I will eviscerate your sister while you watch and then I shall do the same to you."

The phone clicked dead.

She stared at it with her heart pounding in her ears.

Quinn emerged from the office. He was actually smiling beneath his dark sunglasses. "That woman was really helpful. Who knew asking for directions could actually be a good thing?"

She didn't reply.

"She gave me all of these pamphlets." He handed three tri-fold brochures to Janie. "And on top of that, she originally thought a ghost might represent a psychic fair, but then she changed her mind when she remembered that there's a closed-off ghost town called Semolina that's a little north of here." He paused. "Janie? What's wrong?"

She shoved the pamphlets in her purse without looking at them and stared at him, wondering how she would do it. Wooden stake? Silver bullet? She felt her eyes moisten and squeezed off her emotions so she wouldn't cry. Not here. Not like this.

"A ghost town," she repeated. "Well, that makes sense."

He studied her with concern shadowing his expression. "Who was on the phone? Why do you look like somebody just died?"

"Nobody died." *Not yet, anyhow.* "It's nothing. Let's go."

She got into the truck and sat there with every muscle

in her body tense. Her boss hadn't been kidding. If he said he wanted evidence of Quinn's death, then he wanted hard proof. There was no wiggle room for deception. Besides, his damn seers would know if he was really dead.

She had no choice. She had to slay him and she had to do it before she got to Vegas.

Just another vampire to add to her list of kills. It had to be done. But she could wait a bit longer.

First she wanted the Eye.

Then Quinn would have to die.

Ah, a rhyme, she thought. *Lenny would be so proud.*

Chapter 12

Ghost towns were called ghost towns for a reason, and that's because they were deserted and run down. Semolina was no exception.

However, Quinn finally got to see his tumbleweed.

Time well spent, he thought absently.

The tumbleweed blew past a sign in the road that blocked off access to the heart of the ghost town.

It read: DO NOT PASS—DANGER—PRIVATE PROPERTY.

He shifted into park and glanced over at Janie. "Now what?"

She turned to look at him and blinked. "What?"

She'd been acting really strange ever since he'd come out of the tourism office. As if something big and dark was hanging over her head that made it hard for her to concentrate. He wondered who'd been on the phone and what they'd told her. He was willing to bet it had been this boss of hers, whom he hated more with every passing minute.

He nodded at the sign ahead of them. "What should we do?"

She took a moment to look at the sign. "We have to drive around it. The map leads north of the town, and that's where this road seems to go. Otherwise, we might get off track."

"Can't we just figure out what the next landmark is?"

She studied the map, tracing a finger along the lines. "It's looks like a tree. Or a huge black monster."

"I hope it's a tree."

"There's writing under it that says *Asesino del Monstro*."

"Yeah. I saw that already. My Spanish is rusty, but doesn't that mean 'the killer of monsters'?"

"Something like that."

"Sounds like a fun tree."

She nodded at the small collection of dilapidated buildings. "Let's go."

Quinn backed up and maneuvered the truck around the sign. He began driving toward the town on the very bumpy and rocky dirt road.

It looked very similar to what he'd expected. The buildings were all brown and tan from the dust and sand in the area. Very little vegetation other than a few cacti. Old wagon wheels as tall as the truck were up against the sides of the buildings. He half expected Clint Eastwood to emerge out of one of the doors, wearing a duster and a cowboy hat, a cigarillo clenched between his teeth.

He remembered learning about the gold rush back in public school before his father had pulled him out to homeschool him using humorless, personality-deficient tutors who couldn't have cared less if Quinn understood what they were teaching him or not.

So he knew that this is where, more than a hundred years ago, the town would have been erected to support all the men who had gold fever. Searching the mountains and caves and riverbeds for their fortune. They either found it or they didn't, but sooner or later they grew weary of Semolina, and it was deserted, ravaged by nature for the next century, and left as this sad, rather eerie shell.

A shiver went down his back. He didn't like it here. Not at all. It felt almost as if someone was watching him from behind the dirty, broken windows of the ramshackle buildings in the middle of the town.

The creepy feeling was getting worse. What did the sign mean by "Danger," anyhow? He understood "Do Not Pass" and "Private Property." But "Danger"? For a ghost town?

Once they'd rolled into the dead center of town, the truck chugged and coughed and came to a rolling stop. Quinn tried the ignition, which produced only a sad, metallic chewing noise.

He looked at Janie. "You don't know how to fix cars, do you?"

"Of course I do."

He couldn't help but feel surprised. He'd rarely met a woman who would willingly pump her own gas, let alone fix a broken truck. He was impressed.

"I need to call Lenny first." She opened her door and got out, pulling her cell phone out of her pocket. She looked at the screen. "No service?"

"Call him after the truck's fixed."

She glared at him. "I already have a boss ordering me around, thanks."

"This isn't my fault, you know," he said, stifling a grin

at her over-the-top annoyance. "Next time I steal a car I'll have the transmission checked out first."

"This isn't funny."

"No, it definitely isn't." He shielded his eyes from the relentless sun. "Do you think it's possible that it's brighter here than anywhere else on earth?"

She glanced up. "Whatever. I'll be over there."

He adjusted his sunglasses and jogged after Janie, trying to ignore the nagging feeling that somebody was watching them. She still had the map. He wasn't letting her out of his sight.

NO SERVICE

"Terrific," she said aloud. "Just terrific."

She hadn't had a moment alone since speaking with the Boss. She desperately needed to ask Lenny what she should do. Obviously, she wasn't thinking straight since Lenny wouldn't have any problem at all with the prospect of offing Quinn, but he was a good sounding board.

She wondered if Lenny and Barkley had reached Vegas yet. She felt at her neck. She never took off the turquoise necklace, and she felt naked without it on. It was her touchstone to the past, to Angela and to a much, much simpler time. Every time she was stressed out or nervous, she'd run her fingertips over it, which helped to immediately calm her down.

She could really use it right about now.

Quinn marched up next to her and just stood there without saying anything. Dammit, being so near him was way too distracting—and not only because she found him painfully attractive, but because she now knew she had to end his life despite how she felt about him.

"Any luck?" he asked.

"Luck must be something I left behind at the motel along with my moisturizer."

"I'll take that as a no?" He glanced over his shoulder, then turned back to face her. A frown wrinkled his brow above his sunglasses.

"What?" she asked.

"Did the brochure happen to mention any reason why Semolina is blocked off to tourists?"

"You got the brochures, not me."

He nodded at her. "Read it."

She sighed, dug out one of the rolled-up brochures he'd given her earlier out of her handbag, and flipped forward through the pages. "It says that it was blocked off to outside access twenty years ago due to unusual disturbances in the area."

"Unusual disturbances?"

She nodded. "It says that in 1870 the town was abandoned when two men after the same treasure killed each other in a gunfight. Soon after that, everyone else living here just packed up and left." She shoved the brochure back into her bag. "What difference does it make?"

He shrugged. "Do you think a ghost town might actually have real ghosts in it?"

"It's called a ghost town because it's abandoned. Not because of any excessive paranormal activity."

"You ever done any ghostbusting in your career?" he asked evenly.

"Not my area of expertise."

He looked at her grimly. "That's too bad."

She frowned. "Why?"

He nodded back in the direction of the truck. "Because I think that would help right about now."

She looked over and blinked hard. Their truck was hovering five feet off the ground as if raised by an invisible hand. A *big* invisible hand.

She started toward it.

"Stop," Quinn shouted, but when she didn't stop, he followed her.

She looked at the car and reached out to touch it. "That's so strange."

"Don't get too close," Quinn warned.

The car suddenly shot up high into the blue sky until it became no more than a black speck.

"Janie, get out of the way!" Quinn yelled.

He grabbed her by her shoulders and tackled her to the ground. He fell down on top of her and rolled the both of them off to the side of the dusty street and held her tight against him.

She heard a whistling sound, and the ground shook as the truck hit the earth, crushed on impact. She breathed through a cloud of dust that surrounded them. If she hadn't moved, she would be a dusty blond pancake. Quinn just saved her life.

What was wrong with her? She was normally way more alert to danger.

"Are you okay?" he asked, looking down at her, pulling her hair gently off her face.

She was about to answer, but somebody else spoke instead.

"What have we here?" the voice drawled. "I think I see trespassers. In *my* town."

Quinn scrambled to his feet, and Janie got up behind

him, looking over his shoulder at the man who approached then. He had a scraggly gray moustache. Brown chaps, a dirty, once-white shirt, and a weathered black leather vest. He wore a cowboy hat and boots that had spurs that jingled as he approached. A shotgun rested over one shoulder.

His face was very white and his eyes sunken with black shadows under them despite the sunny skies above. He was chewing tobacco and spat out a long stream of brown, disgusting goo to one side.

He also had a big red bloodstain in the center of his chest.

"Who the hell are you?" Quinn sounded much calmer than his tense arm against Janie's back told her he really was.

"Name's Jebediah Masters. And this here's my town."

"You're a ghost?"

Jebediah spat again. "You are trespassing."

"We're just passing through." Janie racked her brain for what she knew about ghost hunting. No priests nearby to do an emergency exorcism. No Ouija boards. And they definitely didn't need a medium to help relay the message from beyond, since the ghost was speaking to them as clear as day in the middle of the street. Without true experts on call, the best thing to do with ghosts was to reason with them. But since most ghosts were completely unreasonable, that didn't exactly give her a sense of comfort. "Did you do that to our truck?"

He glanced over at the decimated vehicle. And spat again. "I sure did, little missy. But you wouldn't be going far without no horses to draw your strange wagon, now, would you?"

"It's not a wagon—" Quinn began.

"Silence, trespassers! Ain't nobody come here trying to take my gold. That's why you're here, in't?"

Quinn eyed him. "Come on, Janie. He's just a ghost. He can't do anything to us. Let's get out of here."

He took her arm, and they turned their backs on the ornery prospector.

The sound of a bullet hitting the wall right next to them, blowing off a chunk of stone, froze them in their tracks.

"Who said you could leave? There's only one way I'm letting you leave, and that's after you're dead."

They turned around slowly. Quinn moved so that he was completely blocking Janie's view. "Stay behind me."

"I don't need you to protect me, you know."

"Shh. A gunshot won't kill me unless it's silver, but it'll kill you."

"But he's a ghost," she whispered. "He's incorporeal, right?"

"That bullet wasn't incorporeal. Now be quiet."

He was protecting her? From the big bad gun-wielding ghost? If she didn't think his dominating alpha hero actions were so offensive to her as an independent woman, she might think it was rather sweet.

Stupid. But sweet.

Would he still try to protect her if he knew she'd been instructed to kill him herself?

"Wait a minute." Janie said to Jebediah as she moved out from behind Quinn to instead put herself between him and the gun. "Why don't we talk about this for a second?"

He lowered the gun and looked her up and down. And spat.

"We don't get pretty little things like you much here in Semolina."

"Oh?" She glanced at Quinn.

"No. We had Miss Greta and her whorehouse for a while, but she found the men here not to her liking. But you are much prettier than any of them whores." Jebediah approached, his attention focused on Janie's body. "Yes. Real pretty thing. Must be my lucky day. Tell me, pretty, do you like gold?"

She held her ground. "I prefer cash."

He was uglier the closer he got. He reached out and was about to touch Janie's face with his dirty hand, when Quinn's hand shot out and caught his wrist. Actually caught him, as if he was solid and not just a ghost.

"Don't you dare touch her," he growled.

The gun moved to press against Quinn's temple. "Nobody tells me what I can and cannot do."

Janie bit her bottom lip and was afraid to move in case the ghost pulled the trigger. Bullets didn't kill vampires, that was very true. There had been an assignment she was on last year, hunting down an insane vampire, and all she'd had was a Glock filled with lead bullets. She'd shot him ten times. Ruined his frilly shirt, but didn't even slow the vamp down.

However, she hadn't been aiming for the head.

Decapitation was another way to kill a vamp. Not pretty and very messy, but it did the trick. A shotgun wound at this range would probably do just that.

She could let the ghost kill Quinn—it would save her having to do it later.

"Don't hurt him," she finally said.

He turned and smiled, showing brown, broken teeth. "And what can I expect from you if I spare his life?"

"Anything," she said quickly.

"Janie—" Quinn breathed. "What are you doing?"

Jebediah hooked his middle finger into the top of her tank top and pulled the material down, exposing more cleavage and the edge of her lacy black bra.

"Yeah," he breathed. "Miss Greta was nothin' compared to you."

"Jebediah Masters!" another voice called out from the other side of the street. A feminine voice that sounded very pissed off. "You good-for-nothing bastard, take your hands off that dirty whore!"

His hand shot back from her shirt and he cringed. Quinn's hand tightened around Janie's waist and he pulled her against him and back a step.

"Mary-Ann, I told you not to bother me no more."

A woman emerged onto the street from a wall of the dusty building marked "Saloon." She was wearing an outfit very similar to Jebediah's, only she had a long brown skirt on instead of pants. She did hold a matching shotgun and sported a matching red stain on the front of her white blouse. She scowled at him.

"I curse the day I ever married you, you whoring, thieving, sheep-loving, back-stabbing—"

"Be quiet, woman! What do I need to do to shut your mouth once and for all?"

"Take your filthy eyes off her bosoms."

With a frustrated growl, Jebediah turned away from Janie's bosoms and stormed off the street and walked right through the solid wall of a building.

Mary-Ann approached. "I'm sorry for my husband's behavior. He was obviously brought up in a barn."

Janie looked at the woman warily.

Mary-Ann laughed at her expression. "Don't you be worrying. I mean you no harm. Just got to keep my man in line." She glanced over at what was left of the pile of twisted metal. "Sorry he did that to your truck."

Janie and Quinn shared a look.

Mary-Ann laughed harder. "Oh, he's not entirely sure what's going on, but I'm well aware that I'm stuck haunting this town 'til the end of time with that worthless man." She shrugged. "That's what greed gets you. Better'n hell, I suppose."

"Is the other prospector still around?" Quinn looked around the main street. "The one who was in the gunfight with Jebediah?"

She waved at her red-stained blouse. "That would be me. Both of us were good shots, don't you think?"

"You shot each other? Over gold?"

"We both wanted it. We fought hard to get it. And when it came down to him or me having the gold, then we fought. Didn't even occur to us to share, even with our wedding vows."

"And now you're stuck together," Janie said.

Mary-Ann gazed off in the direction of her husband. "Forever and ever, amen. And now that he keeps scaring off the tourists, it's just the two of us."

Janie took the story in and tried not to see any parallels between her and Quinn. They were both after the same thing. She had been instructed to kill him to get it. Did he feel the same way? Would he fight her for the Eye? Would he try to kill her when it came right down to it?

Just then, Quinn slid his hand down to grab hers. She looked at him with surprise, but he was focused on Mary-Ann.

"So you're not going to shoot us?" he asked.

She raised an eyebrow. "Not unless you give me reason. And as long as your woman keeps her filthy paws off my husband—"

Janie made a face. "I wasn't even touching him!"

"—then we don't have a problem. You can be off now. I won't try to stop you."

As if Janie would touch a creepy old ghost with a ten-foot pole. "Great. Well, since the truck is now beyond repair, I guess we're on foot." She glanced at Quinn. "Just got to find the *Asesino del Monstro*."

Mary-Ann gasped. "You're looking for the *Asesino del Monstro?*"

Janie nodded and grabbed the map out of her purse. "Yeah, you know it? I figure it's a few miles north of here, right?"

Mary-Ann held up a hand to block the map from her view. "Leave now. Go. And don't come back."

"Can you tell me—"

Mary-Ann faded away until she was completely gone.

Janie turned to Quinn with a frown. "That was rude."

"At least she didn't try to shoot us."

He was looking at her funny.

Her frown deepened. "What?"

"Why did you tell Jebediah that you'd do anything if he didn't hurt me?"

Good question, she thought.

She looked away. "Because if he shot your head off you wouldn't be much good to me, would you?"

"It's not like you need me. You could find the Eye all by yourself."

"Are you trying to give me ideas here?"

"No. Just stating facts."

"Yeah, well, don't do that. And thanks for pushing me out of the way of the falling truck. I was obviously doing my impression of 'deer in headlights.'"

"You hurt your head." He reached up to push the hair off her forehead. "You're bleeding."

She felt at her forehead, pulling her fingers away to see that he was right. Her head stung a bit, but it felt like a minor injury. "Well, don't go getting any ideas for an early lunch. I'll be okay."

His hand twisted into her hair and he gazed into her eyes. "Good."

She put a hand on his chest and could feel his heart beating—slowly. Vampires's hearts beat much slower than humans, but they still beat.

She wanted him to move away from her immediately. Being this close to him made her mind fog up. She couldn't forget what she had to do. Find the Eye and—now that she hadn't let Jeb do her dirty work—kill Quinn, whether or not she wanted to.

But he didn't move away from her. Instead he lowered his face and kissed her forehead. Her body clenched at the feel of his lips against her skin. Then he backed up a step.

"Because if you're not okay, I'm not carrying you," he continued, giving her a wicked grin before he turned to walk out of the ghost town.

She trudged after him, her body tingling from where he'd touched her, cursing her lot in life to have fallen for a man whose life she'd have to end to save her sister's.

Chapter 13

*H*e *had* to get rid of Janie as soon as possible. She managed to do things to him, without even touching him, that other women had to work very hard at. Just one look in her beautiful blue eyes and all he wanted to do was protect her.

But Janie Parker didn't need his protection.

Well, maybe from the falling truck, but that was about it.

The way she'd stood up to the ghost? She'd protected *him*. He wasn't used to that. Nobody usually protected him from anything.

He damn well liked her way too much. Forget infatuation. Forget lusting after her body. Those things were too simple for what he was feeling.

He *liked* her. As a person. And that "like" was growing stronger every moment he spent near her, growing into something larger and deeper and much scarier than anything he'd faced before.

The last woman he'd thought himself in love with told him that he was fooling himself. That his feelings for her were simply those of gratitude for friendship and kindness during a rough time in his life. He'd convinced himself he was in love with her, and he had been. A little.

But *this*. He knew this was much different, and it felt way more complicated.

Shit.

She walked ahead of him on the road. Conversation had slowed to nothing at all, and they trekked along the dusty trail. They'd been walking for nearly an hour since leaving the ghost town and seen nothing at all except mountains and cacti and dirt. Not even one car had come along.

He watched her move along at a clip. She never complained about her feet, or that she needed to take a break. She now carried her jacket, and he focused exclusively on her perfect ass in her tight black jeans as she moved along ahead of him.

The ass of the enemy, he thought absently. Which suddenly stopped in its tracks.

She got the map out and looked at it.

He'd been so focused on watching her walk that he hadn't even noticed the big black tree they'd come up to.

It was well over twenty feet tall, with a thick trunk leading to hundreds of sharp branches. The whole thing was the color of coal, and it bore no leaves, as if it had been on fire once and died but still refused to give up. It was surrounded by a low fence, and a plaque was attached to the trunk.

ASESINO DEL MONSTRO

Legend has it that this tree was enchanted by a Navajo tribal chief as protection against forces of evil that could threaten the land that surrounds it. While the tree does not show any outward signs of life, it continues to grow at a rate of one inch per annum, which makes it a true Arizonian mystery.

"Pretty," Quinn said.

Janie was looking at the map again. "According to this, we need to go west toward the bird thing. If it's to scale based on what we just walked to get here, I figure it's about fifteen miles away. And then past the desert ridge we should get to the big rectangle with the X on it. Simple."

They could hear a humming sound.

Quinn listened. "The highway must be over there."

"We can hitch a ride." Janie looked at her cell phone again. "I can't believe there's still no service. I seriously need to go with another service provider."

Quinn walked around the circumference of the tree. "Sure is ugly."

"It fights evil."

"So it says. I wonder how it works."

A scorpion moved toward the park bench to the far right of the tree. They were the scariest bugs he'd ever seen, and they seemed to be everywhere in the state. He turned to look at Janie instead of at the ugly tree behind him. She made for a much better view.

He forced a smile. "So, now what?"

She just stared at him, her eyes growing wider by the second.

"Janie?"

"Quinn," she said quietly. "Walk toward me right now. Don't turn around."

"What?"

He felt something brush against his leg, and he looked down.

It was black and thin, and hard as a rock, and twining around his ankle. It looked like a branch from the tree. Another branch did the same to his other ankle.

He looked over his shoulder and his heart thudded against his rib cage. The Asesino del Monstro had leaned over in his direction, all of its sharp branches now pointing at him. The thinner branches had grown and escaped from the fenced-in area to touch him.

Monster killer.

He tried to yank away from it. "I can't move," he said, looking up to meet Janie's wide-eyed gaze. She had her gun out. The branch tightened at his ankle.

Another branch wound around his chest as if it was an anaconda, the sharp tip of it rising to eye level. It seemed to be assessing him. The branch around his chest felt dry and brittle but still strong enough to snap him in half if it chose to.

"Quinn!" Janie shouted.

Then the branch reared back and thrust at his shoulder, piercing his flesh. He yelled out in pain.

He was going to die. The tree was going to tear him apart.

Janie shot once, and the branch around his chest dropped to the ground. Another shot and his right leg was free. A third and his left was free. He scrambled away from the tree as fast as he could, holding a hand to his wounded shoulder.

The tree seemed to hiss and growl at them, and Janie felt a tingling magic sweep through the air. It hurt like hell. And then the tree was still and as dead as it looked when they first arrived.

There was a bench to their left, and Janie helped Quinn over to it. She felt as shocked as Quinn looked.

"I told you to move." Janie's words were sharp and curt. "When I tell you to do something, you should do it."

"Noted."

She pulled his black T-shirt down and away from his shoulder and inspected the wound. She let out a long exhale. "It's just a scratch."

"Sure as hell doesn't feel like just a scratch."

"You're damn lucky. It must have only been checking you out."

He snorted. "To find out how much of a monster I was. Well, it sensed it, didn't it? That I'm a vampire? The tree was programmed right. You should have let it do what it had to do and kill me."

She slapped him. He looked at her with shock and held a hand up to his face. "What the hell was that for?"

Her face felt flushed, and she knew her eyes must look glossy from the tears she was holding back. "Don't talk about yourself like that. You don't deserve to die that way."

"Of course I do. I'm a monster, Janie."

"You're a vampire. That's true. But you're not a monster. I've seen lots of vamps—and a hell of a lot of humans too—that deserved death more than you do." Every word she said was the truth. He didn't deserve to die. Not from the tree, and not from her boss's orders. "Why do you have to be so stubborn?"

"How can you say that after what happened last night?"

She turned away. "I wanted that to happen. I told you to bite me."

He shook his head. "The tree knew—"

"The stupid tree doesn't know anything. Not a damn thing. The way it loomed behind you, all of those sharp wooden branches." She swallowed hard.

He tried to smile. "Thought you'd be rid of me once and for all?"

That earned him another slap.

"Ow." He frowned. "I think I've had enough violence for one—"

Then, without allowing herself to think twice about it, she grabbed his face and kissed him hard on the mouth. He seemed stunned by this unexpected action before he grabbed her and pulled her against him, raking his fingers along her back. She traced her tongue along his lips and then kissed his face, his cheeks, his forehead, his chin, before focusing on his mouth again.

After a minute, they parted, and she shot up to her feet and paced back and forth. Her cheeks felt even hotter than before.

"Goddammit!" she yelled. "I so don't need this right now!"

He just looked up at her. "Janie—"

"No." She held a finger up to stop him. "Don't say anything. Not a word."

He pressed his lips together.

"I don't like you," she said. "Just for the record."

"Understood."

"You're in the way of what I want. And if you knew what I'm supposed to do . . . dammit." She stopped talking.

He finally got to his feet. "Janie—"

"You're a vampire," she cut him off. "Not exactly a good thing for me, considering the business I'm in. And that isn't even taking into consideration my current assignment."

"Got it."

She pressed her hands against her burning face. "I mean, Lenny writes poetry for me. *Poetry.* It's bad poetry, sure, but he means it. He likes me. I wish I could like him back the way he wants me to, but I can't. And now this? You're a pain in the ass, Quinn. I don't care what you were like when I was a kid, or what I thought of you then. Times have changed."

"Of course they have."

She let out a long, shuddery sigh. "I have to find Angela."

He nodded. "You're a good sister."

"Damn right I am. And when we get that Eye, none of this means anything. You hear me? It means *nothing*."

He kept nodding and stood up from the bench.

If she kept talking, would she forget that all she wanted to do was kiss him again? When she kissed him, nothing else seemed to matter.

"So I think we better go," she said. "Like I said before, as soon as we get the Eye, then it's every man or woman for him- or herself—"

He kissed her again, and she tried to decide if she should slap him again, but then she just sighed shakily against his lips and kissed him back, holding him as tightly to her as it was possible to do while still fully clothed.

And it was true. For a moment, nothing else mattered.

"Excuse me, ma'am?" Something tugged at her shirt. "Could you take our picture?"

Quinn broke off the kiss with a loud groan of annoyance, and Janie looked down. A little girl, about six years old, looked up at her with a smile. The girl held out a pink disposable camera to her. Janie looked behind the little girl at two adults who were examining the now benign tree.

She forced a smile. "Of course."

Quinn let go of her, and she noted that his eyes held a mixture of desire and regret. Regret that they'd been interrupted, or regret that they'd kissed in the first place?

The little girl pushed her camera into her hand and skipped over to her parents and the tree. They followed, but Quinn froze in place before he got any closer.

Janie noted his stricken look. "Wait here."

She squeezed his hand before she went over and got the family to pose in place, taking their picture in front of the thing that had nearly torn Quinn into pieces.

Quinn stared at the monster-killer tree while he waited for Janie and reviewed what had happened in his mind over and over.

She'd kissed *him,* right? Or had he just imagined that?

He eyed the tree warily.

Some tourist attraction.

"Our car broke down," he heard Janie say. "We had to walk a couple of miles to get here."

"Well, that's not a very nice way to spend such a beautiful day," the mother said. "We'd be happy to give you a ride back into the city."

"We would really appreciate that." Janie smiled and glanced at Quinn. "Isn't that nice of them?"

"Terrific."

The family took some more pictures and a bit of video, and then everyone crawled into their rented trailer. The couple's names were Bob and Sue-Ellen. The little girl was Sabrina.

Sabrina sat next to Quinn, staring up at him in a way that made him very uncomfortable.

"You were kissing her," she said.

"Hmm? What did you say?"

"You were kissing her," she said again. "I drew a picture."

She showed him a notebook that had two people kissing. Well, it looked more like two blobs with eyes. One was green and one was blue. Quinn wondered which one he was supposed to be.

"Nice," he said.

"I draw all the time. Not much else to do. No TV in here. I get really bored."

"Drawing is a good use of your time." He looked at Janie. She was sitting in the front of the trailer, talking to Bob and Sue-Ellen. He had a funny feeling she was trying to avoid him. Maybe he should ask for a copy of Sabrina's drawing, since it would probably be his only reminder that their kiss ever happened in the first place.

No, this was good. Get to the city. Then rent a car or, better yet, get the map and run far away from Janie.

No, not run away. He wasn't trying to escape her. He

wasn't afraid of her. She had no power over him. None. Zero.

"See?" Sabrina said, flipping through her drawings. "I drew a mountain. And a bear. That's a cactus—"

"It's a red cactus," Quinn noted.

"It was during a sunset." She looked at him like he was stupid before her attention went back to her sketch pad. "Here's my mom and dad. That's a bird."

Before she turned the page, Quinn stopped her, trying to get a better look at the bird she'd drawn. It looked awfully familiar.

"Janie!" he called.

Her shoulders tensed and she slowly looked over her shoulder with a frozen smile on her face. "Yes?"

"Do you have the map handy?"

"The . . . the map?" She blinked.

"Yeah, the one that's hiding in your purse. I need to see it."

She made her way to the back of the trailer. "I think I'll hold on to it if you don't mind."

"Look." He pointed at the drawing.

She nodded. "That's a very good picture. You're very talented, Sadie."

"My name's *Sabrina*, lady."

Quinn sighed. "Look closer."

She peered down at the sketch before her eyebrows went up. Then she scrabbled through her bag, pulling out the map.

"It's just like the bird symbol," she said. "Almost exactly. Sabrina, sweetie, why did you draw that?"

She shrugged. "I like birds."

"But why did you draw this one in particular? Did it

come to you in a vision? Like magic? You can tell us. We believe in that sort of thing. Where is it? Can you lead us to it? Close your eyes and try to remember. It's very, very important."

"Mommy!" Sabrina called. "These people are weird!"

"Be polite, Sabrina," her mother said.

Janie crouched down in front of her. "Now, if you don't tell us, Sabrina, a lot of people are going to get hurt. Puppies and kittens are going to die and it will be all your fault. Do you understand me?"

"Janie—" Quinn murmured. "I don't think that's necessary."

She frowned. "I don't know how to reason with kids."

Sabrina rolled her eyes. She reached underneath a pile of books and magazines and grabbed one of the same Arizona tourism brochures that Quinn had picked up earlier. "I thought it was pretty, so I put my paper over it and traced it."

Quinn looked down at the cover of the brochure.

"Shit," he breathed, then looked up the little girl sheepishly. "I mean, *shoot.*"

Between the two of them, they couldn't figure out what even a little girl knew. It wasn't his proudest moment.

The bird symbol on the map to the Eye represented a Phoenix. And it was used on the City of Phoenix sign outside of City Hall.

Which is where, a half hour later, they had Bob and Sue-Ellen drop them off.

Janie consulted the map again, then looked around, shaking her head and sighing with frustration. "According to this, our next stop is a desert ridge. But how can that be in the middle of a city?"

"I've learned my lesson," he said. "Sometimes it's a good idea to ask for directions."

Quinn grabbed her hand and pulled her toward a cab idling at the side of the road. The driver was out getting a hot dog from a street vendor.

"Can you help us?" Quinn asked him. "This is going to sound crazy, but we're looking to visit a desert ridge. We're told it's around here somewhere. Does that sound at all familiar to you?"

The cabbie took a bite of his hot dog, chewed slowly, swallowed, wiped the side of his mouth with a napkin, and then nodded.

"Sure, get in."

They got in the back of the cab and waited impatiently for the driver to finish his meal.

With every passing moment Janie felt more frustrated with their search. Time was running out, and they seemed to be getting no closer to finding the Eye.

Her chest hurt just thinking about it, and she let out a shaky sigh and looked out of the window at the driver, who was now eating his second hot dog. "My sister is going to die."

Quinn touched her shoulder, turning her around to face him. He was frowning. "What do you mean your sister is going to *die?*"

She bit her bottom lip. "I told you that my boss knows where she is. If I don't bring the Eye to him, he's going to kill her. He'll make me watch, and then he's going to kill me, too. He mentioned something about evisceration."

Her throat felt thick. She wasn't going to cry. She wasn't.

Quinn didn't say anything for a moment. "That's not going to happen."

She shook her head. "We're never going to find it. Maybe it was just a wild goose chase Malcolm's had us on. Maybe he's had the real map all of this time and he's playing us for fools."

"We're going to find it. And even if worst-case scenario, we don't, nothing is going to happen to your sister. Or you, for that matter. We'll go to Vegas and find her and protect her."

"You don't know my Boss."

"I don't give a shit about your Boss."

She snorted quietly at that. "Brave words for somebody who's never even met him before."

"Call Lenny. See if they've made any progress yet."

"They're probably not even in Vegas yet. They're in a Mustang, not a teleporter."

"Call him anyhow."

She looked down at the cell phone and laughed, just this side of hysterical. "Well, I probably have service now, but the battery's dead." She shook her head. "Nothing is going right today. Nothing."

"We're here," the cabbie said as they came to a stop.

"Here where?" Quinn asked.

"You wanted to go to desert ridge, right? That's where we are. That'll be ten bucks."

Quinn paid him and they exited the taxi, looking blankly at where they'd been dropped off.

Desert Ridge Marketplace. Which happened to be a huge outdoor shopping mall, complete with a multiscreen movie theater flanked by tall, groomed palm trees.

Chapter 14

A half hour later, Janie and Quinn had searched Desert Ridge Marketplace and had come up with zero clues about where the Eye might be. They stopped very briefly at an outdoor café, where Janie choked down a sandwich since she hadn't eaten all day.

Quinn hadn't ordered anything at all. He simply sat there waiting patiently for Janie to eat.

"Let's go." She slapped enough money on the table to cover the meal and a generous tip, and walked away from the restaurant, the food sitting heavily in her stomach.

If she was the praying type, she would pray that Barkley and Lenny found Angela. Her throat felt tight. Why hadn't she tried to contact Janie in the past five years she'd been missing? What was wrong with her? Didn't she think her sister had been worried about her?

Maybe she knew Janie was a coldhearted Merc who was no better than a hired killer.

She glanced over her shoulder at Quinn. Was that how *he* saw her?

Her boss snapped his twig-like fingers and she came running. She always thought it was out of fear, but maybe she was just as evil as he was.

However, she did have nicer skin. And when it came to fashion, there really was no comparison at all.

"Janie . . ." Quinn said from behind her. She stopped walking and turned to look at him.

"What?"

He was frowning. "That's strange."

"What is?"

"I thought the Eye would be hidden somewhere. Maybe buried like the stone in Malcolm's backyard."

"And you think it isn't?"

He pointed behind her. "Take a look at that."

She turned. The building next to the Marketplace was the Phoenix Native Art Museum. The structure, she noted, had a rectangular shape similar to the last drawing on the map.

But so did a lot of other buildings. Like, all of them.

She shrugged. "So?"

He raised an eyebrow at her. "X docs mark the spot."

On the side of the building, a shape was designed using colorful red and orange tiles that shone under the bright sun. It was in the shape of a large, unmistakable X.

"Huh."

"Yeah."

She shook her head, hardly believing what she was seeing. "If I ever meet the person who drew that map, I think I'm going to beat them senseless."

"I will hold them down for you."

She turned to look at him. "Do you really think it might be in there?"

"Only one way to find out."

They stared at each other. This was it. Were they supposed to race for it now? Fight for it? All bets were off? Whoever got the Eye first was the winner?

He voiced her thoughts. "Let's just find it and take it from there."

She nodded. "Sounds like a plan."

They walked up to the building and went in through the front doors. There was a five-dollar charge to get in.

The museum was practically deserted. Only one employee was out front. The Phoenix Native Art Museum didn't have many artifacts, but what they did have were widely distributed to fill the large building. The museum wasn't even mentioned in the tourism handbook.

Quinn and Janie walked through the halls and into the adjoining rooms. There was an overview of the Grand Canyon, which included a scale model. Some arrowheads and other objects were kept under glass with long descriptions nearby. It was a learning experience. And Janie wasn't in the mood to learn anything at the moment.

She entered another room that contained a huge stuffed black bear, reared up on its hind legs. She eyed it curiously.

"Janie, check this out."

Quinn stood next to a glass table that had the Phoenix and surrounding area in miniature relief.

He pointed down. "Look familiar?"

She was surprised to see that it was the drawings on their map. A ghost shape, a monster tree, and a phoenix. Each of the symbols was explained on small gold plaques. Semolina, the ghost town. More information on it in another room, including the treasure that Jebediah and Mary-Ann fought to the death over. The *Asesino del Monstro*. A sample of its branches was available to be inspected close up in another part of the museum. And there was a huge history and historic overview of the city of Phoenix available in the museum, too.

No rectangle, but then again, she supposed they were standing in the middle of that landmark already.

"Bizarre coincidence?" he asked.

She shook her head. "We're close."

She felt something stirring within her. Where she'd almost given up, that empty, sick feeling was being replaced by a small amount of hope. Follow the vampire, the Boss had said. That's what the seers had told him.

Seers were rarely wrong. At least, not if they wanted to see another day. No pun intended.

"Maybe we could ask somebody." She looked around. Other than the two of them, the place was totally empty. She didn't even see any video cameras or security guards watching over the museum's contents.

"Tribal magic," Quinn said. He was reading another inscription next to the map. "That's why the symbols are so simple. Because they weren't drawn by hand; they were drawn with magic by a tribe that once worshiped the demon who owned the Eye."

"Magic, shmagic. Does it say where we can find it?"

He looked up at her and over her shoulder. "Holy shit."

She turned around. Enclosed in a glass case was a mannequin dressed in Indian wear, including a full ceremonial headdress. In its raised hand was a golden wand with a globe top. The plaque next to it read:

The Eye of Radisshii
The Radisshii tribe worshipped the demon Radisshii
until he was vanquished. The tribe died off as a whole
shortly after, and all that remains is this golden wand,
which was recently unearthed from the sacred lands.

She blinked. She could hardly believe her eyes. Right
there. Right in front of her. She didn't even have to check
the drawing she still had shoved in her back pocket. That
was the Eye. She glanced at Quinn.

"It can't be that simple, can it?" she breathed. "Why is
it right here? Right where anybody can see it?"

"Malcolm told us. It might have always been here, but
cloaked to anyone specifically searching for it. If we'd
come here before the map was revealed, we probably
wouldn't be able to see it at all. It would have been invisible to us."

"That is messed up."

He nodded. "So, what's the plan? Should we wait until
they close and then sneak back—"

With a well-placed roundhouse kick, she shattered the
glass case. An alarm immediately began to sound. She
reached through and grabbed the Eye, taking the mannequin's arm off in the process.

"—in tonight and grab it?" He blinked. "Or that's
good, too."

The alarm rang in Quinn's ears as he stood facing
Janie.

She stared at him. "I have the Eye."

"Yes, you do. And we should probably get the hell out

of here right now." He bit his bottom lip. "Why don't you give it to me?"

She grinned. "Yeah, right. Remember, handsome, I'm the one who has the gun." She reached under her jacket to her holster and frowned. "It's gone. My gun is gone."

"Did you drop it earlier?"

She shook her head. "I could have sworn I had it before we came in here."

He eyed her warily, a distinct feeling of uneasiness coming over him. This wasn't right. None of it. "Janie, we need to get out of here. Right now."

"Oh, you must stay," Malcolm said as he turned the corner. He had a gun in his hand—and Quinn was willing to bet, somehow, that it was Janie's. "We really didn't have much of a chance to catch up last night, did we?"

Quinn's stomach sank down to his feet at the sight of the old man. He'd thought he'd never see Malcolm again. Or maybe that was wishful thinking.

"You cut things short when you staked me and left me for dead."

Malcolm smiled. "We do what we must to protect that which we desire."

It was hard to concentrate with the alarm blaring in his ears. "Have you been following us this whole time?"

His smile widened. "I didn't have to. I made a copy of the map. I've been waiting here for you. I knew you'd eventually show up. I am very patient."

Quinn's shock and surprise faded away and were replaced by hot anger, which he fought back. He needed to keep his head clear. "Why didn't you just take the Eye and be done with it, then?"

Malcolm's brow furrowed. "Because I wanted to give you another chance, of course."

He glanced over at Janie and then back at Malcolm. "What?"

The old man smiled at him. "I know you weren't thinking clearly yesterday." He eyed a scowling Janie. "She's very attractive. I can see why you might be taken by her, but there are bigger things for us to think about. I may have overreacted last night to your betrayal."

"You staked me."

"You're still alive. And as long as you're alive, every day presents new opportunities. I'll give you one last chance to change your mind."

"And if I don't?"

He raised the gun. "I will kill her. Right here, right now."

"Quinn—" Janie said.

Quinn went very still. He had no doubt that Malcolm would do it if he made one wrong move. Said one wrong thing.

"Don't hurt her," he said evenly. "What do you want me to do?"

Malcolm grinned. "I knew you'd see logic eventually. I think you'll be pleased with the next step in my plans."

"Killing vampires?"

He shook his head. "This time it shall be the hunters. I have plans to take care of a great many in one fell swoop."

"Sounds like you have it all worked out."

"I've been planning this particular event for some time. Just waiting for the right opportunity and the right place. And I will share this victory with you in a forum we both know all too well."

Quinn's gaze flicked to the gun again. "What's the plan?"

Malcolm paused, and the alarm continued to ring. Quinn was surprised that the police hadn't shown up yet. What was taking them so long? What would they make of this little showdown in the middle of a downtown museum?

"The annual vampire hunter convention is in Las Vegas as we speak. That is where I will begin putting my master plan into action."

Quinn's mouth went dry. "The hunter convention."

"Yes. It is being held this year at the El Diablo casino—a fitting name for such self-involved devils. I look forward to watching them all burn."

Quinn let out a long breath as he worked through how best to handle this delicate situation without getting Janie shot.

"I appreciate the second chance," he finally said and then looked over at Janie. "Bring the Eye to me."

"Forget it," she managed, clutching the artifact tightly to her chest.

"Don't be stupid. Bring it to me, or Malcolm will kill you."

"And how long do you think it'll be before security runs in here with the alarm going off?"

"Probably a long time," Malcolm said. "I killed the sole employee. No one is here except for us. I also disconnected the alarm from its connection to the police station. It's a mildly irritating noise, but no one will be coming to check it out for a very long while."

Quinn felt a chill go through him. "Janie." He beckoned to her.

She approached slowly, warily. "Don't do this, Quinn. Please."

"Why? Either he has it or you have it. And at least he's willing to share with me."

"But my sister—"

"Janie . . . please."

When she got close enough, he snatched the golden wand out of her hand.

A smile spread across Malcolm's wrinkled face as he regarded the Eye. "Very good." Then he turned to look at Janie, who was literally shaking with anger. "Quinn, please wait for me outside, and I will finish her—"

Quinn swung the Eye, clobbering Malcolm on the back of his head. Another swing made contact and the gun clattered to the ground, followed by Malcolm's body. Unconscious.

Again.

Quinn frowned as he saw something slip out of Malcolm's pocket and roll toward his feet. It was the ruby-like stone that he and Janie had dug up in Malcolm's back yard. He quickly bent over to snatch it from the ground and slipped it into his pocket.

Janie didn't notice this. She had her stake out in a flash, and she fell down to her knees, pushing Malcolm onto his back. She gritted her teeth and raised the stake above her head.

"Wait!" Quinn held up his hand to stop her. "Don't do it."

"He was going to kill me."

"Just . . . just don't do it." He let out a shuddery breath and looked down at the old man, who had been so nice and kind and understanding once upon a time. "I know he's no good, but I don't want him to die. Not like this."

Her eyes narrowed. "That makes one of us."

"Come on." He grabbed her arm to help her to her feet. "We have to get out of here."

Without another word, they ran out of the museum and into the sunshine. Quinn wondered how long it would be before the victim inside would be found or the alarm was noticed. What would they do with Malcolm?

It didn't matter. The old man was in his past now.

Distracted with thoughts of Malcolm, he didn't notice Janie grab the Eye out of his hand until it was gone.

"You dented it." She inspected it, turning it over in her hands.

"It's fine."

Or was it? He frowned. He'd seen sketches of the Eye that his father had collected over the years. He could have sworn that it was not just gold, that it had a jewel in it. In fact, if he thought about it hard enough, he would swear it was a red jewel.

Just like the one in his pocket. He glanced at the wand and saw where the stone was missing. An empty slot where the stone in his pocket would fit perfectly.

Well, Malcolm, he thought. *You didn't tell me everything, did you?*

Luckily, Janie didn't seem to notice any discrepancy. She beelined to the first pay phone she saw.

"I need to call Lenny," she told him.

He nodded. "Tell him we're going to be staying at the El Diablo when we get to Vegas."

She raised an eyebrow at him. "Are you sure about that?"

He nodded and didn't offer any more information on the subject. Malcolm said he had plans to kill many hunters at the annual convention. The last thing Quinn wanted to do was to be there, but he couldn't exactly sit back and mind his own business.

He'd check things out. Make sure Malcolm hadn't already done irreparable damage, and then they'd get the hell out of there.

He waited awkwardly on the sidewalk, with arms crossed, thinking the situation through.

He looked over at Janie on the telephone. He'd help her find her sister. Once he knew she was okay, then he'd leave. With the Eye.

But not before.

After a minute, she hung up. "They're in Vegas. The Boss contacted Lenny, since he couldn't get through to me anymore. He's on his way there now, too."

She noticeably shivered. It made Quinn mad as hell. Who was this asshole boss of hers who had such power over her? Janie wasn't the type to be afraid of anyone or anything. If it was the last thing he did, he'd make sure not only Angela was okay, but Janie, too.

Then he'd leave.

And the sooner they took care of it, the better.

"The Boss will be there this evening," she said. "Barkley's still trying to get a fix on Angela—he and Lenny are going to get a room at the El Diablo. Do you really think he can do it?"

Quinn nodded. "I know it." He hoped he sounded confident enough. "We'll go rent a car right now. Hopefully they won't hold my last rental against me. It was a rather hefty security deposit."

"We?"

"Yeah. That okay?"

She raised an eyebrow. "You're not going to fight me to the death for the Eye now that I have it?"

He shrugged. "Like you said, it's dented now. I only fight to the death over mint collectibles. You should see some of the Star Wars figures I have in storage. People have been hospitalized trying to keep me from a perfect boxed Boba Fett."

She laughed. "I'll remember that."

He looked away. "There's got to be a way everyone can get what they want."

"I hope so." She looked sad. "I really do."

So did he.

Chapter 15

Welcome to El Diablo." The valet, dressed head to toe in red, gave them a big smile as Quinn and Janie got out of their rented Toyota Camry. "I hope you enjoy your stay with us."

"I wouldn't count on it," Quinn said as he gave the guy a five-dollar bill and the keys.

As they entered the casino hotel, Quinn glanced at Janie out of the corner of his eye. Conversation had died down to a bare minimum in the car over the past five hours. Not much to say. She still had the Eye in her possession, and it made him more than a little nervous. She'd tucked it into her jeans and under her jacket so it was barely visible along the line of her clothing.

He motioned for her to go through the revolving entrance ahead of him.

She eyed him. "Such a gentleman."

"I do try."

She snorted. He wasn't sure if she was laughing at him

or with him. What the hell was it about this woman that made him so uncertain and unsteady?

Didn't matter. This was almost over. The odds of them spending any time together in the future were slim to none. The thought was surprisingly unsettling.

"Welcome to El Diablo Hotel, Casino, and Convention Center!" a pretty brunette behind the check-in counter said brightly. She wore all red and had tiny sequined devil horns pinned into her hair. "Do you have a reservation?"

Quinn shook his head and produced a credit card. "No. We need two rooms, please."

"I'll see if we have anything available." She took the card and tapped on her keyboard. "Mr. Quinn, I believe you're mistaken."

He frowned. "About what?"

"We do have a room reserved for you already."

"Really?" His frown deepened. Had Barkley done that for him? He did know they were on their way. "Well, great. My friend here will need a room, too."

The clerk gave Quinn a key card and instructions on how to get to his room on the seventeenth floor. He looked down at the receipt and saw his own name along with another name he recognized.

His father's.

Before he'd died, Roger Quinn must have reserved an extra room for his son so they could attend the convention together. Which would explain why the room was so damned expensive. His father preferred the best of everything.

Thanks, Dad, he thought morbidly.

Quinn glanced nervously around the El Diablo lobby, decorated to look like a scene out of Dante's *Inferno,* including smoking dry ice and large black iron gates to hell—leading directly into the casino area.

Janie nudged him aside and got her own room. The clerk ensured they'd be on the same floor.

Terrific. Just what he needed.

They walked away from check-in and past a poster propped on an easel:

El Diablo welcomes members of the VHA for their 42nd Annual Convention.

He started to laugh and slapped a hand over his mouth before he drew any attention. Or risked showing his fangs.

VHA stood for the Vampire Hunters of America. He was still a member in good standing. It had seemed like a good idea coming there. Now that they'd arrived, he wasn't so sure.

Low profile. Check things out. Then leave first thing tomorrow. Or earlier if possible.

The VHA liked to get together annually to hold workshops and seminars. They'd decided fifteen years ago to hold their events in a more public forum. As long as they went by the acronym and kept the workshops members-only, the general human population would never know what they were up to—ignorance for their own safety.

"Are you okay being here?" Janie touched his arm as they got on the elevator headed to the seventeenth floor. "You look like you just swallowed a puppy."

"I wish."

She laughed weakly at that.

He frowned. "This isn't funny, you know."

"Come on. I'll protect you from the mean hunters. Don't worry."

"I may take you up on that offer."

The elevator dinged and the doors opened up. Two large men got on the elevator with them, pressing Quinn on either side. He tried to pretend that he was invisible. He didn't recognize the men, but they looked like hunters to him. Hunters who had gone a little too long without a shower.

"I think you should give the Eye back to me," Quinn whispered to her.

She raised an eyebrow. "I'm sure you do."

"For safekeeping."

"It's perfectly safe with me."

"I can just take it from you. I don't have to ask."

She gave him a wicked grin and then reached forward to tap one of the hunters on his huge bicep.

"Excuse me—" she said. "Are you here for the convention?"

He looked around at her. "That's right. How'd you know?"

"I can spot a gorgeous vampire hunter from a mile away."

He elbowed his friend. "A groupie."

She fluttered her eyelashes at them. "Maybe I am."

The hunter eyed her from top to bottom, pausing for way too long on the middle part. "You should come to the awards tonight. There's a party afterward, and we can all get to know each other better. I might even let you touch my stake."

Her smiled widened. "Really? That sounds like fun."

The elevator stopped at the fourteenth floor, and the men got off and waved at Janie before the elevator doors closed behind them.

Quinn eyed her. "Let you touch his stake?"

"Vampire hunters love the double entendre."

"So what *was* that?"

"Just me being friendly. And a reminder that if you mess with me to get the Eye, number one, I'd kick your ass. Number two, I can always holler for one of those hairy mammoths to come save me."

"You wouldn't really do that, would you? After all we've been through together?"

She looked away. "Just try me."

The doors opened on the seventeenth floor and they got out and walked down the hall.

Quinn stopped in front of his door, swiped the key card, and turned the knob. "Fine, be that way."

She raised an eyebrow, probably surprised he was giving up so quickly, and brushed past him.

He grabbed the back of her jacket and, before she was able to say a word, pulled her into his room and slammed the door shut.

Quinn stood with his back against the door, aka: her only means of escape.

"We need to talk, Janie."

Her heart pounded hard. No, they did *not* need to talk. What they needed to do was have some time apart so she could figure out what she was going to do next. Her Boss's threat never left her mind: kill the vampire or else.

She didn't want to kill Quinn. The thought of him dead made her heart ache.

And yet she wasn't too thrilled with the "or else" part of that threat, either.

"Isn't talking what we've been doing for the past day

and a half?" she finally said. "I think we've run out of topics."

He shook his head. "There's a way we can both get what we want."

She clenched the Eye in her right hand. "Get out of my way or I'm going to beat you to a pulp."

His lips twitched.

Great, she thought. He found her amusing. She'd been way too soft on him. He had no concept of how mean and nasty she could get when she had to. She might not look it at first glance, but she was like a dangerous animal cornered—

She glanced around at the room.

—cornered in a VIP suite that absolutely *rocked.*

It seemed obvious that the El Diablo had a devil theme throughout the hotel. This room was no different. It was huge and decorated in rich fabrics, shades of red and gold and orange. A blazing fireplace took up the majority of one wall, and paintings of naked or scantily clad women filled the other walls. Instead of looking cheap or cheesy, they added a sensual flavor to the space. Another wall was entirely taken up by a window that looked out and down to the Bellagio Hotel's fountains next door.

Sure as hell beat the Sleepytime Inn.

"If you don't let me out of here I'm going to . . ." She trailed off as another gorgeous element of the room stood out to her. The bed! It was huge. And round! It was also draped in a gauzy red canopy. She was willing to bet it was a million times more comfortable than any of the hard and lumpy motel beds she'd stayed on for way too many weeks to count.

Niiice.

Quinn followed her line of sight.

"You're going to . . . curl up and have a nap?" He raised an eyebrow and grinned, showing the edge of his fangs. "You know, you're more than welcome to share my mattress anytime you like. However, I really should have a shower first. It's been a long day."

She glared at him.

"Ouch," he said. "If looks could kill."

"If only that's all it took. But we can do it the hard way if you'd prefer."

"That sounds interesting, too."

"I don't have time for this, Quinn. Please get out of my way."

His grin vanished and was replaced by the strained expression lying just underneath the surface. He wasn't enjoying himself. He was just as stressed out as she was. They had reached an impasse, and somebody was going to lose.

She was out of options and getting very close to being out of time. Maybe if she got the Eye to the Boss, that would be enough. He'd forget about his orders for her to kill Quinn. It wasn't much, but it was all she had as a plan to keep him alive.

She swallowed past the lump in her throat. "I'm sorry, Quinn."

He frowned and met her eyes. "You are?"

"If there was another way . . . then maybe we could work something out. But I have to get this to my Boss as soon as he contacts me."

"So he can use it."

She nodded. "I suppose so."

"What if it doesn't work for him?"

Her stomach turned over at the suggestion. "It will. Of course it will. Why wouldn't it?"

He rubbed his chin and suddenly wouldn't meet her eyes.

She frowned deeply and closed the distance between them to grab his arm. "Why wouldn't it work?"

He didn't say anything for a moment. "Have you looked at the drawing recently?"

She fumbled in her handbag and pulled out the drawing of the Eye the Boss had given her when first giving her the assignment. It looked exactly like the one she had in her possession.

Almost exactly.

The Eye she had was missing something. A red stone, like a ruby, that sat just beneath the enclosed crystal globe top. Why the hell hadn't she noticed that before?

If the Eye didn't work when she brought it to the Boss, he wouldn't take it well. He'd most likely take his disappointment out by killing everybody within a three-mile radius.

She swore and pushed Quinn up against the door. "You knew? All this time and you didn't say anything?"

"Hey, take it easy. It's the stone that Malcolm had buried in his back yard. The one he said was useless after it revealed the true map."

"He was lying to us?"

"You think?"

"That son of a bitch. Why didn't you let me stake him?" She punched the wall for lack of a better thing to punch. Her hand immediately screamed in pain. "Dammit! That bastard still has it, and I have no idea where he is now."

"Why do you assume he still has it?" Quinn asked.

"Well, of course he has it. Who else would—" She

stopped talking and looked at him. He didn't look cocky, but he sure looked relaxed. "*You* have it."

"Maybe."

"Where is it?" Her gaze raked down the front of him.

"Feel free to search me again. That was kind of enjoyable this morning when you were looking for the map."

"Damn you, Quinn!" She punched him in the stomach.

He hissed out a breath and grimaced. "Okay. *Not* enjoyable." After a moment, he straightened up and walked over to sit on the edge of the bed. "I have a proposition for you, Janie. Are you going to listen to me or not?"

Her arms were crossed so tightly that her hands started to feel numb. "I'm listening."

"I have the stone. You have the Eye. One won't work without the other."

Her face had become extremely hot, and it wasn't just because of the huge fireplace. "Understood."

"You want the Eye so your Boss won't hurt your sister, right?"

"Correct." *Among other reasons,* she thought.

"If she's safe, it wouldn't matter if he got the Eye or not."

She thought about that for a moment. "Maybe."

"I'm going to help you find her. Tonight."

"There's not enough time."

He shook his head. "If she's in Vegas, then we'll find her. When we find her, we'll take her somewhere where your Boss can't touch her."

"And then?"

"And then you'll let me have the Eye."

She shook her head. "No, that won't work. He'll be furious if I don't bring it to him."

"After I'm finished with it, you can have it back. He doesn't have to know it's been used."

"He'll know when he tries to make a wish."

"Or maybe he'll think it simply doesn't work for him. He won't blame you."

"You don't know him. He'll kill me."

"I'll protect you."

She laughed at that dryly, then looked out of the floor-to-ceiling windows down to the Vegas Strip. The vague reflection of a dirty, windblown, frustrated blonde looked back at her. She glanced over her shoulder.

"You want it that bad."

"Haven't I proven that to you by now?"

"All this just to be human again."

He shrugged.

"Human isn't all that great," she said.

"I know. Wasn't that long since I was one."

"So what the hell is the big deal? Why this single-minded obsession to not be a vampire anymore?"

She waited, but he didn't answer right away. She turned around again to fully look at him. His throat worked like he was trying to swallow and was having a hard time with it.

"I've been a monster all of my life, Janie. I just never realized it. Now I *literally* am one. It's my punishment for being a hunter all those years. But if I can be human again . . . I can change things. I can try to redeem myself. I can help people. I know I can."

"You really think it's that simple?"

He crossed his arms and walked over to the window to stare outside. "No, of course not. Nothing's simple. But if I was an evil human, I have no idea how horrible a vampire I'll become if given enough time. And if I have much more blood—" His voice broke. "I can see myself becoming like Malcolm. An immortal, indiscriminant murderer who doesn't even realize what he's thinking and doing is insane. I don't want to hurt anyone, Janie."

She put her hand on her hip and studied him for a moment. "And you think getting the chance to make this wish is going to change all of that."

He moistened his lips with the tip of his tongue. "If it doesn't, then I'm out of options. I won't live this way. I won't. One way or the other—I either live as a human or I'll . . . I'll die as a vampire."

Her heart clenched. "What are you talking about? You wouldn't kill yourself over this, would you?"

His silence answered her question.

She moved closer to him, wanting to wrap her arms around him and hold him tight. To tell him it was going to be okay.

But then she changed her mind.

The immediate sympathy she felt that he'd had to come to this horrible decision was pushed away by a big wave of anger. "I think you might be the dumbest guy I've ever known."

He blinked at her. "Is that so."

"Yeah. Dumb. Moronic. Idiotic." She shook her head. "Honestly, you're such a tool, Quinn."

"This is making me feel so much better."

"Sorry, but I'm not on the high school cheerleading squad. Never was. Honestly. If you're willing to kill yourself over something like this, you deserve to die."

"You're probably right."

She hissed out a long breath. "You know what? You

seemed so cool and cute and together back when I was a kid with a crush. Little did I know what a difference a dozen years would make. Pathetic."

He frowned at her. "Maybe I won't wait to end it later. Got a spare wooden stake lying around?"

She shook her head as she tried to figure out what to do. If she didn't let Quinn use the Eye, he was going to be looking for ways to kill himself. If she did let him use it, her Boss would probably kill him. They were screwed either way.

"Fine," she finally said through clenched teeth.

"Fine, what?"

"Fine, we'll look for my sister. If, and that's a big fat *if* we find her, then you can make your loser, cop-out wish and I won't try to stop you."

And then she'd figure out what to do about the Boss. There had to be another way out of this situation.

Christ. Maybe she should have just killed Quinn earlier when she had the chance.

The thought was almost funny. Almost.

He looked at her warily, perhaps waiting for the catch. "Okay."

"Okay." She shook her head again. "I'm going to find something to wear that doesn't smell like sweaty desert. Had I known this assignment was going to take more than a day, I would have packed a bigger bag. I need a vacation so bad."

He cleared his throat. "So, meet you in the lobby in half an hour?"

"Fine." She left the room and headed down the hall to her own room.

She felt something wet on her face and reached up to touch her cheeks. Wet. Clear, warm liquid.

Oh, Christ. She was crying.

When the hell had that happened? Yeah, she was crying over the stupid vampire's lack of intelligence and common sense. Not to mention her own lack of judgment when it came to him.

She wanted to beat it into him that he was great, vampire or not. That he was nowhere near evil. She'd met evil guys, and Michael Quinn wasn't one of them. Had he made some mistakes in his life? Sure. Who hadn't? Was it something worth dying over?

Was he someone worth killing just because her Boss said so?

No.

She'd figure it out. Nobody had to die today. Not if she had anything to say about it.

She ran the back of her hand over her eyes to dry things.

Haven't cried in years, she thought. *This. This is what triggers it?*

I must be premenstrual.

She needed to buy something expensive to wear. Immediately. That would help take her mind off things. She took the elevator down to the shops, shoving the Eye into her handbag. Then, checking to make sure she was still Visa-endowed, she disappeared into one of the stores to spend as much money as necessary on as little designer fabric as possible.

Quinn went into the washroom to splash some water on his face and tried to compose himself.

Good thing he wasn't trying to impress Janie with his manly ways, because he'd just messed up royally.

Revealed a little too much of that soft white underbelly. Women like her did *not* go for signs of weakness.

He wished he could say he was just playing her to get what he wanted, but he was too bone-weary tired to play any more games. This was him. Warts and all.

Take it or leave it.

Janie, quite obviously, preferred to leave it, as she'd hot-tailed it out of the room as soon as she could. Disgusted by him.

Good thing he didn't care what she thought.

He didn't, right?

He looked up at the bathroom mirror. Yet another one that refused to reflect his pasty face. Seemed to be a trend with mirrors. He brought his hand up to his face and touched his cheek, his nose, his eyebrows to make sure he hadn't just faded away completely into nothingness.

When and if he got to be human again, he'd be able to see himself. Stare right into his own reflection and the person he hated most in the whole wide world.

He thought he resented his father for making him into the man he was?

Misplaced blame. Big-time.

Maybe being human again wouldn't solve all of his problems. Not even put a dent in them, but it was something. If he didn't have that goal . . . then what did he have? His life was completely and utterly devoid of meaning.

Except for finding Janie's sister.

After that, finding this Boss and kicking his ass. There was no way he'd let the guy lay a finger on Janie.

If he could accomplish that, then that was something. Something real that wasn't entirely self-serving.

He splashed some more cold water on his face and then left the room.

The fact that he was in a hotel that he knew currently held at least three hundred vampire hunters did not leave his mind for a moment. In addition to the fear—which he of course was feeling in spades—he also felt amused by the irony. He'd been a hunter, and now he was one of the hunted.

He tried to think back to what he would have done at a convention if he'd found a vamp at the hotel.

Called my friends and had a little fun, he thought with a sick feeling.

Best to keep as low a profile as possible. Later he'd do a little digging around and make sure everything was running smoothly without any Malcolm-induced surprises hiding in the woodwork.

According to the hunters they'd briefly met in the elevator, the awards were that night. They were called the awards, but really it was a chance to pat each other on the back and plan for the next year. Quinn already knew that the overall leader of the hunter community, Gideon Chase, was to give a brief motivational talk about his plans for the coming year. Quinn's father, Roger, had been a leader, but even he'd had somebody to answer to. And that man was Gideon.

Gideon was to the hunter community as Donald Trump was to Manhattan real estate. Big bucks, from a long line of hunters. He enjoyed it. Found the glamour his father and grandfather before him had shunned. This was his night to shine. In fact, Quinn knew that he was going to be receiving a special award for his work not only behind the scenes financially, but as a field operative who'd taken out a record number of vamps in the East Coast area over the past year. He and Quinn had even briefly been friends back in the day.

Briefly.

Yeah. Quinn would definitely be staying away from him.

He kept his eyes on the ground and made his way toward the lobby.

"I thought you said you'd only be a half an hour," he heard Janie say.

His downcast eyes landed on a pair of shiny black stiletto heels leading to long, bare legs, then a red dress that began several inches above the knee and fit her body like . . . like a really sexy tight red dress should. His gaze skimmed over the cleavage displayed by her plunging neckline. The halter-top straps framed her pale neck and throat, which were otherwise unadorned. Her lips were the color of her dress . . . red. Blood red. Her ice blue eyes were rimmed in smoky black liner. Her long blond hair fell across one shoulder, softly draping over her right breast.

"Uh . . . I . . . I . . ." His mouth was literally watering at the sight of her. He wasn't entirely sure if it was because of her exposed neck or the rest of her exposed skin. Probably a combination of the two.

Her red lips curled into a small smile at his lack of verbal skills. "Thanks. I just bought it. You like?"

She spun around slowly and slid a hand down over her hip.

He finally found his voice. "You went shopping? Don't you have more important things to think about right now?"

Her smile fell.

Good, Quinn. Insult her. Chicks love that.

Or . . . he could have told her hell, yeah, he liked it. And he was ready to rip it off her and take her up against the nearest slot machine.

One or the other. An insult or a come-on.

This was definitely his night to make a royal asshole out of himself.

"We need to find Lenny," she said. "I left a message on his voice mail that we'd arrived. Where the hell is he?"

She turned away from him so she could look around the casino. His mouth went very dry as he noticed that her dress was bare to the waist, revealing the smooth line of her back.

Lenny. Yeah, that would help. More testosterone. That's what he needed. Help to clear his head and remember what the hell was really important. And it wasn't Janie's annoyingly sexy red dress.

She chewed her bottom lip in a way that betrayed her nervousness. "We normally don't get assigned to Vegas. Or Atlantic City. Lenny has a bit of a problem."

"A problem?"

"Gambling is an issue for him."

Quinn managed to laugh softly at that. That hulk of a guy had a gambling addiction? Steroids, sure. But gambling?

"Then maybe he's at the tables," he suggested.

Her eyes widened slightly, and she took off. He had to move swiftly to keep up with her. The woman was hell on heels.

They moved past the banks of slot machines—everything from one-cent to ten-dollar bets. Quinn had never gambled much in his life. He didn't see the thrill in it. He'd always gotten his excitement by chasing danger. Shoving money into electronic devices or onto green felt tables seemed rather anticlimactic to him.

Lenny wasn't too hard to spot. He was hunched over a blackjack table on the opposite side of the floor, with the ever-present, ratty-looking poetry notebook at his side.

"Hit me," he told the dealer as they approached.

"Hit you?" Janie repeated. "I'd say that would be a pretty good start. What the hell are you doing?"

He craned his neck to look at her, and his eyes did a bugging-out thing that Quinn swore he'd only seen before in Bugs Bunny cartoons.

"Janie, that dress . . ." he managed, then grabbed the drink next to his notebook and downed it in one gulp.

She chewed her bottom lip. "Maybe it was a bad idea."

Quinn raised an eyebrow at her.

"Janie, I'm glad you're here," Lenny said. "I'm winning. My unlucky streak must be over finally. After all, it has been seven years."

"Lenny broke an enchanted mirror seven years ago," she told Quinn. "They say it's bad luck to break any mirror, but that isn't really true. However, enchanted mirrors owned by vain witches are a different story."

"Vain witches?"

"Don't get me started." She turned back to Lenny. "Come on. We have to leave. We're going to locate my sister tonight before the Boss wants to see us."

"Good luck," he said. "Barkley did say he had a line on her. He was pretty excited about it. I think he's got a bit of a psychic sweet spot for your sister."

"*Good luck?* No. We need your help."

He shook his head. "You'll be fine without me. Besides, lucky streak? Hello? I can't leave the table. I don't know how long this is going to last."

"Where's Barkley right now?" Quinn asked.

Lenny didn't look up, but he fished into his pocket for a key card. "Here. He's upstairs in the room."

"You're sharing a room?"

"Do you know how expensive this place is? Besides, I didn't even know if we were going to stay very long. I left him up there with some room service and a pay-per-view."

"He didn't feel like gambling, too?"

"Yeah," he said distractedly. "Something like that."

Janie snatched the card out of his hand and started walking away without even waiting for Quinn. "I'll talk to you later, Lenny."

"Wish me luck."

She wished him something under her breath that Quinn didn't quite catch, but it sure as hell wasn't luck.

Chapter 16

Janie slid the card into the lock and opened the door on the fifth floor. The lights were off. The only light in the dark room came from the television screen, which, while on mute, was prominently displaying a porno movie.

She shook her head. Men. Were they all the same?

She glanced over her shoulder. Quinn was right behind her and he raised his eyebrow. He nodded at the TV.

"Seen that one already," he said and then actually grinned. "It was very well acted."

Yup. All the same.

He brushed past her and walked into the small room that contained two double beds, the decor again all in shades of red. Adequate, but not quite the luxury of Quinn's VIP suite, that was for sure.

"Barkley?" he called. "You in here?"

"Don't you think it's strange that Lenny would just leave him up here?"

"Maybe he's not feeling so hot."

The door to the bathroom nudged open then, and a big black wolf padded into the room. It walked over to one of the beds, hopped up on it, sat down, scratched behind its floppy ear with its left hind leg, turned around three times, and lay down.

And whined.

"You are kidding me," Janie said.

"I don't think they allow pets here." Quinn peered closer at the wolf. "Having a bit of a problem maintaining human form, are you?"

Barkley whined again. Then his tongue rolled out of his mouth and he panted.

Janie shook her head and tried to ignore the sinking feeling in the pit of her stomach. Since the sinking was on par with the *Titanic*, it was a little hard to ignore. Finding her sister so easily had sounded too good to be true. Turns out it was. "Well, I guess that settles it. I'm going to try to make contact with my Boss right now. I want to get this over with as soon as possible."

"Janie—"

She held up a hand. "Just forget it, Quinn. I gave you a chance. One chance. And since that chance is currently covered in fur, our deal is null and void. You're going to have to give me that stone."

He turned toward the wolf again. "Lenny tells us that you might know where Angela is. Is that true?"

Barkley sat up and woofed.

"Is that supposed to be a yes?" Janie asked.

"It sounded fairly positive, don't you think?"

She sighed. "Just give up."

"Not yet."

Quinn sank down to his knees next to the bed so he

and Barkley were at eye level. "I'm going to assume that you can understand me. So here's what we're going to do. One bark means yes and two barks mean no. Understand?"

"Woof."

Janie crossed her arms. "I don't believe this."

"Do you know where Angela is right now?"

"Woof."

"Is she here at the El Diablo?"

"Woof *woof.*"

Quinn turned to Janie and raised an eyebrow. "See?"

"This is like twenty questions only much, much stupider."

"Not much of an optimist, are you?"

"Not even remotely."

He turned back to the wolf. "Is she in a hotel on the strip?"

That earned a positive woof.

He named off about ten casinos that were met with negative responses until he came to the Paris casino. That received a positive woof.

"She's at the Paris," Quinn told Janie.

She shook her head and gave another shaky sigh.

"You don't believe him?" he crossed his arms.

"It's not that I don't believe him," she said. "It's just . . . just that there's no time to waste on a wild goose chase. Maybe he means that she's actually in Paris. As in France."

Suddenly Barkley howled loudly and shot up on all four paws. Janie and Quinn exchanged a concerned look.

She took a step backward. "Is that a yes or a no?"

"Not sure."

Then Barkley collapsed on the bed, and in a matter of seconds his dark, shaggy, wolf-life form morphed into that of a human male.

A very naked human male.

He stretched full length out on the bed and, after a moment, propped himself up on an elbow. "I really wish I could figure out why that's happening. Because it's becoming rather inconvenient."

"So you have no control at all over it?" Quinn asked.

"None." He scratched his chest, which was covered in a fine layer of black hair, then sat up, swung his long legs over the side of the bed, and stood up.

"Uh . . . Janie," Quinn said. "We should probably go now."

But Janie wasn't looking at Quinn. Even with thoughts of her sister's imminent safety weighing heavy on her mind, she was enjoying the show a little more than she knew she should. She'd never seen a werewolf shift to human before, and Barkley wasn't all that hard on the eyes. She had to say that she preferred him in human form. It was much more . . . interesting.

"Janie," Quinn said again, louder. "Are you listening to me?"

"Yeah, of course. Go. We should go."

The werewolf had a *great* body. Maybe it had been much too long since she'd seen a naked man up close and personal. Everything still seemed to be in the right places. Her gaze traveled down the length of his tall, leanly muscled body.

Yes, very, very nice.

"Janie," Quinn repeated more sharply. "Let's go find your sister."

Janie snapped back to reality and blinked hard. "Right. My sister."

Quinn glared at Barkley. "Put some clothes on."

He shrugged and seemed completely unaffected by being nude in mixed company. "I'm coming with you. Just give me a minute to find some jeans."

"You want to come?"

"Dude, Angela is my soul mate. The mate of my soul. As soon as she sees me, I know she's going to feel the same way. My psychic connection to her is that strong. That doesn't happen just every day, you know." He turned to look at Janie and raised an eyebrow. "Janie, that dress is smoking. Maybe *you're* my soul mate. Damn, you're beautiful." He shook his head. "Sorry. I can't help it. I'm always horny when I shift back to human form."

Janie raised an eyebrow and glanced at Quinn, who looked utterly annoyed.

"Clothes?" Quinn snapped. "Now?"

"All right, all right."

Barkley ran into the bathroom and was finished dressing in about thirty seconds flat. He held Janie's were-loom necklace out to her.

"Thought you'd like this back." He grinned. "I think it was really helpful."

She took it from him gratefully and put it back on around her neck, where it belonged. It didn't exactly go with the dress—diamonds and gold would have been the more logical choice—but she immediately felt a bit better having it back on.

Less than ten minutes later, Janie stood with the two men outside the Paris Las Vegas Resort and Casino, which looked as though the Eiffel Tower had been launched over the ocean and landed in the middle of the Vegas Strip.

The whole town was surreal that way. At one end of the street was the New York Hotel, which looked like a mini New York City skyline, and the Luxor, which was shaped like a huge black glass Egyptian pyramid. At the other end was the Venetian, which sported a working canal complete with gondolas and Venice-style streets. Around the world in less than two miles.

Angela's in there? Janie thought as she stared up at the replica Eiffel Tower. *Could it really be this easy?*

Maybe it was. Maybe everything in her life didn't have to be a constant struggle. It would actually be a nice change.

Her jaw tightened as she thought of the reunion they'd finally have. She'd worried herself sick for too long, thinking that Angela had been kidnapped or murdered. If she'd been hanging out at a Vegas casino all this time without giving a thought to her concerned older sister . . .

Dammit. As long as she was safe and sound, that's all Janie cared about at the moment.

The yelling could wait until tomorrow.

She turned to Barkley. "So you're sure that you saw her here. In your vision?"

"It was another dream. I can't really get official visions. I've tried. I have to be asleep, and I see images. I saw the tower. And some strawberry crêpes. And a guy wearing a beret. And I saw Angela."

Janie glanced at Quinn.

He shrugged. "The crêpes sound like a solid lead to me."

"Okay." She took in a shuddery breath. "Let's go check it out."

They entered the hotel and headed straight for the casino area.

Janie scanned every face she could see until her eyes hurt.

Dammit, she thought. *What am I even doing? There's no time for this. I'm putting all my faith in a psychic werewolf? What is wrong with me?*

"I don't see her." The strain showed through in her words.

Quinn touched her arm gently. "We're going to find her, Janie."

"But what if we don't?"

His expression stiffened. "Then I'll give you the stone and you will give your Boss the Eye. I won't try to stop you. Not if it means your sister's life. I'm not that much of a selfish bastard."

Then he touched her face, stroking his thumb across her cheek, and the world suddenly seemed to stop. For a moment she couldn't hear the clanging and ringing sound of the slot machines. She didn't notice the swell of people around them in the casino.

He gave her a small smile. "Why are you looking at me like that?"

Because I think I just fell more in love with you than I already was, she thought.

Before she could say anything, Quinn's gaze left her face and he pulled away from her. "Barkley! Where are you going?"

Barkley had started walking off in the opposite direction. He seemed to be sniffing along one of the walls, past a blackjack table, and then he disappeared behind a corner.

Quinn's forehead creased into a frown. He grabbed her hand, and they started walking quickly to catch up to the werewolf. "Maybe Barkley *is* barking up the wrong tree—pun fully intended—but we need to keep him in sight."

"I wouldn't be surprised about any incorrect barking at this point."

"Well, I am absolutely positive that he was right about one thing."

"What's that?"

He grinned and his gaze glided down the front of her. "That dress is worth every penny you paid for it."

Despite the huge amount of worry she was working through—to say nothing about the fact her heart was beating a mile a minute because of Quinn's selfless offer a moment ago—she couldn't help but feel pleased at the reaction the dress had received so far. Especially from Quinn. Sure as hell felt better than dusty jeans and a sweaty tank top.

"It's Gucci. You should see the boutiques they have here. I'm going to be paying it off for months." She paused, thinking hard. "That is, if I live through the night."

An excited scream rang out as someone hit the jackpot on the progressive slots.

His appreciative gaze suddenly snapped back up to her face. "I want to meet this boss of yours. When you meet with him later, one way or the other, I want to come. I'm going to make sure he doesn't hurt you."

She laughed at that and didn't like how nervous it sounded. "You make it sound so easy."

"It is."

"It isn't. He's not a nice guy, Quinn. I'll deal with him the best I can. If you stick your nose where it doesn't belong—"

He stopped walking and grabbed her arms. "I won't let him hurt you."

"You're hurting me."

He let her go. "Sorry. Vampire strength."

She tried to smile but found that she couldn't. She watched Quinn out of the corner of her eye as they continued to follow Barkley through the casino.

Could she kill him?

No. She *couldn't* kill Quinn. She *wouldn't* kill him.

However, could she kill Quinn if it meant saving her sister? What if that was the only option the Boss gave her?

She swallowed so hard it hurt.

Quinn glanced at her with concern after her long silence. "I mean it, you know. I will kick your Boss's ass if I get the slightest chance."

She shook her head at him and managed to smile a little.

"What?" he asked.

"You're . . . something, Quinn."

He frowned, perhaps not knowing what to make of her statement, and she touched his tense arm, sliding her hand up to his shoulder. She really wanted to hug him, which, for her, was a very strange thing to want. She wanted to kiss him again like she did when they were at the monster-killer tree.

But she didn't want him to meet the Boss. He'd tear Quinn apart in two seconds flat with or without Janie's help.

And if *she* wasn't going to kill him, then nobody else got to. She'd make sure of it.

Barkley scampered back to join them.

"Am I interrupting anything?"

"No." Janie tore her gaze away from Quinn's handsome face.

"I'm finished checking things out," he said. "My nose is worn out from sniffing everything. By the way, I did find those crêpes if anyone's hungry."

What little hope Janie had for success slipped away. Luckily, it wasn't much of a surprise. "Listen, I appreciate you giving it your best shot, but it's time we head back to the El Diablo."

He looked back over his shoulder. "Oh, no, I found her. She's in the VIP room playing high-stakes roulette. Am I drooling? Because she's even more gorgeous than in my dreams."

Janie's eyes widened. "You . . . you found her? Seriously?"

He nodded. "Come on."

Janie's heart pounded hard in her chest as she followed the werewolf through the casino.

Quinn smiled and squeezed her hand. "See? I told you we'd find her."

"You didn't really believe it, though, did you?"

His smile widened. "No comment."

She grinned back at him, feeling completely stunned. What was she going to say to Angela? She was relieved but at the same time incredibly apprehensive. The most important thing was her sister's safety. Period.

Barkley stopped walking and pointed into an intimate, richly decorated room roped off from the main casino floor.

Janie's heart lurched. There she was.

She touched her were-loom necklace. Angela still wore hers, as well, the turquoise stone standing out vividly blue-green against the rich red color of her hair and the alabaster of her skin.

The last time Janie remembered seeing her, she'd been eighteen years old wearing ripped jeans and an orange halter top, hair back in a ponytail. This Angela looked different.

She'd be twenty-three now, Janie thought, as she watched the beautiful woman lean over the roulette table to place her bet, a smile curling her full lips, as her eyes—the same ice blue as Janie's—caught the light with a mischievous twinkle. Wearing a low-cut black dress that showed off ample cleavage, she was the only woman playing, and the other six men surrounding the table watched her every move.

Janie frowned. That was strange. Her sister had always been flat-chested.

She shook her head slowly.

Unbelievable, she thought. *The girl had time for a boob job, but not enough time to let me know she was okay.*

But even with that thought, Janie couldn't suppress her own happiness at seeing that her sister was alive and well-endowed. It was as if a heavy weight on her heart had lifted.

But still. There would be words.

The roulette wheel spun, and Angela gave a big smile as it landed on her number. The other men cheered for her, despite their own losses. She added to the large pile of chips surrounding her.

"Very lucky, *mademoiselle,*" the dealer said. "Congratulations."

A man next to her, who wore an expensive-looking tailored tuxedo and had black hair, silver at the temples, leaned in and whispered something to Angela. She laughed lightly. He slid his fingers into her long red hair and pushed it off her neck so he could kiss her.

"Hey!" Barkley protested under his breath from over Janie's right shoulder. "That dude is kissing *my* woman."

"Take it easy," Janie said. "You guys stay here, okay?"

"If you need us," Quinn whispered in her ear in a knee-weakening way that almost made her forget the redhead in the next room actually existed. "We won't be far."

"Thanks," she managed.

She entered the room and felt half the men's eyes shift to her.

Oh, right. The dress.

Worth every damn penny.

Angela didn't even look up from her paramour and her winnings.

There was a plush red seat vacant next to her, and Janie slid into it.

"Angela," she whispered

Angela was kissing the older man now, rather passionately.

Janie tapped her on the shoulder. "Angela. Please, look at me."

Angela stopped kissing the man and turned a bit to look over her shoulder.

"Oh, my God." Janie couldn't help the smile that blossomed on her face. "I am so happy to see you!"

"I'm sorry?" Angela crooked a well-defined eyebrow

above her beautiful eyes rimmed in smoky black liner and gave her a blank look.

"Yeah, sorry would be a good start." Janie grabbed her wrist. "Come on. We have to get out of here right now."

Angela wrenched her hand away and glanced at the man before looking back at Janie. "I think you must have me confused with someone else. Who are you?"

Janie let out a nervous laugh. "I'm the Easter Bunny. Now move it."

She grabbed Angela's wrist again, but she twisted away.

The older man frowned deeply. "I think we may need security over here."

Janie shook her head. "This is my sister. She's been missing for five years. I don't know what she's trying to prove right now by pretending she doesn't know who I am, but it's not very funny."

"Is this true?" The older man's frown deepened and he stood up from his seat. "What is going on here?"

Angela shook her head, her expression one of confusion. "I don't know. This woman is obviously crazy. Just sit down and don't make a scene."

The muscles in the man's jaw tensed. "A scene is exactly what I *don't* want."

"Are you together?" Janie asked. Although she supposed that was fairly obvious. She just wanted it confirmed.

"We . . ." the man began and then closed his mouth and sighed before he turned toward the entrance. "I wanted this to be discreet. I wanted something simple. This isn't simple anymore, and it's not just this."

Angela stood and grabbed at his jacket. "Where are you going?"

He wrenched the material out of her grasp, but not before there was an audible ripping sound and a expression of disdain crossed his face. "I had a feeling there was something strange about you. I ignored it these last few months, but this is the final proof I needed that you're a liar. You won't even acknowledge your own sister?"

"Bernard! How can you say that?" Angela looked at Janie and then back at him. "This person walks in here and tells you that I'm not who you think I am and you believe her? Just like that?"

"Angela." Janie's frown deepened. "The necklace. Look at your necklace and then look at mine. They match. We bought them together. Don't you remember?"

Angela glanced down at the were-loom. "Obviously just a coincidence."

The man shook his head. "I expect my wife to lie to me, but not my mistress. I'm leaving."

Angela's cheeks flushed almost as red as her hair. "I haven't lied. And this . . . this is all it takes? Some stupid woman spouting crap about me? Where's the trust, Bernard? Where?"

He shrugged. "Let's just say it's the straw that broke the camel's back. Besides, I know you've been unfaithful."

"But you're *married!*"

"Except for my wife I've been completely faithful to you."

"You son of a bitch. Fine. Leave."

His lips thinned, and his gaze tracked down the length of Janie. He produced a card. "Perhaps *you* should call me sometime. I'm in town through the end of the week."

Angela threw three red chips at him. They hit his back and fell to the floor.

"There's the money for my new boobs, you bastard. The ones *you* wanted me to get. Don't say I don't repay my debts."

Bernard kept walking.

The room had gone completely silent.

"Place your bets," the dealer said after another moment.

Angela's face was almost as red as her hair, and she leaned forward to place a small pile of chips in the middle of the table on seventeen.

"Well," Janie said, slightly stunned. "At least he didn't say that you'll always have Paris."

Her face was tight. "I don't know who you are, but I think I hate you. No, scratch that. I definitely hate you. Do you have any idea who that was?"

"Should I?"

"Only if you watch the news and are not completely ignorant of politics."

"Then I definitely don't know. Nor do I care. Listen—" She took a step toward her sister.

Angela backed away a step and held up her hand. "Go away or I'm going to call security."

The wheel spun.

"Black seventeen!" the dealer announced. "The lady wins again."

"Whoop-dee-shit," Angela said, decidedly not thrilled by the whole situation as she gathered together her large pile of chips in front of her. "I'm out of here."

Janie's stomach churned. "You *seriously* don't remember me?"

"Why should I?"

"Oh I don't know. Because I'm *Janie*. Your *sister*. You disappeared five years ago and I've been searching for you. I thought something terrible had happened to you."

"I'm sure if I had a sister and she was you it's not something I'd just forget. Now get the hell away from me. Capische?"

Janie's mind was reeling, and she took everything in. It was all making sense. Angela didn't remember her. Of course, that's why she hadn't been in contact for years. Her sister had amnesia!

This piece of news was actually an odd relief, all things considered, but it didn't lift the heavy ache of disappointment she felt at how poorly the reunion was going so far.

Janie grabbed her wrist again. "Listen, I know this is strange to you, but you have to come with me. You're in terrible danger."

"*You're* in terrible danger if you don't let go of me."

Janie looked to her left toward the entrance to the VIP room but couldn't spot Barkley or Quinn. Just then, a large man wearing an earpiece and a casino vest entered the room and headed straight toward them.

"Is there a problem here?" he asked.

"I'll say there's a problem," Angela hissed. "This woman is harassing me. I thought the high-stakes rooms here were better supervised."

He shook his head. "I'm sorry, madam, but I wasn't speaking to you." He nodded at the dealer. "Is there a problem?"

The dealer's expression was sour. "I'm not sure. This . . . this young lady has been at my table for over an hour now and has won every round."

"I'm having a lucky night," Angela said.

"Every round for an entire hour?" The dealer shook his head. "I would rather not outwardly accuse you of cheating to the casino manager, but—"

"Cheating?" Angela blustered. She started scooping the chips off the table in a hasty and rather nervous motion. "Of all the nerve! I've never been so insulted in my life!"

The man nodded for security, and two even *larger* men in tuxedos and matching earpieces came to join them. All the men who had been ogling Angela and Janie moved out of the way, their gazes now firmly fixed on the patterned carpeting or the ornate gilded ceiling instead of the ample displays of female cleavage in the room.

Before Angela could grab any more of her winnings, one of the security guards grabbed her firmly by her upper arm.

"I think I'm going to be very fair about this whole situation," the casino manager said. "I will not call the police. I will simply ask you two ladies to leave the premises and not return. If you step foot inside this casino again, you will be dealt with much more harshly. Do you understand?"

Janie frowned. Did he say *two* ladies?

The other security guy's hand clamped around her arm. Her first thought was to fight him off, possibly by breaking his arm and shattering his kneecap, but she decided that might be a bit excessive.

She craned her neck searching the area. Didn't Quinn say he'd be nearby? Where the hell was he?

They were thrown out of the casino and onto the cold sidewalk outside. In the nicest, most civilized way possible.

Janie brushed off the front of her dress. The Eiffel

Tower loomed tall above them. A couple of tourists side-stepped to get past her to reach the entrance.

"And I usually do the bouncing," she said. "That was a new experience."

Angela glared at her. Then she turned around and started walking away on her very high Ferragamo heels. Across the street, the Bellagio fountains danced and sprayed around. The stars were out in the night sky, but the Vegas strip blazed bright as day.

"Hey!" Janie called after her. "Where do you think you're going?"

"Why are you still talking to me? Shut up!"

Quinn and Barkley ran up beside her. "What happened?"

"Where were you? I could have used your help in there."

Quinn gritted his teeth and gave Barkley a dirty look. "Wolf-boy got us kicked out. Saw a leg he couldn't help but get . . . friendly with."

"It's a compulsion." Barkley looked away. "I'm so ashamed."

"I'm sorry I wasn't there," Quinn continued. "Is everything okay?"

Janie waved in Angela's direction. Her throat felt thick. "I think she's got amnesia. She doesn't remember me at all."

Angela turned around. "I don't have amnesia." She looked at Quinn, her heavily made-up eyes widening slightly and then taking their time to take him in completely from head to foot. A smile spread across her features as she approached him. "Well, hello there. And what's your name?"

He glanced at Janie, then back at Angela. "Uh . . . you can call me Quinn."

Angela took his hand in hers and turned it over. "You know, Quinn, I can tell a lot about a man by his hands." She ran a French-manicured fingernail along his palm. "Your lifeline is very long."

"Well, I am currently immortal."

She laughed.

Janie couldn't believe it. Her sister was flirting with Quinn.

And he didn't seem to be stopping her.

"So you *were* cheating in there," Janie said. "And not just with that guy."

"I wasn't cheating." Angela's pleasant expression soured.

Barkley stepped forward and cleared his throat. "Matthew Barkley, at your service, Angela. It's a pleasure to finally meet you."

She raised an eyebrow at him. "*Finally* meet me?"

"I've been having visions about you. And, may I say, you are a vision tonight. Of loveliness, that is."

Janie wrapped her arms around herself to keep the desert chill away. "We don't have time for this."

Angela's expression brightened. "You've been having visions about *me?* You're psychic, too?"

Barkley nodded enthusiastically. "I think I'm in love with you. Am I moving too fast?"

"Hold on, Romeo," Janie said. "One thing at a time. Angela, listen to me and listen to me carefully. You have amnesia. You are my sister. You are in danger. You have to leave Las Vegas immediately. Like, *now*. There's no time to waste."

Angela turned her back on Janie to look Quinn. "Can I ask a favor?"

Quinn nodded. "Of course."

"Will you see me back to my hotel? I'm staying right next door at the Aladdin. Like the genie in the lamp?" She moved close enough to him to run a hand down his arm. "And you do know what happens when you rub the lamp properly, right?"

Quinn actually laughed but managed not to show off his fangs. Janie shot him a look.

He nodded. "They say that you get a wish."

"That's right." Her hand moved to his chest. "Any wish you want."

"Believe it or not, that's already my goal tonight." Quinn grabbed Angela's hand and removed it from his person. "Unfortunately, I already have my wish in mind. And . . . it's not what you're thinking."

She pouted. "Well, damn."

"You're leaving Vegas tonight," Janie said, louder this time. Was she being ignored on purpose? "There is somebody who wants to hurt you, Angela. He will kill you if you're not out of this town as soon as possible."

Angela raised an eyebrow. "Are you actually serious?"

"Deadly serious. Now, if you'd like to ignore what I'm telling you and pretend it's all just a big joke, then be my guest. However, if you'd like to keep yourself from being eviscerated—which, FYI, is the same as disembowelment—while you're still alive, I strongly suggest leaving."

Angela's mouth now gaped wide open in horror. "Who would want to do that to me?"

"Other than your boyfriend's wife?" Janie said dryly. Her sense of humor had gone from nil to nonexistent in record time. "A very bad man who does very bad things to anybody he pleases."

She nodded slowly. "I think I may leave town tonight. I'm sick of Vegas, anyhow."

"An excellent idea." Janie glanced at her wristwatch. "It's getting late. The Boss is going to be looking for me. Dammit. I don't want to leave you alone. How am I supposed to know you'll be safe?"

Angela frowned. "Who are you again?"

"I'm your sister!" She let out a groan of frustration.

"You have totally screwed up my night."

"I'll go," Barkley said firmly. "It would be my honor to protect you, Angela. With my very life. I will guard your beautiful body."

Angela eyed him briefly and then looked at Quinn. "I'd rather *you* guard my body."

"Uh . . ." Quinn glanced at Janie.

Janie bit her bottom lip. "Barkley it is. Congratulations, Barkley. You're my sister's bodyguard. Go to her hotel, get her packed, and go anywhere but here."

"Yes, sir!" Barkley hooked his arm around Angela's waist.

"Be careful," she told her sister.

"Go to hell," Angela called back and kept walking.

Janie nodded. "I think I hate her."

She turned around and couldn't believe that Quinn was smiling.

"I hate you, too," she informed him.

"You're just saying that."

"She was totally hitting on you. Even with amnesia."

"Hey, when you got it, you got it." His smile grew.

A long limousine drove past behind him, and Janie felt

a chill go down her spine as if somebody just walked over her grave. Was that the Boss? Did he just get into town?

Angela and Barkley were moving with the rest of the constant Vegas crowd. Everyone else was heading to a club, to a casino or a show. At least Angela was heading somewhere safe. She felt relieved. Not much, but enough for the time being.

She shook her head and turned for a last look at the casino and forced herself to relax as much as she could. "I wonder how long she's been doing the psychic gambling thing?"

Quinn glanced up at the replica *Arc de Triomphe* to the right. "Probably not very long. She doesn't seem very good at keeping it quiet." He turned his gaze to meet hers. "So now what?"

"A deal's a deal." She chewed her bottom lip for a moment. If that really was the Boss, then that meant things got even trickier now. "We go back to the hotel and you make your wish. I'll give the used Eye to the Boss and cross my fingers that he takes a faulty magical artifact in stride. Soon this will all be over, one way or the other."

His throat worked as he swallowed. "With any luck you'll be rid of me by tomorrow."

She looked at him for a long moment before turning away.

But what if I don't want to be rid of you? she thought, feeling those now annoying familiar tears prick at the backs of her eyes.

She focused on putting one foot in front of the other to get back across the street to El Diablo. "Then let's get this over with."

After he made his wish to be human again, it would be

over between them. He had what he wanted. She had what she wanted.

Everybody would be happy.

She was hoping the happy thing would kick in later, because she sure as hell wasn't feeling it right then.

Chapter 17

Quinn decided that he had a few problems to deal with.

He and Janie were currently taking the El Diablo elevator up to the seventeenth floor. The glass walls looked down into the red and orange casino floor. Devil-costumed waitstaff strode the area delivering complementary drinks to the gamblers. A steady line of what could only be hunters filtered into the Hell's Gate Theater for the beginning of the hunter awards.

Every single one of Quinn's problems seemed to, he decided, revolve around the beautiful blonde in the sexy red dress standing across from him. The one who had the ability to make his thoughts go a thousand different directions at one time.

He sighed.

To recap his original plans: find the Eye, make the wish, be human again. Move on from there.

It had seemed so simple. The perfect answer to all of his fanged problems.

Nothing seemed simple anymore.

He leaned back against the elevator wall and tried to appear as relaxed as possible. "Can I ask you a question, Janie?"

She tucked an errant strand of long hair behind her ear and then crossed her arms. "What?"

He noted that her fingernails weren't long and sculptured like some of the helpless women he'd known in his life. Janie kept hers short, practical, but a dark, dark red. He was pretty sure he'd heard that color was called "Vamp."

Rather apropos.

He suddenly imagined those nails raking erotically down his naked back.

Yes, thoughts in a thousand different directions. Had to focus.

"What?" she prompted again.

He cleared his throat. "This boss of yours—"

"What about him?"

"I don't understand why you don't quit. If he's so bad. Just leave."

She stared at him for a moment and then laughed humorlessly. "I can't do that."

"Why not?"

The elevator reached their floor and the doors opened. They walked down the hall to Quinn's room and entered.

"My boss," she began, "He's . . . well, we're not supposed to talk about this, but he's got these contracts. I signed the contract to work for him in blood."

Quinn felt cold at that admission. "Who the hell is this guy?"

She shook her head. "I honestly don't know. Let's just say I won't make the same mistake again."

"What? Signing your freedom away to a black magic practitioner who holds your life in his hands?"

"No. Actually I meant that I didn't read the small print. I haven't had a raise in three years." At his look, she smiled weakly. "Look, it's really not that bad. I don't always have to do shitty things for him."

"You're lying."

"But it sounds believable, right?"

"How do you get out of the contract?"

"I'll have to die." She shrugged and then frowned hard. "At least, I'm pretty sure that will release me, but maybe not. Again, I really should have read the fine print."

His stomach lurched. "Janie—"

"So, shall I go get the Eye right now and you can make your wish?" Her gaze moved over the contents of Quinn's suite, from raunchy paintings to floor-to-ceiling brocade drapes. She walked over to the window and looked out at the brightly lit Vegas strip. "I'll bet you a thousand bucks there's a message in my room from Lenny about when we're meeting with the Boss." Her heels clicked against the half moon of orange and red ceramic tiles by the window as she turned around. "Definitely not going to get my raise tonight, am I?"

"How can you sound so calm about all of this?"

"Do I sound calm? Obviously the screaming is only going on inside of my head."

"Janie . . ." He studied her for a moment longer and then looked away.

Shit. If he made his wish to be human again, how was he supposed to protect her from this bastard of a boss? And how was he supposed to do anything at all to stop Malcolm's let's-create-a-vampire-super-race plans?

Quinn had been the one who made the decision not to kill the old man when they had the chance at the museum. A stupid, sentimental decision. He hadn't even had enough time to check out the convention to make sure Malcolm hadn't done any damage there yet. He had said he'd been planning for a year for this event.

He looked up to see that Janie looked back at him with concern in her eyes. "Quinn, what's the problem?"

"I wish there was a better answer." He shook his head slowly. "I . . . I just don't want to be what I am."

She frowned hard at that, but then understanding filled her expression. "You're *not* a monster, Quinn, if that's what you think."

"That's not what I think, that's what I *know.*" His voice cracked on the words.

"You think you are. But you're not. You're . . . you're better than that. Much better."

"Don't lie."

She let out a gasp of frustration. "Why do you have to be so stubborn about this?"

He stared at her for a moment. With anger suddenly coloring her cheeks she looked even more beautiful than she had before.

"I don't know what to do, Janie."

"What you need to do is listen to me. Look at me. Even if you're stuck as a vampire for the next twelve centuries, you're not a monster and you'll never be one. You have to be a monster in your heart, and your heart is pure." She rolled her eyes. "Okay, that sounded dumb, but you know what I mean. Even when you were a hunter, you approached it with that purity. You always wanted to do the right thing. You're the coolest guy I've ever known.

You hear me? And I don't say that to just anybody, either."

He shook his head and began to look away, but she grabbed his chin and made him look directly at her.

"Do you think I'd let any vampire bite me like you did last night?" she said, and then a smile lit up her beautiful face. "And just for the record, I didn't want you to stop. Any of it. Do you think I'm lying *now?*"

She now stood close enough that he was able reach forward and brush the long blond hair out of her eyes.

He swallowed hard. "No, you're not lying."

"Of course I'm not," she said. "We made a deal, and now the Eye is all yours."

"But your boss—"

"I'll deal with him."

No, Quinn decided. They'd *both* deal with him when they took him the Eye intact. There was no way in hell he was going to risk Janie's life just so he could make his self-serving wish. End of story.

"Now, you get the red stone ready. I'll go to my room and get the Eye." She glanced around the room. "I'm going to make a couple calls and find out what the status on the Boss is. Wait here for me, okay?"

Before he could say anything in reply, she pulled him against her and kissed him hard on his lips. Then, just as suddenly, she turned and left him in the room, as his heart pounded like crazy in his chest.

Okay, she hadn't meant to kiss him.

It was just one of those highly inappropriate things that sometimes happened when emotions were running high.

Damn. The man had lips like a Greek god.

She'd let herself in to her dark hotel room and now was trying to regain her composure in front of the vanity mirror. She flicked on a sidelight to look at her reflection.

Nice dress.

Not a bad outfit to die in. And when the Boss found out what happened to the Eye, that was exactly what would happen.

Hopefully Barkley and Angela would be well on their way out of town by then.

She already had the plan all figured out. Quinn would make his wish to be human. Then, knowing him, he'd insist on coming along to confront the Boss. That couldn't happen, especially not if the wish worked and he lost his vampire strength and extra healing abilities.

Nope. She'd knock him out, throw him in a car trunk, and get Lenny to drive him out of the state, where he'd wake up and start his newly rehumanized life.

Give him a couple of days and he'd forget all about her.

"That's not something to cry about," she sternly told her reflection. A tear had begun struggling to make its way through her perfectly applied eyeliner. She grabbed a tissue and gently dabbed at it.

Thank God she hadn't totally fallen in love with Quinn. Imagine how she'd be feeling *then.*

The thought just made the tears come faster, because she knew it was a damn lie.

Two days? How the hell had she managed to fall in love with him in only two days?

She sighed heavily. Now she'd have to wash her face and reapply her makeup before she went back to see him. Terrific.

But first she had to get the Eye out of the safe and check her messages. Priorities. It was all about priorities.

She took a very deep breath and let it out slowly, studying her reflection.

"Pull it together, Janie," she told herself.

Then she crouched down in front of the room safe and dialed in the combination, opened the small door, and pulled out the Eye.

The Eye of Radisshii, the museum had called it.

The Eye of Radish.

Normally this would amuse her greatly. She managed to smile wryly at the thought.

Then she stood up, turned away from the safe, and gasped.

Malcolm Price was sitting on the edge of her bed, studying her.

He shook his head. "I thought you were much more observant, my dear. You didn't even sense me in your room?"

She hadn't. Not even a little. She glanced back at the mirror, which, of course, reflected everything but Malcolm.

Damn vampires.

Her heart thudded loud and fast.

But then she forced herself to relax. She wasn't some weak floozy who fainted at the sight of blood or danger. She was a Merc, a hired monster hunter, and she ate guys like Malcolm for breakfast.

Not literally, of course. Because . . . *gross.* The guy was old.

After another moment, a small smile curled up the side of her mouth. Quinn wasn't around to stop her from paying the old freak back for almost killing her twice.

"Malcolm, how did you know where to find me?"

He matched her smile and rose from the bed. "As a hunter, one acquires many skills related to tracking one's prey."

"Oh, I know that."

"You are not a hunter, though."

She shook her head. "Always thought they were a little overzealous. I like to diversify, otherwise I get really bored."

"You're a mercenary."

"I work for an agency right now, but you could still call me that."

She felt behind her on the vanity table. She'd slipped a wooden stake in there earlier before her mini shopping spree.

He raised an eyebrow. "Your weapon isn't in there, dear girl. I've been here for quite some time waiting for you. I had a chance to look around."

"Did you?" She found that keeping her voice steady wasn't all that hard. After all, she wasn't *completely* freaked out by this situation. A little, but not completely. He'd taken her by surprise yesterday with the cane to the back of her head, which still, despite the healing balm, was a little sore. She sure as hell wasn't going to be surprised today by him when he was standing right in front of her.

She could take him easily, even with her bare hands. She glanced down at her feet. The stiletto heels would certainly be useful. A sharp kick to the throat and . . . well, the maids wouldn't be very happy about the mess, but she'd just have to make sure she tipped extra.

Unfortunately, since Malcolm had been made a vampire only less than a decade ago, there would be the inconvenience of a body. She preferred doing battle with older vampires, because their dead bodies disintegrated so conveniently. She usually kept wet wipes in her purse to deal with such a situation.

"Yes. Quite the little arsenal you have hidden in here." Malcolm looked around the room. "Not much, but enough to take out a few belligerent foes. I suppose it's appropriate with this being the hunter convention. You fit in quite nicely, I think."

Her smile widened, artificial as it was. "That's always been my goal, Malcolm. To fit in."

"Oh, I find that hard to believe." He studied her for a moment. "You know, I think I like you."

"So sorry, but the feeling isn't exactly mutual."

"Perhaps not right now. I have been under the false impression that Quinn was to be my ally in my new plans, but I believe I have changed my mind."

"He has his uses."

He laughed. "You have brains, beauty, and strength."

"Thanks. Most guys can't get past the boobs. A little inside information? They're actually my secret weapons."

His lips twitched. "If you would hear me out, I would like to offer you greatness."

"Which means what?"

He nodded at the Eye. "You will give that to me and join me on my quest to create a more perfect world."

"Sounds tempting."

"It does?"

"No. I'm just kidding. Malcolm, don't take this the wrong way, but you're a disgusting old coot who obviously thinks he has charm when really it's just . . ." She paused trying to find the right word. "*Sad and pathetic.* No offense."

His smile vanished. "Sad and pathetic, am I?"

"Very much so."

"Quinn is the one who is sad and pathetic."

"That's debatable. However, he isn't quite as crazy as you, at least not yet. He's also a great deal hotter."

"I see. Then I retract my offer."

"Yeah, good idea."

"I will have to dispose of you, then."

She smiled brightly at that. "You can try, sweetie. You'll be the fifth vamp I've taken down in the past year and by far the one I'll enjoy the most."

She placed the Eye down on top of the vanity table and approached him with the confidence she'd earned over the last few years. Her job wasn't pleasant, and it was a rare occasion that she really felt right about what she was doing on her assignments. This was one of those rare occasions. He'd threatened her. He was scum.

He was going to die.

She grabbed the front of his shirt and found it a little surprising when he didn't resist.

"I thought you wanted to fight."

He smiled at her. "You're the one who likes to fight. I prefer to take care of things in a more civilized manner."

He lifted his left hand, which, she realized too late, held her stun gun. She felt 200,000 volts of electricity rip into her. Her muscles convulsed, and she crashed to the floor in a boneless heap. She blinked up at the old man stupidly, still twitching, but unable to move or speak.

He nodded at her. "Brains over brawn, my dear. You might want to consider it sometime."

He threw the stun gun onto the bed, stepped over her prone body, and snatched up the Eye. Just before he reached the door, he paused.

"Rude of me, isn't it?" A strange smile twisted his mouth. "Presented with such a lovely treat and I turn my back?"

He retraced his steps until he was over her. Then he grabbed the front of her dress with both hands, hauling her to her feet, and roughly threw her onto the bed.

She felt his weight press down on top of her, and couldn't stop him as he wrenched her head to the side and tore his fangs into her neck.

Chapter 18

What was taking her so long?

Quinn paced back and forth in the suite and glanced at his watch again. It had been almost ten minutes since Janie left to get the Eye. Her room was only four doors down the hall.

A couple phone calls and get the Eye. That's what she said. And then she'd be back.

Women.

He looked at his watch again. Surprisingly enough, it hadn't changed since the last time he checked.

He walked over to the ridiculous, round, red-draped bed and threw himself on it and stared up at the ceiling for all of five seconds.

Then he slammed the backs of his arms into the mattress, growled, and got up again. He couldn't relax. There was too much to think about, too much to do.

And not enough time to wait around while she powdered her nose or whatever seemed to be taking so long.

He felt in his pocket where he'd put the stone for safe-keeping, and then he left his room and walked briskly down the hall, pausing in front of her door, and placed his palm against its cool surface.

He knocked.

"Janie? Any time now. That would be great."

There was no answer.

Just as he was about to try the door to see if it was unlocked, it opened and he looked up, completely stunned to come face to face with Malcolm. Quinn's eyes widened.

"What the hell—?"

Malcolm glanced at him with dark, dark eyes, and then a slow smile spread across his features to show off his longer-than-average fangs.

"Janie and I had a little talk, and we've finally come to an understanding about this whole situation. She's sweet, that girl. Very, very sweet." His tongue slithered along his bottom lip.

"Where is she?" Quinn managed.

He shrugged. "Now, if you'll excuse me."

As he brushed past Quinn, he noticed that the old man held the Eye in his right hand. Quinn grabbed his shirt and pushed him against the wall hard.

"What are you doing here?" he growled.

Malcolm shrugged. "Just some business, my boy."

Quinn gritted his teeth.

"Where's Janie?" Hot fury raced through his veins just as he heard a small sound.

A whimper?

Tearing his gaze away from the white-haired vampire, he nudged the door open to look inside.

Janie was sprawled on the bed on her back, her limbs askew.

Malcolm shoved him then, and began moving quickly down the hallway. Quinn was about to pursue, but he turned back to the room.

Janie wasn't moving. The red of her dress seemed to have spread to the white sheets of the bed.

No. No it wasn't the dress. It was blood. *She was bleeding.*

He was at her side in a second.

"No," he managed. "What . . . what did he do to you?"

Her eyes were open and glassy, and she stared up at him. Only she wasn't really staring *at* him, it was more like she was staring *through* him. Her face was pale, corpse-like, and turned to the side so her throat was completely exposed.

His stomach lurched and he let out a strangled cry. Malcolm hadn't been gentle with her. It looked as if she'd been attacked by a wild animal, the fang marks on her neck uneven and raw.

Quinn grabbed at a pillow and ripped the case from it, trying to make a bandage. He held it against her neck to try to stop the bleeding.

"How long?" he asked her. "Dammit. How long was he here?"

Her mouth moved, but no sound came out.

Too long, he thought. Malcolm had drunk from her for too long.

Janie was going to die. The victim of a vampire. The combination of too much blood loss and the vampire toxins from Malcolm's fangs were a deadly combination.

That bastard *meant* for this to happen. He meant to leave her to die alone.

Why had Quinn waited so long before he came over to check on her? He could have prevented this.

His throat hurt so much he could barely form words. His eyes blurred. "Please, hold on. You can't die on me. Not like this."

Keeping the bandage pressed against her throat he reached toward the phone. He could call an ambulance. Call hotel security. Something. Anything.

But then his hand curled into a tight fist, and he turned away from the phone and back to Janie. Whoever he called wouldn't understand what just happened. And besides, it would be too late before anyone arrived to help even if they knew how to treat such an injury. He'd seen vampire attacks like this before. Witnessed men twice Janie's size succumb to blood loss much quicker. There was no hope for them.

There was no hope for her.

He swore loudly and got up from the bed, grinding his fists into his closed eyes. His stomach twisted painfully, and he felt as if he was going to be sick. He looked down at her and pressed the back of his hand to his mouth.

"No," he said again, and it sounded so strangled that he realized he was crying from frustration and grief. "I'm not losing you. Goddammit, Janie. Do you hear me?"

He crawled onto the bed next to her and gathered her into his arms. The life was leaving her eyes. He had no time to think things through. No time to worry if he was doing the right thing or the wrong thing, if she'd thank him or if she'd hate him.

She could hate him. She could want to kill him. He didn't really give a damn. At least she'd be alive.

He was pretty sure she couldn't hear him anymore, but

he kept talking anyhow. "You've been trying to convince me that my being a vampire doesn't make me a monster. I'm really hoping you were serious about that."

He brought his wrist to his mouth and, without taking his gaze from Janie, slit his flesh with the sharp edge of a fang. He felt so numb that he didn't even register the pain.

"I'm sorry, Janie." He pressed his bleeding wrist to her mouth. "Call me selfish. It's true. But I'm not losing you like this."

And then he prayed. Something he hadn't done for . . . he didn't even know how long. He'd been Catholic once. A good Irish Catholic boy. His mother once took him to confession. It was a fuzzy memory, since she'd died when he was only six, but it came to him right then. Lighting the candle, his mother smiling down at him, mussing his hair; then he'd gone and spoken to the priest about the tiny sins that little boys commit.

Things had changed greatly since then. He had a lot more to confess if he ever went back.

"Please, God," he murmured. "This seems like an odd situation to ask for your help with, but I'm begging you— don't let her die. Please. I'll do anything. Just get her through this. I know exactly what I'm going to do. I'm going to find that asshole Malcolm and get the Eye back. Then I'll make the wish. I'll wish Janie human again so none of this will matter and she'll be okay. But I have to do this and, please God, let it work. Let her live."

It felt as if it took forever before she began to respond to his blood.

He worried that his own lack of strength and lousy nutrition of late would come back to haunt him now. The only blood he'd had recently had been Janic's. When he'd been injured last night, his own blood had run thick and unnatural and inhuman. But what came from his wrist now was red and filled with life.

It was Janie's, after all. She'd given him his life back. Now he was returning the favor.

Finally she began to drink, and the feel of her mouth at his wrist was such a relief he felt tears stream down his cheeks, but he didn't bother to wipe them away. He held his wrist to her mouth and with his other hand stroked the long, tangled blond hair off her face.

He watched as the color slowly came back to her cheeks. Her gaze fixed on his as she drank, and the intelligence and awareness returned to her eyes. Her forehead creased as she realized what was happening, but she didn't release his wrist.

"That's right." He managed to smile down at her and then kissed her forehead, her cheeks, and the side of her mouth softly. "You're going to be okay."

A tear slipped down her temple, and he wiped it away with his thumb. Finally she closed her mouth and lay back on the bed.

"Janie?" he asked, holding his wrist tightly to stop the bleeding.

"Thank you," she murmured and then drifted off to sleep.

Janie pried one eye open and then the other.

So this was the afterlife, huh? Looks a lot like my hotel room.

She propped herself up on her elbows and looked around.

It *was* her hotel room. Two double beds. A bathroom.
A closet. A portrait of a strung-out Courtney Love on the
wall . . .

No, wait. That was her reflection in the mirror.

She reached up to touch her face and wipe at the mess
of smeared eyeliner and lipstick.

She turned her head and saw Quinn. He'd just emerged
from the bathroom. He froze in place when he saw she
was awake.

"Is that a wet towel in your hand," she managed, surprised at how croaky her voice sounded. "Or are you just
happy to see me?"

His lips twitched, and she was pretty sure she saw relief in his dark blue eyes. "I'm very happy to see you. But
this is also a towel. For your neck."

She nodded and grimaced. Her neck. Vampire chew-
toy central. Seriously. Was she wearing a sign on her back
that month that said "Bite me"?

She reached up to touch the wound, but Quinn closed
the distance and grabbed her hand. "It's pretty bad."

"Have I told you about the time when a zombie tried to
eat my intestines on an assignment?" she asked weakly.
"First of all, intestines can't possibly be a tasty treat. Ever.
Even if you're a rotting corpse. Very disgusting. But you
should see my scar. Some people think I've had a tummy
tuck. I can cover it up with a bikini, but still. Not a pleasant experience, so I'm sure this can't be worse than that."

"So I'm guessing that the zombie *didn't* eat your
intestines."

"Good guess."

He handed her the towel and she pressed it to her neck.
Damn. Hurt like hell.

She nodded over at her purse. "There's a tube of ointment in there. Can you grab it for me?"

He did as she asked and brought the small tube over to her. "What is that?"

"Healing balm. Should do the trick and get rid of these . . . wounds."

His lips were very tight, and he nodded. "Can I help?"

"Sure. Smear a little on my neck. I'll be good as new before you know it."

She saw his throat work. "You're very brave."

"It's in my job requirements."

Very gently, he dabbed some of the ointment on her neck. He was close enough that she could see that his eyes were red. She didn't ask him why. She already knew.

She was a vampire now. Just like Malcolm. Just like Quinn.

Simple. It was so simple. But just because something was simple didn't mean that it was easy. Her head hurt too much to go over what this meant for her. Not now. Not yet.

When he was done, he looked up at her. There was no humor in his expression. "I'm sorry, Janie."

"What?"

"I . . . I'm so sorry—" His voice caught on the words. "If there was another way—"

She shook her head. "Don't be sorry."

"Do you remember what happened?"

"Vaguely. The main parts." Her jaw clenched. "Malcolm was waiting for me in the dark. He used my own stun gun—my *own stun gun*—on me. I don't know why I didn't see that coming."

"I should have let you stake him at the museum."

"You think?"

He covered his face with his hands. "This is all my fault."

"Spilled milk, Quinn."

"This is hardly that simple."

"I don't have time for this to be complicated."

"Do you . . . do you feel okay?"

She slowly and carefully got up off the bed. "I've felt better, that's for damn sure." She eyed herself in the mirror and grimaced, glancing at the bite marks, which had, thanks to the healing balm, already started to heal with a tingling sensation. They still looked like she'd played the raw steak to Malcolm's pit bull, though.

"You should sit down."

She sighed at her reflection, which didn't include Quinn's. "I guess I better get used to not looking in mirrors anymore, huh?"

Quinn made a strangled noise.

She turned around and raised an eyebrow, feeling grim. "And when should I expect my fangs? Tomorrow? Next week?"

He turned away and walked quickly toward the window to look outside without answering.

Okay. So she was a vampire. Which blew. But now that it was done, there wasn't much she could do about it, was there? Janie had always tried to roll with the punches, and this one . . . this was one of the heaviest hits she'd taken.

No, scratch that. *The* heaviest hit. She'd never had to reassess her species before.

Vampire. She shook her head.

Well, it beat dying, she supposed.

She glanced at Quinn. Looked like she was handling her new life status a little better than he was. By the looks of him, he was seconds away from throwing himself through the window.

Of course, he thought being a vampire was the equivalent to being a monster.

She honestly wasn't sure he was completely wrong about that, but for the time being she felt very normal. Very herself.

"That son of a bitch stole the Eye," she told him. Perhaps a slight change in subject would be a good thing.

He shook his head. "He won't go far. He can't."

"Why do you say that?"

"I still have the stone."

She noticed that he held his injured wrist tenderly and frowned at him. "Come here."

She grabbed the healing balm and applied some to his wound. She was almost out of the stuff. That meant she'd have to go see that witch in New Orleans who made it. That bitch always made her lick a toad as part of the payment. The toad always seemed to enjoy it a bit too much.

Were-toad. Had to be.

"Thank you," he said when she finished, still refusing to look directly at her.

"How's your stake wound from last night?" she asked, then frowned.

"It's fine."

"I should have given you some of this then, but I wasn't thinking straight, I guess."

"And you are now?"

"Surprisingly, yes. Now, don't be a baby. Let's see."

He grudgingly pulled up his shirt and let her apply the balm to his already healing wound.

"God, I almost forgot all about that evil tree thing

scratching your shoulder. She ran her fingers lightly over his ribs and abdomen and then pulled the shirt up even higher, before he pushed her hands away.

"I need to go." He stood up and turned away from her. "I have to find Malcolm before he gets too far."

"And what are you going to do when you find him?"

"Tear him apart with my bare hands."

"Sounds like a good start. I'll join you."

"No. You . . . you stay here. Just rest."

"I'm already rested enough. Look, we'll find him. I have a right to get my hands on him, too, you know. The asshole almost killed me. I don't take kindly to stuff like that."

He didn't say anything.

"Quinn—" She grabbed his arm and tried to search his blank expression. "It's really okay. I don't blame you for any of this."

He nodded with a firm jerk of his head. "Good."

"We'll get the Eye back. I know you want to make your wish."

"Forget the stupid wish." He said it so harshly that she cringed. Immediately his expression softened, and he closed the distance between them to touch her face very softly. He stared into her eyes. "I thought I'd lost you."

"I'm hard to lose."

"Good to hear." His face was a jumble of emotions that she couldn't read. He pulled back from her and turned away, frowning. "I'm . . . I'm going to grab the stone and . . . and we'll go find Malcolm."

She nodded. "Okay."

With a last look, Quinn turned and left the room.

She let out a long breath, feeling very shaky, and she wasn't entirely sure it was from blood loss.

Okay, so being a vampire doesn't make you a great deal more confident. Then again, she was barely a real vampire yet. She was no more than a *va*. Maybe a *vam*.

Maybe the confidence came with time.

A hundred, maybe two hundred years should do it.

She glanced at herself in the mirror again.

He'd saved her. Quinn had saved her life and was now racked with guilt over what he'd done.

How could she prove to him that she was very, very grateful?

Quinn was shaking by the time he got back to his room. The stone wasn't there like he'd told her. It was still in his pocket, but he'd needed a few minutes to compose himself before he'd be able to do anything else. He glanced at the clock to see it was nine o'clock. She'd been unconscious for almost an entire hour.

Too much to think about.

Shit. He'd just sired Janie. He couldn't believe it.

He'd sworn that he'd never drink from another person, be they human or vampire. He'd crossed that line. He'd never even imagined he'd cross the next line, that of actually making another vampire.

She was bound to him now. That's what he'd heard. That sires and their fledglings had a deep bond that could be broken only by death.

Something stirred deep within him. Knowing that she was bonded to him felt right somehow.

Why the hell could something so wrong feel so right?

There was a soft knock at the door behind him, and he spun around to see Janie enter the hotel room.

"I'm almost ready," he said after clearing his throat. He patted his pocket. "Got the stone."

She nodded. She'd washed her face, which was now clean of makeup. Brushed her hair until it was long and silky straight. She still wore the red dress, but her heels were gone and she stood in front of him in bare feet, looking painfully beautiful and strong and . . . and *alive*.

His eyes flicked to the neck wound, which was healing faster than he ever thought possible. Damn, what was that healing balm made of?

Magic.

He felt at his stomach and could barely tell where Malcolm had pierced him with the stake. He looked down at his wrist, which tingled pleasantly. Just a thin red line left.

Before too long he could almost forget anything at all had happened.

"You saved me," Janie said softly. "You saved my life."

"I don't know if you could call it that."

"Nobody saves me."

"I find that hard to believe."

She shook her head. "Why didn't you let me die?"

"What?"

"The way you feel about vampires . . . I just don't understand why you didn't let me die."

He didn't say anything. Couldn't say anything.

She licked her lips. "You said that you'd rather be dead than be a vampire. And yet you'd make me into one that easily? I don't get it."

"I . . . I don't know what to say."

And he didn't. Well, he could tell her the truth, he supposed. Tell her that the thought of losing her—even after being with her for only two days—nearly killed him. And that he knew that there was a chance she'd hate him for making her into a vampire, but he couldn't let her die because he was madly in love with her.

Yeah. Something like that.

"I don't think I properly said thank you," she said.

"You don't have to."

"Thank you." She bit her bottom lip and looked down at the carpet.

"We need to go. Hopefully Barkley and your sister are well out of town by now, but your boss . . . Malcolm . . . we've got to take care of some things."

"In a minute." She nodded and turned back to the door, pushing it closed with a click.

He watched her warily. "What are you doing?"

She turned back to face him. "Thanking you."

And then before he could register what was happening, she walked directly toward him until they were almost touching. She reached down and took his right hand, bringing it up to her mouth.

"Janie," he breathed.

"Thank you." She kissed his palm—"Thank you"— and then her lips slid over his injured wrist.

His body stirred, and he felt his heart rate pick up. A lot. Obviously she wasn't thinking properly after her loss of blood.

She released his hand and pulled at the bottom edge of his shirt, moving it up to reveal what was left of his stake wound again. Before he could protest, she leaned over and ran her tongue over it.

He gasped, and his brain stopped working. The blood was immediately needed elsewhere.

"The healing balm tastes like strawberries," she said absently. "Weird."

"Uhh?" was all he was able to say in reply.

She drew up to look into his eyes. His shirt remained raised, baring most of his chest. The front of his pants strained tightly against his arousal.

"Is that all you have to say?" she asked.

"Janie—"

"Yes?"

He cleared his throat. "I thought you were recovering from your recent diagnosis of vampirism."

"It's a rumor that fledgling vampires take a long time to recover from being turned. As long as they get what they need from their sire right away, there's no problem."

"And, believe me, I'm definitely willing to give you anything you need," he managed, trying to sound flippant, but the raspy, husky tone to his words betrayed him "But right now we really need to—"

She cut him off. "Really need to *shut up,* I think."

Just as he was trying to think of a witty reply, she kissed him. She had to raise herself up on her tiptoes to do so, since she was currently high-heel deficient, but she managed.

God, her mouth. Just like the balm, she tasted of strawberries, he thought, as her tongue darted between his lips. He groaned at the feel and taste of her.

He grabbed her upper arms and crushed her against him, letting her go only long enough for her to pull his black T-shirt up over his head. She ran her dark red fingernails down the front of him, and he shivered at her touch.

She kissed down his neck and over his chest, running her tongue down the center of him, from the hollow of his throat, down his chest, and past his navel to the edge of his khaki pants. He drew her back up to meet her lips again. She was driving him insane—his body was literally shaking with desire for her.

When did I lose control over this situation? he wondered absently.

Screw it.

He grabbed the bottom of her new red dress and pulled it off of her, hearing a rip at the last moment.

She stiffened. "There was a zipper, you know."

"Oops."

"Do the words 'designer' and 'expensive' mean anything to you?"

"Will you take a check?" His gaze took in every inch of her perfect, mouth-watering body now clad only in black thong panties.

Yup. He would have guessed that lingerie choice, and he approved greatly.

His mouth felt very dry.

"I have an idea." She bit her bottom lip. "Why don't you just pay me in sex?"

He raised an eyebrow and grinned. "It's a deal."

Then they were on the bed. Quinn kneaded Janie's bare breasts in his hands, taking one nipple in his mouth, working it to a hard peak while his right hand slipped down her body and traced the edge of her silky panties.

"You better add these to my tab." He tore them off her and threw them to the ground.

"Quinn . . ." she moaned. "Please. Make love to me."

"You're so polite," he breathed into her ear and met her lips again in a hot, open-mouthed kiss while his hands freely roamed her body.

Suddenly, he felt her hands at the front of his pants, fumbling with the zipper. Just as he was about to help her with the situation, she slipped the khakis over his hips and he felt her hand close around him. He let out a shuddery moan and looked down at her with surprise. She raised her eyebrow at his look of shock, giving him a very wicked look.

"Janie—"

And that's when he lost all decorum. The feel of her touching him, of her writhing beneath him, was enough to send him right over the edge of sanity. He'd been standing pretty close to it up until then.

He found her mouth again and kissed her deeply. Strawberries. His absolute favorite flavor as of that moment.

Before she'd managed to work his pants the rest of the way down his legs, he stopped her. He grabbed her wrists to move them up above her head and then, with one deep thrust, he drove himself into her.

"Quinn!" She gasped and then pulled her hands away to grab at his shoulders and his back as he began to move inside of her.

"Janie . . . *Janie* . . ." he said over and over, trying not to lose control but failing miserably.

She arched her back and cried out. He felt her spasm beneath him.

Nothing had felt this good to him. Nothing at all. Nobody. He'd waited his whole life for her.

He loved her. Oh, God, he loved her. He couldn't believe it himself, but having her in his life was the best thing that had ever happened to him. Why hadn't he realized it until just now? Had it taken the possibility of losing her to make him realize what she meant to him?

"I thought I'd lost you," he managed. "I couldn't lose you. Not like that."

Her silky hair ran through his fingers. She found his mouth again, and he kissed her deeper and harder, almost violent in his need for her lips and her body . . . and for *her*. All of her.

After another minute, he cried out against her mouth and then fell against her and the soft sheets and the firm bed and her fragrant skin that surrounded him, filling his senses completely.

When he was able to think—which wasn't right away—he pushed up on his elbows, searching blindly for her mouth and finding it. He kissed her for a very long time, just exploring her lush lips and tongue, and then pulled back and looked into her beautiful blue eyes.

"Well, hello," she said.

A smile played at his mouth. "You say 'thank you' really good."

"You think?" She ran her fingers through his hair.

"How much of the dress have I paid off?" he asked.

"Not much. You have a great deal of work ahead of you."

He arched an eyebrow at her and grinned. He was definitely up for the challenge. Like, *immediately*.

He leaned forward to kiss her again.

"That was simply beautiful," a voice said from behind him. *Malcolm.*

Quinn tensed and he looked at Janie, whose eyes had widened. Then he looked over his shoulder at the intruder.

Chapter 19

I *thought* you'd sire her," Malcolm said, with a wry grin. "You really should consider locking your door before getting intimate. It's common practice in polite society, you know."

"You son of a bitch." Quinn's eyes narrowed. "I'm going to kill you."

Malcolm didn't look concerned. "I've returned for the stone. I know you have it. Give it to me."

Quinn glanced at Janie, who stared back at him with a mix of anger and uncertainty. He swung off the bed, pulling on his khakis.

"You think I'm going to give you anything after what you did to her? I should have killed you myself when I had the chance."

"But you didn't," Malcolm said. "A decision I actually found rather weak, my boy. Very Hamlet, in fact. The young prince who overthinks his actions to the point of never achieving anything at all. To his own detriment, in the end."

"Never cared much for Shakespeare."

"I believe it is our deep emotional bond that keeps you from attempting to kill me."

"Just shut up, old man." Quinn's eyes narrowed. "You think you can walk in here after everything you've done and get it from me? Not damn likely. Where's the Eye?"

He pulled it out of his jacket pocket. "Right here."

Quinn glanced down at it, every muscle in his body tense and ready to strike.

Malcolm didn't back down. "I'm sure you think you can take it from me, right? Well, let me remind you of one thing, Michael Quinn. My plan? Do you remember what I shared with you?"

The conversation he'd had with Malcolm in the country bar replayed in his mind. The gist had essentially been, "Kill them. Kill them all." Fist pump.

"What about it?"

Malcolm smiled thinly. "I'm not surprised that you came here to the very casino where I told you my plans would begin in earnest. Your first thought is to save others, even when they are scum who deserve to die."

Quinn stared at him in stony silence. He'd had so many chances to kill Malcolm. Yesterday at his house when he'd first knocked Janie out. In the alley after he'd staked Quinn and left him in the country bar. Even earlier today in the museum. Three opportunities to end a creature who'd given up his right to live by being the epitome of evil—the very thing Quinn had always hoped to save others from, even when it was misplaced.

All because the old coot used to be nice to him as a kid.

Not good enough.

Quinn shrugged, attempting to look in control. "I think all three hundred hunters in attendance here might disagree with you. And I very much doubt they'll have a problem taking you out if you try anything."

"Is that so?" Malcolm raised an eyebrow. "So many of them and only one of me. And yet tonight I shall still begin my true plans with a . . . bang."

"What the hell does that mean?" Janie snapped from behind Quinn. She gathered the sheets to cover herself and stood up.

Malcolm smiled and raised his index finger to his mouth. "Shh. Do you hear that? Three hundred hunters now gathered in the theater for their ego-stroking awards. All of them in one place. And I will kill them. All of them."

Quinn tried to laugh at that. "You must have a very big gun."

"Or a very big bomb."

Quinn's blood ran cold. "What did you say?"

Malcolm smiled. "I have placed a bomb in this building. It will detonate in . . ." He glanced at his wristwatch. ". . . less than twenty minutes."

"You're lying."

"Why would I lie about something so perfect?"

Quinn glanced over his shoulder at Janie. Why he expected her to look afraid of the old man who almost killed her, he wasn't sure. Instead, her eyes flashed angrily, her teeth clenched, her fury barely contained. He could tell she was having a difficult time restraining herself from killing Malcolm where he stood.

"Now," Malcolm said, rubbing the Eye against his leg as if he was polishing it. "I don't plan to take the ruby from you by force. It would be very foolish of me to try. I want you to give it to me of your own free will."

"Like hell. Where's the bomb?"

"Why should I tell you?"

"Because you obviously want to. If you didn't, you wouldn't have come up here to do your little dramatic presentation. You know that I can kill you easily."

"Perhaps not so easily, boy."

Quinn spread his hands. "Then why don't we find out? You have no idea what I'm thinking right now. How much I hate you. You're disappointed in me? I have no words for the disappointment I feel for somebody I once considered closer to me than my own father."

"As if you are any better than me."

"He is, you son of a bitch," Janie snapped. "There's no comparison."

Malcolm looked at Quinn. "Your whore is defending you."

Quinn backhanded him across his face.

Malcolm raised his fingers to touch his jaw.

"I *am* better than you. And you know why? Because I won't stand here and let all of those men down there die."

"That's exactly what you're going to do."

"You're wrong. You're going to tell me where you put the bomb, and you're going to tell me right now."

"What do you care about their fate? They're hunters who live by the sword and have chosen a dangerous path for themselves by killing indiscriminately. They deserve death."

"I'm curious about something. Did your God complex come before or after you'd been made into a vampire, Malcolm?"

He snorted at that. "God complex? Just because I wish to reshape the world in my own image? Because I know best for all of humanity and I will kill or save whomever I chose? You think that means that I have a God complex?"

Quinn blinked. "Well, that's pretty much the definition of it. So, yeah."

"I've planned this night for a very long time. I won't let anything ruin it."

"Then you're going to have to make a choice. Right here. Right now." Quinn paused. "You can either kill all of the hunters at the awards ceremony tonight. Or I can give you the stone."

"Quinn!" Janie shouted. "What are you doing?"

He didn't turn to look at her. He kept his gaze fixed on Malcolm's wrinkled face. "Tell me where the bomb is and the stone is yours."

"I could tell you it's anywhere, and you would believe me?"

"No. You tell me, and Janie and I will go find it. Disarm it. Then we will meet in a neutral location and I'll give you the stone and you can do whatever the hell you want to do with the Eye."

"Just like that?"

He nodded. "Just like that."

A humorless smile curled his lips. "Well, this is a rather interesting turn of events. I honestly didn't predict this, my boy."

"And you can stop calling me that. I'm not your boy."

"No, you're not." He rubbed his chin as he appeared to think things through. "Very well. It's a deal."

"It is?"

"Yes. I have years ahead of me to execute my plans."

"That's the spirit."

"I will tell you where. And you will meet me in twenty minutes downstairs at the entrance to the theater."

He nodded. "Sounds fine. Janie, grab your dress. We're leaving."

She raised an eyebrow. "My ripped dress, you mean?"

He turned and met her gaze. Despite everything, he almost smiled. "You have other clothes, right?"

She sighed. "I really liked this dress."

Malcolm raised his hand. "She stays with me."

"What?" she exclaimed.

"She will be my insurance that you will not just leave after you take care of my present for the hunters. That you will return and follow through with your end of the bargain."

Quinn glanced at Janie, who looked suddenly stricken. "I'm not leaving you alone with her."

He laughed. "So protective. Get over it. When she dresses, she comes with me."

"Forget it. The deal's off."

"Quinn," Janie said. "Just . . . just do as he says. I'm fine with it."

His throat felt tight remembering what the old man did to her an hour ago. "I don't like this."

"I'm not exactly doing cartwheels over the chance to spend time with that crazy old asshole, myself. But it's the only way."

"Such a sweet, charming girl." Malcolm raised an eyebrow. "Then it's settled."

Quinn played out all scenarios in his head as fast as he could.

He could take Malcolm down right now. Then he'd have the Eye, and Janie would be safe, but three hundred hunters plus several innocent bystanders and a good chunk of the hotel would be blown up when the bomb went off.

He could say yes to Malcolm's plan and take off after the bomb, but Janie would pay the price, both from Malcolm and from her Boss when she didn't come through with the Eye.

He tried to think of a third option but came up empty.

His only hope was to buy some more time. Disarm the bomb, then figure a way out of giving Malcolm the stone. He didn't know what the old man wanted to wish for, but he was confident that it wasn't world peace.

"Fine," he said finally.

Malcolm smiled. "The bomb is beneath the speaker's podium of the hunter awards. It would be interesting to witness a vampire risking his life to save hundreds of his enemies. Would they do the same for you, do you think?"

"Enough talking." The muscles in Quinn's right arm were twitching. If he could make his wish right now, all he'd wish for would be a wooden stake. Extra sharp.

Malcolm studied him. "I know you so well, my boy. Eight years and you still wear your emotions on your face. You are thinking of killing me. But perhaps I am lying. Perhaps I've told you the wrong location? You won't know for sure until you check it out for yourself, will you?"

"I hate you," Quinn spat out.

Malcolm's smile widened. "Best be off, now. You're wasting time. We will meet you downstairs by the tournament slot machines."

Quinn picked his shirt up from the floor, casting a worried glance at Janie.

"I'll be back."

"Is that your Schwarzenegger impression?"

"Hadn't planned it, but sure."

"Good luck."

He moved toward her with the sudden desire to kiss her again. For luck or just to touch her, to reassure her that he meant that he'd be back. But Malcolm grabbed his arm.

"Leave. My patience wears thin."

Quinn scowled at him.

"Go," Janie said. "It's okay. Don't worry. I can handle fang breath here."

"Who, me, worry? Ridiculous."

With a last look, he tore his gaze away from her and left the room, his heart thudding like a wild animal in his chest, to go prowl among the hunters who would love to make it stop.

The moment Quinn left the room, Janie had tried to kill Malcolm with her bare hands. She flew at his throat, losing the bed sheets wrapped around her in the process. He'd managed to bat her away like a pesky mosquito.

She was weak from loss of blood. She'd felt great for a while, but the events of the night were catching up to her. She couldn't overexert herself, and killing vampires was hard work.

When she got her strength back, first she'd stake him, she decided, as the elevator descended to the ground floor. Then she'd hold his head under a vat of holy water. It wouldn't do anything, but it would be fun to watch him flail around. Then she'd probably decapitate him. Or burn him.

Possibly both.

The violent thoughts helped to calm her a little.

Then her thoughts moved to her sister, and a knot formed in her stomach. She'd be okay. Out of everything that had gone on tonight, at least Angela would be safe.

She twisted her were-loom necklace and glared at Malcolm.

"For some reason you look terribly displeased with me," he said.

"Bite me."

He smiled. "But I already did that, didn't I?"

Decapitation, burning, staking, *and* electrocution. Maybe she could find some hungry rats, too.

She'd made him take her to her room first so she could grab her jeans and tank top. They'd seen better days, but the dress was unwearable. Well, it was fine if she didn't mind baring her left breast while walking through the casino on the way to where they were to meet Quinn.

She kept getting flashes of Quinn making love to her. It was very distracting, to say the least. She would have been very happy to have spent the rest of the night in bed exploring him much more thoroughly than their passionate but much too quick session before. She bit her bottom lip.

She looked at Malcolm and her eyes narrowed. He'd had to interrupt them just when things were getting good.

She spent the rest of the elevator ride thinking about even more imaginative ways to end his life.

The doors opened. She made a move to get off, but Malcolm raised his arm to stop her.

"Don't try anything," he said.

"What do you mean?"

"Don't try to get anyone's attention or warn anyone. This is between you and me and Quinn. Do you understand?"

"I understand that you're a sick, twisted freak."

"You're a fledgling now," he said. "And during their first hours, vampires are so easy to kill. I could do so with the slightest effort."

She rolled her eyes. "Blah, blah, blah. You don't scare me, jerkoff."

"You don't care about yourself?" He raised an eyebrow. "Then give me any problems and—" He fished into his pocket and pulled out small black box that Janie sinkingly recognized as a remote detonator. "—I can end this very quickly. Quinn's body will be destroyed, but I can hunt through the ashes later for the red stone."

"And you think I give a shit?" she tried to sound more confident than she felt at that moment. "Maybe I've been playing him all this time, too. Did you ever consider that? After all, I want the Eye, too."

He nodded and raised the detonator. "Very well, then."

"No—" Janie raised her hand. "Just . . . *dammit*. Just don't do it."

He smirked at her and put it back in his pocket. "Just as I thought. Come with me."

They threaded their way through the crowded casino. A devil-waitress in a red sequined minidress and black bat wings brushed past her. The dress was so short that black sequined panties could be seen as she swished across the floor on four-inch slingbacks. If Janie hadn't felt so sick and sore and bruised and worried, she'd feel positively underdressed.

They moved past the tables, and she spotted Lenny, who, not surprisingly, was still at the blackjack table. He had his cell phone to his ear.

When he spotted her, he pushed away from the table and walked directly toward her.

"Janie," he said. "I'm glad you're here. That was the Boss. Said he's been trying your cell phone for an hour and you haven't been answering. He's very . . . *unhappy* is a good word."

She glanced nervously at Malcolm, who held the detonator firmly in his right hand, thumb hovering over the trigger. "Don't you remember? It's dead."

Bad choice of words.

"Oh. Right. I've—" He shook his head. "I've been kind of out of it."

"Have you been here since the last time I saw you? How much have you lost?"

He gritted his teeth. "I was winning for a bit."

"Didn't you write an ode to not gambling once? Why didn't you memorize it?"

He sighed. "So much for my lucky streak." He glanced at Malcolm. "Who're you?"

"Oh . . . this?" She gave him a nervous, sideways glance. "This is Malcolm. Malcolm is an old friend of Quinn's."

Lenny presented his big mitt of a hand. "Pleased to meet you."

Malcolm ignored it. "Janie? Let's go."

Her head ached. "Listen, I'll catch up with you in a bit, okay, Lenny?"

"No, not okay. The Boss wants to see us immediately. He's on his way here right now. I'm really, really hoping that you have the Eye now. Do you?"

"Of course I do."

"Then we're golden."

Golden. That would be the color they'd be before they turned black while the Boss roasted them over his barbecue spit.

She was usually quite good at multitasking, but perhaps that was the old, nonvampiric version of her. This version just felt a dull ache in the pit of her stomach at the thought of facing her boss without the Eye.

One thing at a time.

"Great. Listen, when he gets here, try to keep him busy for a bit, okay? I . . . I have something I need to take care of first."

Lenny frowned. "Janie, are you all right? You look a little pale."

"I'm fine." She made sure her long hair covered the fading bite marks on her neck. They still tingled from the balm.

"But—"

"No, I don't have time right now. You can talk to him. Tell him about your poetry. I'm sure he'd love to hear some of it."

"You really think so?"

She nodded and started backing away from him as Malcolm's grip on her arm grew tighter.

"Where are you going?" Lenny asked.

"Ladies' room."

"With him?"

"I'll be back soon. Don't worry."

Lenny didn't follow. He just looked confused. She hated giving him the task of holding off the Boss, but there was no other answer.

Time had officially run out. Her hourglass had about three grains of sand left in it. She hoped those grains would count and everything would work out okay.

She hissed out a breath through her clenched teeth. Dammit, she wished she knew for sure that her sister was safe. She could only hope that she'd gotten through to Angela about how dangerous it was to stay in Vegas.

At least her sister had Barkley around to protect her like a big furry watchdog. He wouldn't let anything bad happen to her, would he?

She turned toward the slot machines.

"Oh, shit," she said out loud.

The big furry watchdog waved at her.

"Hey, Janie!" Barkley called as she and Malcolm grew closer.

Her stomach flipped over. Could this night get any worse?

"Janie," Barkley said. "I need to talk to you."

"Janie—" Malcolm's voice held a firm warning. Her eyes darted down to the detonator. One click and Quinn was dead.

She glanced at him and then back at Barkley. "Where's Angela? Is she okay?"

"Yeah, about that." He bit his bottom lip and averted his gaze. "So remember that whole thing I was talking about her and me being soul mates, and how madly in love with her I was?"

"What about it?" Her words were clipped.

"I take it back. She's a completely psychotic bitch."

"Janie," Malcolm said again. "My patience wears thin."

He moved close enough that she could feel his hot breath on the back of her neck. She cringed.

"Just a sec, Malcolm. I'm having sister issues." She looked at Barkley. "What do you mean she's a bitch?"

"*Psychotic* bitch. She got me back to her hotel room and attacked me."

"With a knife? A gun?'

"Her body. She tried to molest me."

She rolled her eyes. "There's no time for games, Barkley. She's in danger. What the hell?"

"I know! I tried to get her to pack her things, but she's completely out of control. She obviously doesn't know I'm practically alpha wolf. That means that women are not supposed to throw me on the bed and have their way with me. It takes away from my manliness."

"I don't have time for this, Barkley." Her stomach was now completely in knots.

His shoulders slumped. "And then I turned wolf. Just—*poof*—dissolved into it without any warning at all. I realized right then and there that I turn wolf when I can't handle a situation. I'm like a turtle who retreats into his shell when he's threatened. Only my shell has fur."

"Werewolves are also on my list, along with hunters and vampires," Malcolm said ominously and then glanced at his watch. "Wrap this up, Janie. Now."

She grabbed Barkley's shirt and shoved him up against a Crazy-Sevens slot machine. *"Where is Angela now?"*

His eyes widened and he pointed. "Over at the tables. She wanted to gamble some more before we left town."

Janie let him go and turned around in a circle, scanning the area.

There she was. Angela's red hair was very distinct— enough that she could spot her from a fair distance.

"This could not be worse," she said, mostly to herself.

"You've got to get her out of here right now. There's no time to waste."

He shook his head. "She told me to stay out of her way." He showed her his arm, which had scratch marks on it. "The woman has very sharp nails. Did I mention that I hate her with a fiery passion? And it's not even the hate/love deal where you hate each other and then want to do it like rabbits when you're not fighting. This is just the hate. I know she's your sister, but she is pure evil."

Janie's jaw tensed, and then she turned around in Lenny's direction and waved him back over. He'd been eyeing the craps table.

"You changed your mind?" he said. "The Boss should be here any minute."

"I need you to listen to me very carefully, Lenny."

"Um. Okay. What is it?"

She put a hand on his shoulder and pointed in the direction of her sister. "See her? The one with the red hair?"

He nodded.

"That's my sister."

His eyebrows raised. "Really? You finally found her?"

"Yeah. You know what I told you the Boss said he would do to her?"

He nodded gravely.

"You need to get her out of here right now and make sure she's safe. Do you understand?"

"But what if—?"

She shook her head. "There can't be any buts." Her eyes stung. "Protect her, Lenny. For me. Please."

Lenny nodded. "I'll take care of it. Of her. I promise."

"Thank you. Now go. Do it now."

"Okay." He turned away.

"Oh, and one more thing, Lenny?"

He turned back. "Uh-huh?"

"She won't know who you are. She doesn't know who I am. She'll probably think you're trying to kidnap her, and she'll make a big scene. Can you handle that?"

His brow furrowed. "Well, it does sound a bit challenging." He brightened. "I can handle her. She's little."

Then he took off.

She shook her head. Had to love the big guy. He sure knew how to take orders well, be they hunting down a rampant werewolf or babysitting a kid sister.

She glanced at Barkley.

He let out a long, dejected-sounding sigh. "I'm sorry I couldn't help."

"Yeah, me too."

Swallowing past the large lump of anxiety in her throat, she turned her back on him and without another word, and she and Malcolm made their way to where they were to meet Quinn in five short minutes.

Chapter 20

The first time Quinn ever met Gideon Chase, the leader of the vampire hunters, was when he'd been twenty years old, a fresh-faced young hunter with only a couple of shaky kills under his belt. Gideon was five years older and already close to taking over his father's empire of old money and sharp stakes. Quinn's first impression had been that Gideon was a really cool guy. Somebody he'd like hanging out with, grabbing a couple of beers. Somebody, despite his riches, he would be willing to fight side by side with.

That impression had been short-lived.

They'd gone hunting together. They'd found a nest—a resting place where vampires gathered together for safety and social purposes. Quinn wanted to observe only and return with backup.

Gideon disagreed. There had been a strange gleam in his eyes that made Quinn very uncomfortable. Gideon had run into the nest, and all hell had broken loose. He'd killed rampantly and without mercy. It had been a bad place, anyhow. Even now, the guilt Quinn felt about it was tempered by the fact that he knew it was a gang of vampires, no females or children, who harvested humans for their blood and kept them barely alive in order to keep the supply steady.

But Gideon had gone over the line. The sole vampire Quinn had killed that night was a young male who had tried to flee only to find himself face to face with Quinn. The vamp had wanted to fight to the death.

Quinn couldn't argue. Luckily, even with his inexperience, he'd won.

Meanwhile, Gideon had killed ten vamps all by himself. When it was done, he stood in the middle of the nest, surrounded by a few whole bodies of the young ones and the remains of the old vamps, who'd disintegrated. His face was covered with blood, and it hadn't been his own. He'd turned to Quinn and said, "That was fun." And then he'd laughed.

Quinn's blood had run cold.

Just as it did at that very moment as he watched Gideon, now in his midthirties, standing in the backstage area of El Diablo's Hell's Gate Theater, wearing a tuxedo that was probably custom-made for him.

He was an imposing man. Over six feet, with dark brown hair and piercing green eyes. Chicks were all over the guy, not just for his money—of which he had billions—but for his male model looks that camouflaged the cold, calculated killer beneath.

Quinn had been jealous of him at one time. The guy had everything going for him. He'd gone to Harvard and studied politics and business, graduated top of his class.

Plus Gideon's father thought he was the perfect son who could do no wrong.

Quinn had absolutely no idea what it would be like to have a father like that.

Okay, Quinn thought. *How the hell am I going to get past Gideon?*

Time was running out.

Janie was waiting for him. Counting on him to come through.

He still couldn't believe the turn of events that evening. He was still shaking from seeing Janie drained, then siring her, then . . . doing other things to her. All in a matter of not more than an hour.

The most important things in life always happen the quickest.

He could still taste her. His body still ached to touch her.

He shook his head to clear it. Thinking about Janie right now was not going to help him focus on what had to be done. And that was getting past Gideon and getting to the bomb. He glanced at his watch.

Yeah. And he'd better do it quickly.

He looked up and frowned. Gideon had disappeared. Where the hell had he gone so fast? Out onstage?

He felt a tap on his shoulder.

"Quinn? Michael Quinn?" Gideon said. "Is that you?"

Shit, shit, shit.

He turned slowly to face the number-one most important and dangerous man in the hunter organization.

"Gideon," he said slowly. "Great to see you."

Gideon nodded, and there was a smile in his gaze. "It's been too long."

"It certainly has."

"How have you been?"

Quinn swallowed. Didn't he know? Hadn't word made its way through the grapevine that he'd been turned into a vampire against his will? That his father, a leader in his own right, had been murdered and that Quinn's hands weren't exactly clean when it came to that nasty situation?

He forced a smile. "I've been . . . good. Really good. How about you?"

"Oh, you know. Taking care of business." He slapped Quinn's shoulder.

Taking Care of Business. It had been their theme song for the short time Quinn imagined the two of them as friends. He was surprised Gideon even remembered such a small detail.

"Can't talk long. I have to do my speech." He raised a dark eyebrow. "You know how much I hate public speaking."

Quinn snorted. "Right. Only if the spotlight isn't completely on you?"

"You *do* remember." Gideon laughed loudly. "You're staying to hear me, I hope? I'm going to talk about organization and power in numbers. I've been very busy lately, but I had somebody write it for me. I think it sounds fairly natural."

"Organization?" Quinn couldn't help but find that amusing.

"I know. I was always the gung-ho hunter without the plan, wasn't I? Well, time changes many things, doesn't it?"

You have no idea, he thought. "Listen, do you think I could go onstage for a moment?"

Gideon grinned and looked toward the stage where Quinn was focused on. "Are you serious? You want to say something inspirational to the troops?"

No, I want to grab the bomb that's about to blow your ass straight to hell.

"I'm all for raising morale. If I can do something, then I'd love to be more involved in the organization from now on."

"That's very good of you. I'm sure everyone would love to hear what you have to say. Listen, there's a VIP party afterward. You are welcome to join us. We need to catch up."

"That sounds really"—*incredibly wrong on so many levels*—"fantastic. Thanks for the invite."

Gideon smiled thinly. "Quinn, I have to say I'm rather insulted. You must really think I'm very stupid. Is that it?"

He swallowed and kept his face completely neutral. "What are you talking about?"

Gideon's smile held. "Is this some sort of pathetic assassination attempt? Because I get those all the time. It takes a great deal more to impress me these days."

"Assassination." He frowned so deeply it hurt. "Of course not."

The other man studied him for a moment. "Then I don't get it. Unless turning into one of the bloodsuckers has really fried your mind. You think you could just waltz up to me and pretend that nothing's changed as if I am not made aware of everything—be it big or small—that happens to my hunters?" His smile faded around the edges. "You've made a horrible mistake."

Quinn couldn't help but take a step back from the murderous expression on Gideon's face. He backed up into something large. Two iron vices grabbed his arms to hold him in place. Gideon's bodyguards. Of course a man as important as Gideon wouldn't be without bodyguards close by.

Out in the sun too long today. Lack of blood. Mind-blowing sex. Enough to fry his brain cells. Definitely.

He was dead.

Gideon reached under his jacket and produced a silver knife with a curved blade. It looked extremely expensive. And extremely sharp.

He brought it up to Quinn's throat so close that it bit into the skin. "Tell me why you're here."

"Because I'm trying to save your life. Can you believe it?"

Gideon raised an eyebrow. "Is that so?"

"Yeah. As a matter of fact, in about ten minutes, a bomb that Malcolm Price—who isn't quite as nice as I am—put under the podium onstage is going to detonate, taking you, me, and everybody within a block with us. So feel free to kill me now. It won't really matter in a minute."

Gideon slid the knife into his pocket and grabbed Quinn by his throat. "Are you lying to me?"

"Why don't you go out there and check? Easy enough to do."

He glanced at his bodyguards and with the barest nod of his head, they let Quinn go. Just as he was getting his bearings, Gideon grabbed the neck of his shirt, catching him off balance, and pulled him out onstage.

Quinn blinked at the bright lights. The audience—whom he couldn't see but knew were out there in the darkness—was deadly silent.

A large man in a leather jacket was in the middle of presenting the award for lifetime achievement, and he looked annoyed by the interruption until he saw that it was Gideon. Then he graciously backed off the stage, leaving it clear.

Gideon nodded at him. "Go on."

Quinn focused on the podium. When he got to it he slid the bottom door open.

"Well?" Gideon asked.

Quinn looked at him. "I was wrong."

Gideon's lips thinned, and he nodded at his body-guards.

Quinn continued. "There isn't ten minutes left. There's three."

Gideon moved to his side and looked down at the bomb. His expression didn't change from vague annoyance. "I thought Malcolm Price was dead."

"I wish he was."

Gideon motioned for someone off on the other side of the stage, a tall man with glasses whose eyes widened as he saw the device.

"Take care of it," Gideon barked. Without question, the man immediately fell to his knees and began disarming the bomb.

Then Gideon turned to Quinn. "This is ruining my event."

He shrugged. "Sorry. So are you going to kill me now?"

"Yes."

Quinn grabbed the microphone and addressed the crowd. "There is a bomb in the building. Everyone run for your lives!"

And despite the fact that they were three hundred of the toughest men and women in America, they immediately scattered screaming in all directions.

Gideon turned around in a circle, watching the sudden chaos surround him. When he turned back, Quinn had disappeared into the crowd.

Janie glanced at her watch. How much time was left? Where was Quinn? He should have been back by now.

"He's been killed." Malcolm's voice bit into her thoughts.

"Shut up."

"If he does not disarm it, the bomb will go off in less than two minutes." He smiled cruelly. "I believe we will be fine here, but if you'd prefer, we can leave the building."

"He'll disarm it."

"I still would be happy to take care of you, Janie. I am your true sire, after all. I gave you vampire life; Quinn simply smoothed out the rough edges."

Her fists ached to hit him. Knock out some teeth. Live eternally with no teeth—see how he'd like that.

Not that he was going to live eternally, because she was *so* going to kill him and shove that detonator he'd been waving around right down his vampire throat. She just had to wait to make sure Quinn was safe first.

"Shut. Up." She repeated it with an underlying danger that normally brought perspiration to even the strongest man's brow.

"As you wish."

She couldn't help but let out a small, humorless laugh at that. "Yeah, that's what all this is about, isn't it? The wish? And what are you planning on wishing for?"

"I plan to wish for omnipotence."

She eyed him sideways. "You can get a prescription from your doctor if that's a problem for you."

"*Omni*potence."

"I know what it means, you freak. Absolute power. But you're already a vampire, so what difference does it make?"

"All the difference. You see, right now, while I am a greater being with the potential to live eternally, there are still side effects. Should I not get enough blood, I will die. Should I be staked or shot with silver, I will die."

She eyed his neck. "Don't forget about decapitation."

He raised a hand to touch his throat. "But when I make my wish, none of that will affect me any longer. I can be stabbed with a wooden stake, but it won't kill me. Nothing will kill me. I will have no fears of my end, so I can focus on my ultimate plan."

"Which is?"

"Creating a race of greater beings. Those with vampire strength and stamina but the training and instincts of hunters. And they will answer only to me."

"Maybe you should get a dog. Sounds like you're in serious need of a hobby."

He ignored that. "And you, Janie. You have recovered very quickly from what happened before."

"You mean when you tore out my throat and went all happy hour on me? I'm managing."

"This is why you would make a brilliant addition to my team. Are you certain I can't change your mind?"

"I already work for a twisted psychotic bastard—why would I want to make a lateral move now?"

"You would be hard to control, admittedly, but I see great things for your future."

"I wish I could say the same for you."

There was a rush of activity suddenly as a mass of people streamed into the casino. Janie and Malcolm were off to one side, in a section of slots reserved for an upcoming tournament. There was no one within hearing distance.

"They're coming from the theater." Malcolm frowned as he watched the swell of men and women with panicked expressions milling about, heading for the exit.

Janie's heart clenched. An image filled her mind of three hundred hunters finding a single vampire in their midst—not counting her, since there was no way anyone would be able to tell that she was one of the future fanged at the moment without being told. She shuddered. They would tear Quinn apart limb from limb. Or torture him to get information.

She really wished she had a weapon at the moment. Even her high heels were upstairs. She curled her hands into fists, every muscle in her body tense.

If Quinn was dead—her throat constricted—after what had happened between them . . . then she'd want to die, too.

After she took out a slough of hunters and Malcolm first, that is.

She eyed him to see that he was now clicking the detonator. He looked disappointed. Without thinking, she kicked it out of his hand and it went flying across the floor.

"Don't be a sore loser," she said.

"Just wanted to double-check." He smirked. "But where is your lover now? He may have stopped the bomb, but perhaps the hunters stopped him in return."

"I've got to go find him," she said, under her breath, more to herself than to Malcolm.

And then she saw him turn the corner headed their way.

She felt so much relief that—yes, again—she started to cry.

Premenstrual. Definitely. Was that even possible now that she was a vampire? Would her body change so that she no longer had normal human problems like getting her period? She didn't know. All she knew was that she was a total emotional wreck. Is that really what she wanted when it came to having Quinn in her life? Her emotions in a constant state of upheaval?

If that's what it took, then, yeah.

She sucked in a breath and restrained herself from throwing her arms around him. Had to look strong and unaffected.

"I'm here," Quinn said, glancing nervously over his shoulder.

The PA system clicked on, and a voice that introduced himself as the manager of the hotel calmly suggested that everyone inside the building briefly leave the premises due to a bomb threat.

The voice was calm, but the effect was not. The remainder of the people in the casino gathered their chips and, with panicked expressions, fled to the nearest exits.

"You found my little present for the hunters?" Malcolm asked dryly.

"I did."

"And it was where I told you it would be?"

"It was."

"Then my part of the bargain is complete." He held his hand out. "Now, the stone, if you please?"

Quinn reached into his pocket.

Tension filled Janie's chest. "Quinn, what are you doing? You can't give it to him!"

Their eyes met. He might have looked only slightly strained on the surface, but his eyes held a different story. There was a storm going on inside Quinn. But when his gaze settled on her, a small amount of calm came over his expression.

"I made a deal," he told her.

"Forget the deal."

"I can't do that."

"Do you even know what this piece of shit plans to do with the Eye when he has it? Let me give you a hint. It's not to build children's hospitals in India."

Quinn hesitated. The stone was clenched in his hand now.

"I should kill him," he said.

"*We* should."

"I am standing right here, you know," Malcolm said. "And I don't take kindly to broken promises."

The old man twisted around and caught Janie into a choke hold. He was good. He even knew how to use the pressure points in her throat to render her limbs useless.

Smart guy.

Her? Not so much. She should have seen this coming from a mile away. She could blame it on severe blood loss, species transformation, and/or her mixed up emotions wrecking havoc on her brain, but there was no excuse for letting this bastard take her by surprise yet *again*. If she wasn't so scared, she'd be embarrassed.

Yet, despite his appearance, he wasn't just another old man. He was a vampire. And before that he'd been a high-ranking hunter. The man was death with a very bad haircut.

All the more reason he shouldn't be allowed to get his wish.

"Janie—" Quinn's voice sounded strangled.

"I will kill her," Malcolm snapped. "Have no doubt. She's so fresh right now that a stake would slide right through her flesh and into her heart like butter."

He shook his head. "Let her go."

"Give me the stone."

"Don't give it to him, Quinn," Janie managed.

He frowned at her hard. "Why aren't you fighting him?"

She wasn't even clawing at his arm around her neck. Her limbs were currently useless. It was a rather odd sensation, and not one that filled her with a great sense of girl power.

"If I would, I could. Pressure points? Didn't you learn about them in training?"

She felt Malcolm's fangs graze her neck. "Or I could finish draining her," he said. "Right here. She did taste divine earlier. The *stone*. Don't make me ask again."

Without another word, his eyes fixed on Janie's face, Quinn reached into his pocket and pulled out the red stone.

"Good," Malcolm breathed. "Very good."

"Quinn—" Janie noticed that his gaze left hers to move over her shoulder. She frowned. "What are you—"

Suddenly, Malcolm grunted and his grip on her throat loosened. As soon as the feeling rushed back in her body, she pushed away from him.

She turned to look at Malcolm, who was frozen in place, his arms dropped slackly to his sides. She frowned with confusion as the tip of a wooden stake protruded from his chest, but then it disappeared leaving behind a round blood stain on the front of his now-ruined white shirt.

Her gaze flicked to what stood behind him. It was the Boss, flanked by two helper drones, one who held a blood-covered stake that he'd just plunged through Malcolm's back and into his heart.

Malcolm's eyes glazed over and he fell to his knees, and then forward onto his face.

He was dead.

The Boss motioned down to him, and a drone dropped to the floor beside the old man and searched him, quickly finding the Eye. He stood up and, with eyes lowered obediently, handed it to the Boss.

"Parker," the Boss said, his tone even. "Did I not stress how important this is to me? And yet you failed me again."

Her mouth was as dry as the desert she and Quinn had spent the better part of the afternoon traveling through.

"I . . . I—" She felt a tug at her sleeve and turned to see Quinn behind her, concern and worry etched into his expression. His hand moved down protectively to her waist, and he drew her closer to him.

The Boss's gaze flicked to Quinn. "He's still alive."

She nodded.

"I told you to kill him, and you ignored my orders."

Quinn's hand tightened at her waist. "Janie?"

She turned and looked at him. "I couldn't do it."

The Boss nodded his wrinkled skull. "And now, to make things even worse, you are a vampire?" He shook his head. "Pathetic. Truly pathetic."

She reached to touch her throat, but the marks had disappeared almost completely thanks to the healing balm. "How did you know that?"

"I can smell it on you from here."

She looked at Quinn. He shrugged. "I think you smell great."

The Boss sneered at them. "My seers once told me that you were destined for greatness. Despite your previous shortcomings, I gave you this chance to prove your worth to me. You have failed." His gaze moved to Quinn. "How rude of me not to introduce myself. I am he who shall end your life tonight. Yours and Parker's."

"Oh, yeah?" Quinn growled. "And I am he who shall end yours first."

The Boss laughed, a dry cackle that, as per usual, sounded riddled with disease. "Perhaps earlier I would have found you more humorous, but now I am simply weary and ready for this all to be over." He looked at the Eye. "Finally. After a millennium it is mine again."

"A m-millennium?"

Janie hated that the man made her stutter with nervousness. This is not how she'd envisioned her final meeting with the Boss.

The casino, except for them, was completely vacant. No witnesses. She was living on borrowed time now.

"Yes, Parker. This"—he held up the Eye—"was my staff, you see. And it was taken from me by a tribe of humans who once worshipped me until they betrayed me, a cloak of magic placed over its location for all this time until very recently. They were very good at keeping it from me for so long, but I will have the last laugh."

"Your staff?"

"It is part of me. Part of what little power I still have

left. It represents that which was taken away from me when I was banished."

"Banished?" Janie felt very confused, which wasn't really a big stretch from when she'd been *sort of* confused. "From where?"

"From Hell." His thin lips twisted into a humorless smile. "I was a high-ranking demon at one time. For many millennia. And then my power was taken from me by Lucifer himself. I was punished. Sent here to the earthly realm. They expected me to wither away into nothingness among insipid, vile humans. The only thing that has kept me alive for all of this time has been hate and my deep desire for revenge."

"You're a demon?" Janie repeated, feeling cold at the thought. Why that had never occurred to her, she had no idea. She'd always referred to her "boss from hell." She'd never known she'd been speaking literally.

"Not just a demon," the Boss said, raising his hairless eyebrow. "I answered only to Lucifer."

"And that's what your wish is?" A cold feeling of dread swept over her. "To be a demon again?"

"This fragile body grows weaker by the day. All will soon be restored, and I will get my revenge on all who have betrayed or disappointed me." His eyes narrowed. "And that includes you, Parker."

"But I found the Eye. Doesn't that count for anything?"

"You intended on letting your lover use it. Even with my threats toward your sister. You didn't believe that I would follow through?"

She glanced at Quinn. *Her lover.*

The Boss knew everything, didn't he? The thought was not in the least bit comforting.

Damn seers. She only hoped they didn't have some sort of psychic video connection to YouTube.

She didn't try to deny what he said, knowing it would be wasted breath. "But you have it now."

"Yes." He smiled, and then he laughed in a way that made Janie even more nervous than she already was. "All of these creatures in search of the Eye for all of these years, hoping to find it to use it for their own purposes. *Any one wish* was the rumor, yes?"

Quinn's grip tightened at her waist.

"That's what they say," Quinn said. "Make one wish and the Eye grants it."

"Amusing how information can be twisted over many years to become that of legend and myth. Yes, there can be only one wish. However, *I* am the only one who can make that wish."

Janie was stunned at this news, and then she glanced at Quinn, whose face had whitened. "*You're* the only one?"

He smiled wistfully. "Wait until you see me in demon form. I am a thing of horrific beauty."

She was beginning to think that Malcolm's wish for omnipotence was almost cute compared to her Boss turning full demon.

But the Eye wasn't complete, was it? Not without the red stone that Quinn still had. Did the Boss even realize that?

She turned to look up into Quinn's dark blue eyes. His expression was tense, and he hadn't moved from her side since Malcolm had been slayed.

Did he know what she was thinking?

Yes. She could see it in his eyes. He knew. She didn't have to tell him.

He had to go. He had to run and protect the stone. Take it somewhere that the Boss would never be able to find it. There was a chance that Quinn could escape before the Boss even knew what was going on and what he was missing. A slim chance, but they had to take it.

Quinn's throat worked as he swallowed. He shook his head almost imperceptibly.

She could almost read his mind. *No, I'm not leaving you. Not like this.*

But she didn't give him a chance. She pushed him, hard, away from her and moved toward her Boss and his helpers to distract them. She didn't look to see if Quinn had taken off. She knew he had.

"Parker, what are you doing?" the Boss said, frowning. "You're a bit of a freak, do you know that?"

"I suppose you want to kill me now," she said.

He raised an eyebrow. "It does sound tempting. But that can wait until after."

"After you've made your wish."

"Yes." He looked down at the Eye then, studying its beautiful etched details. If what he said was true, he hadn't seen it in person for ten centuries. His pale, watery eyes appraised its every surface. And then his brow slowly lowered, and he raised his gaze to Janie's.

He'd noticed the discrepancy.

"Where is your lover?"

"Gone."

"He would leave you to face my wrath alone?"

She said nothing.

Then his eyes did the oddest thing. Where vampires's eyes turned black when they were very hungry, her Boss's eyes filled with what appeared to be . . . fire? A red and orange gleam that froze her inside. She hadn't seen that before. Ever.

"Bring her," he said, and his helper drones grabbed her on either side, painfully, and dragged her through the deserted casino.

Chapter 21

Quinn had escaped. He had the stone. He could run away and try to forget any of this had happened with his safety intact, knowing that the demon he just had the misfortune to meet wouldn't be able to make his wish.

He stood outside, next to the fountain of the Bellagio as it did its choreographed water dance to Celine Dion singing about her heart going on.

And on.

Then he swore loudly. Loud enough that the gathered crowd turned to look at him as if he was something to be wary of. Something to fear.

He was.

He'd left her. Just like that. Without even arguing. Without coming up with a better solution.

And now she was going to pay the price. Her boss would kill her for her betrayal.

He never understood why she seemed so ready to follow his orders when she appeared so strong and self-sufficient.

It was because her Boss was a demon. Even in a weakened shell, Quinn could sense his power thrumming just beneath the surface. It had turned his blood cold just to be in his presence.

How had Janie started working for him? He was willing to bet that it wasn't of her own accord. She had been forced to sign that contract in blood. To do his bidding under great duress.

And now she was going to die because Quinn had been unable to protect her.

He let out a soft, humorless laugh at that. Janie would kick his ass if she knew he thought he could protect her. She didn't think she needed protection. But she did.

And he'd failed.

She could already be dead.

The thought tore at his insides.

He shoved his hand in his pocket and wrapped his fingers around the hard red stone. He had to save her. Whatever it took, he wouldn't stand by in the shadows while she was murdered.

I love her.

The thought wrapped around his heart and held on tight. She was everything he thought he didn't want. Too stubborn, too much baggage. Too opinionated. A real pain in the ass, all things considered.

And he didn't want to live another day without her in his life.

He didn't know if she felt the same way. She'd given herself freely to him earlier when they'd made love. She hadn't blamed him for turning her into a vampire. They'd worked together like a well-oiled machine when they weren't fighting.

But that didn't mean a thing.

Okay, he told himself. *Stop wasting time. Go back and find her before it's too late.*

She was going to be pissed at him for doing this. She could be. He was fine with it.

As long as she was safe, nothing else mattered to him.

He ran back to the El Diablo. There were flashing lights of police cars that had just arrived, probably to investigate the bomb threat. All he had to do was sneak in past them.

A man stood with his back to Quinn, his arms crossed in front of him, staring up at the hotel. He was alone.

It was Gideon.

No one was watching. This could be the opportunity of a lifetime. Sneak up behind the leader of the hunters and snap his neck. It would be murder, but could he justify it to himself that it would save so many in the long run? Also, Gideon was well known for being unforgiving to those in the hunter ranks who disappointed him. Torture was one of his tools for getting the information he wanted.

Kill him. Break his neck. It would be fast, and the man who had ended so many with no thought to gentleness or being nice about it would be dead.

He tried to summon something inside himself, that spark of the killer he once was, but came up empty. Quinn wanted never to kill again—not if he could help it. And not like this.

"I know you're there," Gideon said softly without turning around.

"You do?"

"I don't like when things are out of my control. There are few things I cherish, and my power is one of them."

"Could have guessed that."

He turned to face Quinn. There was no friendliness on the man's face, only weariness. He looked much older than his thirty-five years. "Why did you do it?"

"Do what?"

Gideon's lips curled into the ghost of a smile. "Warn me about the bomb."

"I wish I could hang out and chat, but I'm needed somewhere else right now."

"Then tell me quickly."

"Because I don't believe in mass murder. And the man who planted the bomb had a very skewed idea of the world now that he's a vampire."

"And you don't?"

"No. Actually, I see things a lot clearer now."

"Does it make things simpler?"

"What things?"

"Choices. Life and death and all that lies between?"

"Not sure what you mean, exactly, but no. Choices are not any simpler. Clearer, maybe, but not simple."

"And where is the man who planted the bomb now?"

"Dead."

"I see." Gideon nodded. "Can I tell you a secret, Quinn?"

"Make it a fast one."

"I know that vampires are not all deserving of death. It was my father and my father's father, and those that went before, that made the decision that vampires would be our targets—our life's mission to destroy. They were blind to reason, but I am not."

"So what is that supposed to mean?"

Gideon's expression shadowed. "It changes nothing, of course. But it does make me question my own humanity. The fact that even knowing what I know—I won't stop. I'll never stop what I'm doing until all vampires have been wiped off the face of the earth."

Quinn felt cold at his words. "And you think that's going to happen?"

Gideon breathed out a short laugh. "Unlikely. But my life is devoid of challenge. Women are too easy—none excite me enough stimulate my intellect. Other men fear me, and I call no one my true friend. My father was too focused on his work, and now he is dead. There is only me and my mission."

Quinn nodded. "No challenge, huh?"

"I climbed Mount Everest last year. It was disappointingly uneventful."

"Vampires are pretty easy to kill."

His mouth turned up in a cruel smile. "Like shooting fish in a barrel. So few put up any sort of a challenge. They just accept death. It bores me. I thought for a moment that you would present me with an interesting diversion tonight, but even you . . ." He trailed off and sighed. "You offer nothing new."

If Gideon weren't whining about not having enough cool things to kill, Quinn might even feel sorry for him. He supposed that was what it was like, to have everything in the world, any woman, any material possession, the luxury to travel to the four corners of the globe and stay in style. Life would be boring after a while.

Gideon had nothing he cared about.

Quinn had Janie.

That made all the difference at the moment. And he'd do whatever it took to save her.

The helper drones pushed her, wordlessly, into a suite at the hotel that made Quinn's lavish room look like the economy special. The place was still empty of guests. As they passed a window, she saw the flashing lights of police cars and ambulances that had arrived in case the bomb scare had not been false.

Janie was preparing herself mentally for death. She'd done it before. It was a quick assessment of everything she'd lived through. That which she would miss, that which she wouldn't. During her meeting with the Boss the other day, she'd decided that all she'd miss in the world were her new shoes. A lot had changed since then.

Now she knew that she'd miss Quinn. Just the thought made her throat thick with grief. The crush she'd felt for him as a kid had been nothing compared to how she felt now. It had been just kid stuff. Cute in retrospect.

Now she was truly, deeply in love with him. She'd imagined herself in love with other men over the years. High school boyfriends, the creep who'd roped her into working for the Company, and even the evil wizard she'd made the mistake of falling for while on assignment. After his death, she'd sworn off men. Sworn off the chance of having her already cold, hard heart break any further. It just got in the way of doing business.

Until Quinn came back into her life. She couldn't deny her attraction to him. He was very handsome and had a smile—when he chose to use it—that turned her inside out. She couldn't even pinpoint the exact moment when that infatuation had turned into love.

But it had. She loved him. Enough that she cared more about his safety than her own. He was safe. He was gone, and he had the stone. The Boss could do whatever he wanted to her now. She was at peace with her decision and sacrifice.

Well, not completely, but she was working on it.

She wondered if Quinn felt the same for her.

I guess I'll never know, she thought.

At least her sister was safe with Lenny. Her sister who didn't remember her. But it didn't matter. Janie remembered *her,* and she was safe and that's all that mattered.

There was a knock on the door.

The Boss motioned for his drone to answer it.

The drone opened the door and was met with another mindless drone. They nodded pleasantly at each other.

"Hey, Joe."

"Hey, Steve."

"Come on in."

She craned her neck to look over her shoulder, and her body froze at what she saw.

It was Lenny. A very worse-for-wear Lenny. He was pushed into the room, and he slumped forward. His face was covered with cuts. His upper lip was swollen. His shirt was torn and bloody.

"Lenny!" she exclaimed.

He looked up at her, and she saw that one eye was swollen shut. "Janie!"

The drones had Lenny's notebook, and they flipped through it, pointing at page after page, tittering like school-girls. Then they tore pages out of it. Lenny's beloved poetry.

The sight of it was enough to make Janie's blood boil.

The Boss approached and looked up at Lenny. "From

her I would expect betrayal, but from you? I didn't think you were smart enough to be concerned about."

He said nothing.

She was worried about Lenny. He looked very defeated. And what about her sister?

She didn't have to wonder very long, because Angela was the next person to be shoved into the room. She glared at Janie.

"Everything was great in my life until I met you," she snarled. Then she turned her head to look at Lenny and her expression softened. "Lenny! What have they done to you?" She ran over to him and threw her arms around the big guy.

Janie frowned.

Angela tenderly kissed his lips and his injured face. "Are you hurt?"

Lenny didn't pull away. "I've felt better."

Angela glanced at Janie with tear-filled eyes. "You're the one who sent him to me?"

"Didn't work out quite the way I expected, but yeah. What was what, a whole half hour ago?"

"It doesn't matter. He's the only good thing that's happened tonight." She kissed his lips. "He's the man I've been dreaming of all of my life."

"Let's not get dramatic."

"No, I'm not being dramatic. I've literally dreamed of him. My big, beautiful mystery man who fills my nights with true love and erotic pleasure. I thought he was only a dream, and then all of a sudden there he was."

"You've dreamed of him all of your life? Erotically? *Lenny*?"

"Yes. At least the last few years I have. I don't remember anything before that."

Janie let out a long sigh of frustration. "That's because you have amnesia. Like I was telling you? God, you're so annoying."

"Don't talk about her like that," Lenny protested. "I love her."

"Let me guess, you've been dreaming of her, too?"

"No. But it doesn't matter. The moment I saw her, I knew. We were meant to be together. I even read her some of my poetry . . . before we were . . . *interrupted* . . . and she loves it."

"You were reading her poetry when you should have been leaving town? Great. Just great."

Angela glanced at Janie. "The man has a talent with words. He really should get an agent."

"If I may interrupt," the Boss said as one of his drones brought him a martini. "You may wonder why I've gathered you all together here tonight. Well, it is quite simple. I plan on torturing you"—he nodded at Angela—"as part of my punishment to her"—a nod at Janie—"and then I will kill you all."

"Can't we talk about this?" Janie asked.

"No."

"There has to be some way I can make this right."

"There is. Have your lover bring the stone back to me. That is the only solution."

She bit her lip. Hard. "Not going to happen."

"Then I'm afraid the night shall not end well for you." Fire flashed in his eyes again.

Just as he was about to protect Angela, Lenny was pushed down into a chair and handcuffed to it. Front-row seat. The drones grabbed Janie's arms again.

Angela blinked up at the Boss, who approached her

like something out of a nightmare. "I don't want to be eviscerated!"

He hovered his hand over her face, not quite touching. "There is a veil of magic over you. A curse."

"A . . . a curse?" she stammered.

"Shall I lift it for you?" He smiled. "My powers are not vast, but that is within my means. Shall I do that?"

He didn't wait for an answer.

Angela screamed, and Janie wrenched against the men, who held her still.

Her sister went silent, her eyes closed tightly, and then she slowly opened them and looked at her. "Janie?"

Janie's heart lurched. "Angela? You remember?"

She nodded. "Oh . . . oh, my God. I can't believe this. I left and you didn't know where I was all of this time. I'm so sorry!"

"What happened?"

"I went out partying. I wanted to get drunk. I went to a club just to dance and forget everything." She laughed dryly. "I guess it worked, didn't it? A guy started flirting with me. We got along really well. Left together. His girlfriend found us making out in the parking lot. She was a witch . . . said some stuff in Latin. And then everything I knew went away."

"She cursed you."

"The guy wasn't even that cute. I was definitely wearing my beer goggles." She glanced at Lenny.

He swallowed and looked down at the plush carpeting. "So I guess this means that you and I—"

She shook her head. "It doesn't change anything. My heart has known you for years, Lenny. I love you."

"*My heart has known you for years,*" he repeated. "That would be a great title for a poem."

"Which you will never have the chance to write, since you will be dead," the Boss finished. "Now"—he gripped Angela's shoulder and his eyes blazed—"shall we begin?"

"No!" Janie yelled.

The door burst open, and she looked over to see Quinn standing in its outline.

"Am I too late?" he asked.

"Quinn!" she managed, struggling against the men who still held her. "What are you doing here?"

"Saving you."

"How did you find us?"

"The place is empty. It was easy to follow the screaming."

"I'm going to kick your ass."

"That's what I thought you'd say, but I'm still here."

The Boss regarded him in silence for a moment. "I could rip your heart from your chest where you stand."

"That sounds unpleasant."

The Boss's eyes turned to flame.

Quinn held up his hands. "No need for violence. I've brought you what you want."

"Have you? Just like that?"

"Just like that. But you have to release everyone." He glanced at Janie with concern.

The Boss smiled thinly. "Love is a dangerous thing, vampire. You would risk so much for a woman who does not even possess the ability to feel such an emotion? Remember one thing, I hire my employees based on their lack of conscience. On their cold ability to do their jobs without any threat of emotion playing a part. Parker has rarely failed me in that respect. She doesn't love you."

Quinn's expression didn't change. "I'm here to give you what you want and you're arguing with me? Yeah, that sounds intelligent. I can see why you're the boss around here."

The Boss's eyes narrowed. "Do you know that there is a scale on which all life is ranked? Demonkind, of course, is at the top. Humans take up a great middle section, since there are so annoyingly many of them, but within that category they are separated into the weak and the strong. Those who would fight to live another day, versus those who would kneel before their death without raising a finger to stop it. Then there are the others. Those with magic infusing their existences, like werewolves and witches and fey and other lessers. They rank lower than humans, for their souls are not quite as tasty, you see? But at the very bottom, do you know what is there?"

Quinn crossed his arms. "Let me guess. Vampires?"

"No. Actually, angels. They are really annoying. But just above angels are vampires."

"You talk a lot for an evil entity."

"Give me the stone."

Quinn eyed him warily. "Any reason you're not just taking it from me?"

The Boss's lips twisted. "Unfortunately, I cannot take it from you; you must give it to me of your own free will. It was part of my banishment. Rules and regulations even apply to demons."

It was in Quinn's hand in a flash. "Let them live and it's yours."

"You would take me at my word?"

"When you have what you want, you won't give a shit about them anymore. I'm sure you'll have much more interesting things to take care of, won't you? What difference will it make if you spare a few meaningless creatures?"

"Quinn, what the hell are you doing?" Janie said through clenched teeth.

"Silence," the Boss hissed. "Very well, vampire. I will give you my word the only way I can. By giving you my name. The demon Radisshii gives you the solemn vow that you and your friends here shall be spared my wrath."

"*Radisshii?* That's seriously your name?"

"Now, the stone?"

Just as Janie was about to open her mouth to protest, Quinn threw the ruby at the Boss.

Since the Boss was very old and frail, the stone hit him in the face and fell to the floor.

"Ouch," he said.

Quinn cleared his throat. "Sorry. I . . . I thought you'd catch that."

A drone dove to the ground, picking it up and handing it to the Boss with eyes lowered in reverence.

The Boss rubbed his cheek, which now bore a small red mark. He frowned.

Quinn raised his eyebrows. "Remember, you said you wouldn't kill me. Now let my friends go."

"Silence."

The Boss—the demon Radisshii—produced the Eye, running his dry fingers over its golden surface. "I've waited so long. I can hardly believe the time has finally arrived." He raised the Eye to his mouth and kissed it gently. Then, with fingers shaking, he slid the red stone into place on the bottom of the filigreed silver globe. It fused with the rest of the staff with a small burst of light.

Janie glanced at Quinn, feeling such mixed emotions she thought she might be physically ill.

He'd come back for her. He'd gotten out in one piece, but he'd come back to save her.

She never thought she'd have her very own knight in shining khakis, but there he was, standing just a few paces away, his gaze fixed only on her.

On the other hand, his saving her meant the rest of the world was basically screwed when the Boss turned into his full demon form.

While it had been a very romantic gesture for him to return with the express reason of saving her ass, he really hadn't been using that big beautiful vampire brain of his.

She tried to remember what she knew about vanquishing demons. It hadn't really been her specialty. Had she thought for even a moment that her Boss was a demon, she would have gotten a dozen grimoires and read up on the subject. But she hadn't. She'd never liked homework all that much to start with. What she knew about slaying vampires or hunting down werewolves and other nasties she'd learned by doing.

Unfortunately—or rather, *fortunately*, up until now— demon hunting wasn't her deal. Demons usually stayed in Hell or the Underworld, since most of them found the earthly realm much too dull.

The Boss had started to chant something in a language she couldn't place. Something ancient and magical and infused with evil. If a language could be evil, then the one he was speaking fit the bill. There were a lot of consonants.

The room went silent and the air seemed to thicken. She waited, feeling the sweat dripping down her back. It was getting warmer in there by the second. Like a posh, expensive microwave oven.

She had to do something. Anything. She struggled against the men who held her still. "Boss! Let's talk about this. Maybe we can make a deal."

He opened his eyes. "You interrupted me."

"Sorry."

"No, you're not. You're trying to stop me from making my wish."

"That's silly. But maybe you're focusing on the wrong thing. Maybe this is the wrong time. Wait until tomorrow. It doesn't seem like it's working, anyhow. A nice night's sleep will do everyone some good."

"I've slept enough," he said, smiling. She noticed that his teeth had grown sharper. "It is as if I've been unconscious for a thousand years and tonight I shall finally awaken."

The Eye began to glow, a very soft light emanating from underneath the filigree. He looked at it and smiled.

"Let us go," Janie said. "You promised."

"Yes, I did promise, didn't I. It is unfortunate that I lied."

"But you used your true name!"

"I gave you the wrong pronunciation." He smiled thinly. "I will be quite hungry when I change. I shall begin with a light meal of you and your sister. If I still have room, then your lover and partner will follow. For dessert I may nibble on a couple of my servants."

Joe and Steve exchanged a nervous glance.

"Janie—" Quinn said, and she craned her neck to look at him. "I can't move. I'm . . . *shit* . . . I'm frozen in place."

"My power grows even before I make my wish." The
boss's old wrinkled face was filled with demonic joy.
'Shall I tear him apart now or wait for later? It is so very
tempting."

"Don't hurt him!" she yelled.

A sound began, a low buzzing that increased in volume until it filled the room and hurt Janie's ears. She
heard somebody scream and saw it was Angela, covering
her ears and staring around with terror. Lenny struggled
against his bindings.

She had to find some way to stop him from saying the
words. From making his wish out loud.

And then, as if he'd creepily read her mind, he looked
directly at her. "But I don't have to speak it, Parker. I told
you that the Eye is part of me. It already knows what I
want."

Just then, the Eye burst open, the delicate silver filigree that encased the globe-like top parting until the
smooth crystal beneath was fully exposed. It glowed as
hot and bright as a tiny white sun, and the Boss held it at
arm's length as if the brightness was too much even for
him to take. The noise was so deafening that if she'd
yelled something, even if she'd screamed, she wouldn't
be heard.

It was too late. She'd gone into this assignment not
caring what it was he wanted her to retrieve. Not caring
who had to get hurt or who it might hurt once her assignment was over. All she cared about was saving her sister.

Hell, it wasn't even about that at the core level. She'd
cared only about saving her own skin. She thought she
didn't care if she lived or died, but she'd been fooling herself. Self-preservation had kicked in.

And this is what had come of the decisions she'd made in her life.

She wanted to give up all hope, but she still managed to cling to it weakly. As long as she and Quinn were still alive, there was a chance to fix this. To stop this.

The bright white crystal turned red—a swirling red and orange and gold like the fire that she'd seen in the Boss's eyes.

Seeing that globe of fire extinguished the small bit of hope she still had. That fire wasn't filled with light. It was filled with endless darkness.

She had no control over this, no say in the outcome.

Quinn had tried to save her, but now they were all doomed.

The red light extended itself like cobwebs, crawling up the Boss's arm and over his shoulder. Down his neck to his small, frail body. Up his face to slide onto his cheeks like red veins, like the roots of a belligerent tree taking deep root in his body from the outside in.

After a moment he was completely encased with the pulsing veins of fire. Past the incessant loud buzzing sound, she could hear something or somebody screaming. It was her Boss. He screamed with pain from inside that thing.

It was eating him alive.

It was killing him.

But not in the good way.

It was killing what he was now. The small, physically weak man whom she called Boss. Who gave her orders she feared not to follow through with. Who made his employees sign their contracts with him in blood. Who killed those who failed to do their jobs according to his whim.

That wrinkled, scary, pathetic thing was dying.

And then the screaming stopped.

The drones released her, and all three of them dropped to their knees, blinking around at the rest of them.

"We're free!" one said.

The veil had been lifted from them, too, just like the amnesia had been lifted from Angela. It took the Boss's death for them to be freed from his influence, from his magic. They were no longer drones or slaves, but free men.

The thought should have made Janie happy. But she couldn't take her eyes off the faceless, silent red thing in front of her.

"We need to get out of here," she said quietly. "Right now."

The Eye dropped to the floor, and the red thing slumped heavily down next to it in a heap.

"He's dead," Lenny said. "He's dead! It must have killed him."

Quinn shook his head slowly, coming close to grab Janie's shoulder and turn her around. "Like you said, let's get the hell out of here."

"I'd really rather you didn't use the word 'hell' right now."

"Come on!" he yelled, grabbing for her arm.

A former drone quickly released Lenny from his bindings, and he grabbed Angela in his arms and the two ran from the room. The drones followed.

Janie stood, frozen in place, staring at the red form lying in the middle of the floor.

And then it began to change.

It started to grow and shift.

"Janie, are you deaf?" Quinn yelled, his grip on her arm tightening. "Let's get the hell out of here!"

She turned to look at him. His face was damp with perspiration, and his eyes were wild.

"You shouldn't have come back."

"I wish that had been an option for me, but it wasn't."

"Go," she whispered. "I'll try to stop him."

"Like hell you will."

"There's that word again."

"You're coming with me if I have to knock you out and throw you over my shoulder."

"I'd like to see you try."

"We don't have time for this, Janie."

"Then get out of here. Save yourself."

"God, you're so annoying. Fine. Have it your way."

"You're going?"

"No. I'm staying with you. We can fight him together."

She paled. "That's crazy."

"Just what I've been trying to tell you." His face was strained with emotion. "Now, unless you can come up with a plan better than *stupid,* then we've got a problem."

She licked her lips. "I've suddenly come up with another plan."

"That's good to hear. You suddenly remembered how to kill a demon?"

"No."

"Then it's not as good of a plan as I'd like."

She took a step toward the morphing demon.

"Janie—!" Quinn's voice was strangled. "Don't!"

But she didn't listen to him. Couldn't listen to him. There was only one thing she could do. She leaned over and grabbed the Eye off the ground.

"I have to destroy this," she told him. "Let's go."

He nodded and turned to the door; Janie followed, but something thick and wet shot out and wrapped around her ankle. She looked down. It was part of her Boss. His hand, still morphing, still changing. It held on to her so tight that it felt like it would snap her in two. It burned her ankle and up her leg. She screamed.

"Janie!" Quinn turned back.

"Take this," she threw the Eye at him. "Go!"

"You're obviously not a very good listener." He shoved the staff into his waist band and grabbed her hands. "Don't let go."

The floor caught fire from where the Boss lay. The red material on him and surrounding him was actual hellfire. The bed ignited next. Janie's leg felt as if it was burning. Her eyes filled with tears of pain.

"Dammit." Quinn put his arms fully around her and held her against him. Then he kicked at the burning arm. "Let go of her, you bastard."

The demon didn't loosen its grip. If possible, it got even tighter.

Quinn grabbed the Eye and, using the end of it, jammed it into the thing's head. There was a muffled scream and suddenly Janie was loose.

She didn't think. She just ran through the burning room, Quinn clinging to her arm. She took a last look over her shoulder in time to see the huge demon rise to its feet behind them.

Chapter 22

In the elevator, Quinn inspected Janie's leg, yanking at the denim to pull it up. It was raw and red and bleeding, but at least it was still attached.

He felt great relief. "I hope you have some of that healing balm left."

"I think I'm all out." She gently touched his throat where Gideon had threatened him with his blade earlier. "You're hurt, too."

"Just a scratch. We'll both heal before too long. One of the perks of being a vampire."

The elevator shuddered as a roar sounded out that shook the hotel's foundations, and they braced themselves against the railing.

Quinn cleared his throat. "So maybe when this is over we can go for a drink. Maybe see Wayne Newton?"

"Sounds great." She blinked slowly. "How are we going to stop him?"

"You may not believe me, but I actually do have a plan."

"You do?" Her eyes widened. "What?"

"It partly involves us getting out of here very quickly."

The doors opened at ground level, and he grabbed her arm and they raced outside.

Quinn turned slowly to look at the tenth-floor balcony. A large red thing stood there, its hands braced against the railing, looking down at them and roaring so loud it hurt his ears. It seemed to be on fire, as was the room behind him.

He could see its long, sharp teeth as it smiled.

The thing was huge. Probably five or six hundred pounds, ten feet tall. It had large white horns that protruded from either side of its skull.

Basically what he would have expected a demon to look like.

The hotel was on fire, a fire that quickly began to consume the rest of the building.

Janie's grip on his hand was very tight, and they looked at each other.

"Wayne Newton, you said?" she managed. "I'm actually more of a Tom Jones fan. Is he in town right now?"

"We can check it out."

"Parker!" the demon screamed with a sound that painfully reverberated through Quinn's skull. "I will destroy you! I will destroy all of you!"

He felt her body tense. "What are we going to do? When he gets to full strength, he's going to destroy everything!"

He shook his head. "It's already taken care of."

"Why do you sound so damned confident?"

"Do I? I'm not really, but I'm very hopeful."

"That will get us all killed. But it's a nice sentiment."

"I'm a romantic."

"Is that it?" a voice said from beside him.

He looked over at Gideon and nodded. "It is."

A smile spread over Gideon's handsome features. "Nice."

When he'd been faced with Gideon earlier, he'd quickly told the hunter all about the demon who would likely be making an appearance very soon. He was counting on Gideon's passion for adventure and difficult challenges. And he'd been absolutely right. Gideon had salivated at the thought of getting the chance to slay a true demon.

Gideon was flanked with five large men, all of whom looked ready for battle, gazes focused on the burning El Diablo Hotel.

He blinked. One of them was . . . Barkley?

"Barkley, what the hell do you think you're doing?" Quinn managed.

Barkley grinned. "Hey, Quinn. I've joined up. For one night only. I'm a hunter. I'm going to help vanquish this demon."

"Like hell you are."

He shifted the huge gun he carried to his other shoulder. "This is the chance I've been looking for. I'm going to prove I'm not a coward. That I can be alpha. It's a total metaphor for my life. I slay a demon, I'm slaying my own demons."

Quinn looked at Gideon. "He's a werewolf, you know."

Gideon shrugged. "He's crazy. And that's how I need my men to be before going into battle."

And before Quinn could say another word, Gideon

turned, with a grin, and ran into the burning building, not
even waiting for his men to follow him.

Every muscle in his body tensed. "I have to go with
them."

Janie grabbed his arm tightly. "Not a chance."

He turned to face her. "If I can do anything to stop it,
to protect you—"

"You've done enough. Besides, fire and vampires do
not go well together. Any prolonged exposure to flame
and you'll go up like a tiki torch." She grabbed him by
his waistband, and thrust her hand down the front of his
pants—which made him gasp with surprise—and
slowly drew out the Eye. Then she threw it on the
ground and, with a firm step, crushed the crystal. It let
out a flash of light and then went dark. "Hopefully that
might give Gideon a bit of an edge." She picked up what
was left of the golden staff. "Never knew you two were
friends."

"Still"—he looked at the hotel barely visible through
the flames—"I need to go—"

He felt only a short burst of pain as she clobbered him
with the Eye, and he fell to the ground unconscious.

Safe. But unconscious.

She stayed with him until he woke up. It took only a
couple of minutes. She sat on the ground next to him,
holding him in her arms while she watched the madness
surrounding them.

She knew when the Boss was finally dead, vanquished, because there was a sound unlike anything she'd
ever heard before. A piercing, inhuman scream that
seemed to split the air in two. She covered her ears to pro-

tect them, but it hurt as if somebody had beaten her sense-less. Afterward she felt bruised and very tired.

Suddenly she felt a rip through her center, and she grabbed at her stomach and cried out in pain. The Boss's hold on her—the contract she'd signed in blood—was null and void. He was dead, and she was finally free.

If she hadn't felt like a sack of shit, she would have celebrated.

As Quinn blinked his eyes open and looked up at her, she gave him a weary smile.

"Hey there," she said.

"Wh-what happened?"

"We won," she said simply and kissed him lightly on his forehead.

She helped him to his feet.

"You knocked me out." He rubbed the back of his head.

"And I'll do it again if you give me any problems."

He looked angry with her, just for a moment, and then a smile spread across his face. "You are so annoying."

"Right back at you." She placed her hands flat against his chest. "I'm sorry about the wish. I'm sorry it didn't work out the way you wanted it to."

He shook his head. "I was going to wish for you to be human again, anyhow. Not me. So I'm the one who's sorry."

"Me? Human again? But why?"

He laughed a little. "The fact that you ask me why makes me realize that being a vampire might not be as bad as I originally thought."

"You don't think being a vampire sucks anymore?" She grinned. "Get it? Sucks?"

"That joke is so old your Boss probably made it up. As far as being a vampire, I'm still getting used to it. But perhaps things aren't quite as black and white as I thought they were."

"Good way to think of it." She raised his hand up and kissed it. The feel of her lips made him ache. "So what now?"

"Well, that all depends—"

Angela ran over to them and grabbed Janie into a bear hug. Quinn's grip on her fell away.

"Janie! You're okay!"

"I am." Janie pulled back to smile at her sister. "I don't want to lose you again. Promise me you're not going anywhere."

"I promise. Well, wait. I do want to go back to Florida. I miss home so much. As long as the two of us are together again, then nothing else matters."

Janie hugged her tightly. "Florida sounds really good. I would so appreciate getting my life back to some sort of normal. Whatever that is. And Lenny's coming, too?"

Angela nodded and reached out a hand to the big guy, then transferred her hug to him. "My two favorite people in the world are safe. My big sister and my true love."

"I love you, Angela." Lenny leaned over and kissed her passionately.

Quinn felt very envious watching Lenny. Not of kissing Angela. But of kissing Janie. He reached out to her.

"Quinn!" a voice caught his attention, and he turned toward the burning casino. It was Barkley, who was covered in soot from head to toe. "We did it!"

Quinn grinned and slapped the werewolf on the back,

causing a puff of black ash to appear. "Of course you did."

"Don't sound so confident. It was crazy in there. I could hardly see anything. All I could hear was yelling and screaming. But we did it. At least I'm pretty sure we did."

"You did. You should be proud."

"I am." White teeth showed through the darkness of the ash. "And the best thing is, even though I was really scared, I didn't turn wolf to protect myself. I'm not a coward."

"Of course you're not. So are you going back to your pack and fight to become alpha?"

"Hell, no. I'm going to start my own pack. Start from scratch. I don't need to revisit the past. I never felt at home there. Maybe I'm an open-road kind of werewolf. I'm going to prowl around until I find somewhere that feels right. How about you?"

Quinn glanced at Janie, who was still celebrating with her sister and Lenny. "I . . . I don't know what my plans are yet." He turned back to Barkley. "Where's Gideon?"

The werewolf shook his head. "Not sure. He went face to face with the demon, from what little I could see. And then I didn't see him again. I . . . I think he's gone."

Quinn nodded. If he was a betting man, he'd say that Gideon had finally found a challenge worth his talents. But it had been his last one. Even though he knew Gideon was a murderous scumbag, it still hurt a little to know that he'd died to save them all.

It would be only a short time before someone else rose to lead the hunters. Gideon's death would mean nothing in the long run. The world kept turning. Vampires kept being sired. Hunters kept hunting.

He turned to look at Janie again, but he couldn't catch her eye. He heard her say to her sister that she wanted to go back to Florida with her. To their home. To a normal life. Now that Janie was free of her boss, she could do anything she wanted. Find somewhere safe to adjust to her new life as a vampire. It made sense.

He was far from being completely okay about being a vampire, himself. He was a mess. Not something that he wanted to inflict on somebody he cared deeply for.

It started to make sense to him that their short time together had come to an end. Now that the Eye was destroyed, her new life was one that he might not be a part of. Maybe it would be better that way.

He let her celebrate with Lenny and her sister. She didn't even notice when he slipped away into the shadows.

Janie paced back and forth at the airport the next day. She'd tried to get a message to Quinn that she was leaving to go home to Florida. He'd left the night before without saying anything to her—he'd just disappeared. After everything that had happened between them.

That said a hell of a lot to her.

He didn't want her in his life.

Did she blame him? Not really. She had a long way to go before she would be the sort of a woman that any man would want to spend more than a couple of days with. Plus, now that she was a vampire, she needed to devote a lot of time to adjusting to that fact. Her first goal upon getting to Florida would be to find an apartment for her and her sister to share. Then she'd source the local vampire bars and find out where she was going to get her blood supply from.

Blood, she thought. *I'm going to have to drink blood if I want to live.*

So strange.

Oddly enough, the thought didn't fill her with dread. It filled her with an odd sense of excitement. The next stage of her life would be an interesting one. Plus, she wouldn't have to worry about the whole aging process. She'd be eternally twenty-five, with—as Barkley had so enthusiastically put it when she'd met him—the body of a Hooters waitress. A high compliment, she'd come to realize.

Angela and Lenny had left on an earlier flight. They wanted to spend some time alone to get to know each other better. Since they couldn't keep their hands off each other, Janie was happy to allow them as much time as they needed. The last thing she needed right then was to feel like a fifth wheel. She was happy for them, especially for Lenny. As long as she'd known him, she'd never seen him with another woman. She'd been afraid that his crush on her had damaged his chances of being happy with somebody else, but now she'd been proven wrong.

He was in love with Angela. Who knew?

She was sorry that his notebook full of poetry had been destroyed but fully confident that it wouldn't be long before it was replenished with sonnets inspired by her pretty redheaded sister.

Janie had broken the news to him that she was now a vampire. She'd expected that he wouldn't take it well, since he didn't have much love for the fanged members of society.

He'd taken it remarkably well. In fact, he composed a new poem, "Vampires Rock," right on the spot.

She looked around again. It wasn't long before her flight left. Where was Quinn?

And what would she say to him if he did show up?

The time to tell him she loved him had passed. It would seem odd and awkward to make such an admittance now. And if he didn't feel the same way, she'd just look foolish. The Boss had said that he hired based on lack of emotion—and that had been very true. At one time, anyhow. Janie had been a coldhearted woman, with her eyes on the prize and not much else. Being a hired Merc had given her a purpose in her otherwise empty life, filled her time but not her heart.

But she *wasn't* emotionless. She was one big ball of raw emotion at the moment. And it was best that Quinn didn't see her this way.

She adjusted her dark sunglasses, just purchased at an airport kiosk. She'd already noticed that everything seemed brighter to her now that she was a vampire. She wondered what would be the next side effect to take hold. The loss of her reflection, or her fangs?

She wrapped her fingers around the handle of the small bag of new clothes she'd purchased earlier at a casino shop. It was carry-on. She didn't have any luggage to check. She could wait a couple of minutes more. And hope.

When those minutes expired, she turned around, swallowing past the thick lump in her throat.

Good-bye, Quinn, she thought with an ache in her heart. She started walking toward the door leading to her gate.

"Janie!"

She turned around to see Quinn rapidly moving toward her.

I'm not going to cry, she commanded herself.

She forced a smile to her face and felt her nails dig into her palms as he approached.

"You almost missed me," she said evenly.

He glanced at his watch. "Sorry. But I'm here now."

"Yes, you are."

"You're okay?"

She nodded. "Better than okay."

He looked up at the flight screen. "You're going back to Florida?"

"Home, sweet home. Hard to believe after all these years."

"So what are your plans?" He crossed his arms.

"I have absolutely no idea." She gave him a small smile. "I am a woman at loose ends."

"I'm sure you'll find your way."

"Maybe I'll start a detective agency."

"You'd be a great detective."

"Or I could keep being a hired assassin. Totally better money than detective work."

He raised an eyebrow.

She laughed. "I'm kidding."

"Oh." He smiled. "Good to hear it."

"And what about you? What are your plans now that you're stuck as a vampire for the next billion years?"

"You really think it's going to be that long?" He shrugged. "I'm just settling in, I guess. I'll travel. I have money, so I don't need to look for work right away. Maybe I'll take a little while off and relax. Do some exploring."

"So you're not planning on going back to Toronto?"

He shook his head. "Maybe for a visit, but not as a permanent residence. I'll probably end up in New York. That's where I was born and raised, after all. Sometimes I even miss it."

She licked her lips. Her mouth was very dry.

She'd hoped for a sign that he felt something more for her than a passing fancy, but she sensed nothing. Saw nothing in his eyes that told her he wanted her to stay.

Also, even after racking her mind, she couldn't think of any excuse to stay with him if he didn't say something to her to give her a reason.

So be it.

She hoped her love for him would fade with time. She doubted it would, but she did hope.

He watched her, waiting for some sort of signal that would give him permission to fall at her feet. To take her into his arms and beg her to stay. But she was completely expressionless.

After he'd left the burning casino last night, he'd ended up at a low-end motel that didn't even have a slot machine. Barkley was the only one who knew where he went. He was the one who got the message to him about Janie's departure. And it had almost been too late to get to the airport in time.

The whole night he'd tossed and turned, running though the past couple of days in his head over and over and over again.

They'd been two of the worst days of his life.

Absolutely. No question about it.

Then how did they also become two of the best days of his life?

Only one reason for that. And it was the beautiful

woman standing in front of him right now, only moments away from getting on a plane and leaving him forever.

Say something, he commanded himself. *Tell her to stay. Ask her. Beg her. Whatever it takes.*

But he said nothing, fighting hard to ignore the big knot of emotion tightening in his stomach until he felt ill from it. The pain was a great deal similar to not having enough blood. He was starving. He was dying inside.

"Okay, I guess this is good-bye, then," Janie said suddenly. She turned to look at him. "Good luck, Quinn. With everything."

"You, too." How could his voice sound so neutral and emotionless when he was a total wreck? He searched her face for some sign that she didn't want to leave him but found nothing. Her job was done. She was finally free from her boss. She might be a vampire now, but she was strong enough to find her own way, wherever that would lead her.

Without him.

His jaw clenched. *Suck it up.* This was for the best.

A smile played at the edge of her beautiful mouth, and she closed the distance between them to kiss him lightly on the lips, her fingers tracing the edge of his jaw. "Take care of yourself."

He just nodded. She squeezed his hand once and then let him go, turning and walking away from him.

Don't go. Please. Stay with me.

He swallowed so hard it hurt, tears stinging the back of his eyes, and he watched her until she disappeared through a set of opaque glass doors. She didn't look back at him.

He stood in place for five full minutes.

Maybe someday he'd look her up again. When he had

his life under control. Although when that was going to be was anybody's guess.

You should have stopped her, his subconscious scolded.

To do what? See if she wanted to spend her time with someone like him? She had better things to do with her life.

But you're in love with her.

Yeah. Well. Maybe this was part of his repentance. Give up what he wanted most in the world to even the scales of what he'd done in the past. His punishment.

He rolled his eyes at himself. Christ. No wonder she didn't even look back over her shoulder at him. He was such a whiner.

He'd get himself straightened out. Find his true purpose in life. Help those who needed his help. Show her that he deserved her.

It was a lousy plan, but it was the only one he had at the moment.

He made his way to a bank of windows and watched the planes taxi away from the airport before heading toward the runway. Finally, he saw the plane he knew Janie was on. He bit the inside of his mouth so hard that he tasted blood.

And then he turned away.

There was a slot machine right next to where he stood and he fished in his pocket for a quarter, slid it into the slot, and pulled the handle.

He didn't win.

This amused him greatly for some reason.

He sighed heavily, trying to ignore the big empty place in his chest that felt like somebody had very recently ripped out his heart, and turned around.

Janie stood there with her hand on her hip. She looked pissed.

His eyebrows raised.

"Nice try," she said.

He was so shocked all he could say was, "What?"

"Thought I'd forget, didn't you?"

"Forget about what?"

"Honestly. Men are so devious. You were going to let me get on that plane and leave. Luckily, I remembered just in time."

His mouth was dry. "What are you talking about?"

She shook her head. "Sure. Try to renege on the deal we made. I still expect to be paid in full."

He frowned as she waited for a reply he didn't have.

"The dress?" she prompted. "The one you ruined?"

"The . . . the dress," he repeated.

"Don't try to play stupid with me. That was a very, very expensive designer dress. We had a deal. You were going to pay me back in sex . . . and hello? Not even close to being done yet. And you were just going to let me leave without saying a word to remind me. Like I said, nice try." A slight smile betrayed her serious tone.

He felt something flutter in his chest as his heart sped up. "Oh, right. I almost forgot about that."

"Yeah, obviously."

"Uh, how much do I still owe?"

"A lot. It's going to take a really, *really* long time for us to be square on this."

He nodded. "I understand."

"I mean, I'm immortal now. We could be talking about decades. Possibly centuries."

"How much was that dress, again?"

"It was expensive. That's all I'm saying." She approached him and twisted her hands into the material of his shirt.

"I don't turn away from a deal."

"You're sure about that?"

He nodded gravely. "Very sure. But what about Florida? Your sister?"

"I know where she is. She's safe with Lenny. She'll understand that we have a serious matter to take care of between us."

"Serious."

"*Very* serious."

"It probably shouldn't wait much longer, then. Like you said, I have a lot to pay back." He stroked her long blond hair off her forehead and tucked it behind her ear.

"You're okay with this burden, right? I mean, you can always write me a check if you'd rather."

"Well . . ." he said quickly. "I have no idea where my checkbook is. Do you take Visa?"

"Sorry, no."

"Then it's going to have to be a great deal of sex, then."

"So be it."

He met her gaze. "I shouldn't have let you get on that plane."

"No, you shouldn't have. I suppose we have a problem that we're two very stubborn people. Every now and then, one of us is going to have to compromise."

He swallowed hard. "I thought that you were—"

She covered his mouth. "I love you, Quinn. There's nowhere I'd rather be than with you right now."

Her words filled him with a deep, coursing warmth. "I love you, too. So much." His voice broke.

"This is very good to know." She smiled and pulled him to her. He didn't resist, not in the slightest. Their lips met, and she ran her hands over his chest, feeling his heart beat.

He was alive. He *felt* alive. Even if he was a vampire, it didn't matter anymore. He was in control of his future as long as it contained her. This woman whom he had quickly grown to love more than anyone else he'd ever known in his life. His heart wasn't as cold as he thought it was, and if it was, then she'd managed to melt it in record time.

They were together. The thought filled him with some strange sensations—hope, joy, bliss. Emotions he thought he'd never feel again. But he did. And he didn't hate himself for being a vampire anymore. He didn't hate himself for his past as a hunter, because it was just that—his past. There was nothing he could do about it now except do his very best to make the most of his present and his future.

He had fangs, and he needed blood to survive, and he'd live the rest of his days as the very thing he'd always considered a monster. But he *wasn't* a monster. He was certain of that now.

He didn't have a reflection, but he didn't need one anymore. His gaze locked with Janie's as they stood together in the middle of the airport, people milling about on every side, rushing to catch their flights.

Janie was his reflection now.

She looked at Quinn with love in her beautiful blue eyes. He really liked what he saw there.

About the Author

Michelle Rowen is a self-confessed bibliophile and reality TV junkie and is well known for making a mean pot of Kraft Dinner. Her books include the 2007 HOLT Medallion winner for Best First Book, *Bitten & Smitten*, and its sequel *Fanged & Fabulous*. Michelle is currently hard at work on her next fantastical novel.

She'd love to hear from you! Please feel free to contact her through her Web site at www.michellerowen.com.

THE DISH

Where authors give you the inside scoop!

♥ ♥ ♥ ♥ ♥ ♥ ♥ ♥ ♥ ♥ ♥ ♥ ♥ ♥ ♥ ♥ ♥

From the desk of Michelle Rowen

Michael Quinn used to be a vampire hunter. Now, he's a very reluctant vampire in search of a magical cure for what ails him in LADY & THE VAMP (available now). He's nursing a bit of a broken heart after being on the losing end of a love triangle in my first two Immortality Bites titles, *Bitten & Smitten* and *Fanged & Fabulous*. He doesn't know that true love is just around the next corner, and she's got a wooden stake with his name on it. To help this tall, dark, and "fangsome" vampire bachelor on his quest for love, liberty, and the pursuit of a hot, blond mercenary named Janie, here is something that Quinn might encounter in your average, everyday vampire bar.

Top Ten Vampiric Pick-up Lines

1. "I don't drink . . . *wine*. But, how about a piña colada?"
2. "Hey, you! You, in the black!"
3. "Didn't I go to your funeral?"
4. "Baby, you don't look a day over 350!"
5. "You have a beautiful neck, mind if I bite it?"
6. "You look just like David Boreanaz!"

7. "Are you one of the children of the night? Would you like to be?"
8. "Where have you been all of my long, tortured existence?"
9. "You, me, a bag of blood. Whaddya say?"
10. "Is that a wooden stake in your pocket or is it . . . ? Okay, never mind."

Then again, perhaps Quinn should just steer clear of vampire bars for the time being. It's just a suggestion.

Happy reading!

Michelle Rowen

www.michellerowen.com

♥ ♥ ♥ ♥ ♥ ♥ ♥ ♥ ♥ ♥ ♥ ♥ ♥ ♥ ♥

From the desk of Marliss Melton

Dear reader,

It has been said that every novelist draws on what she knows and that her stories are, in some ways, autobiographical. So, reading any author's work is a bit like glimpsing the skeletons in her closet or her underwear hanging out to dry! This often-embarrassing phenomenon couldn't be truer for me than it is in DON'T LET GO (available now), the fifth book in my Navy SEAL series.

I've never been to Venezuela to do mission work like Jordan (the heroine of DON'T LET GO), but I did study abroad in Ecuador during college. I never adopted a child like the little boy Jordan wants to adopt, but I cherished my little Thai foster sister, who went on to be adopted in the United States. I've stood in her sister Jillian Sanders's shoes, a widow with young children, hoping to carry her boys through their grief in the most positive way possible. I've watched a relationship develop between a fatherless boy and a man willing to fill a giant's shoes. But, most obviously, I've loved a man like Solomon McGuire, a man who is passionate in all things, secretly romantic, and sometimes hard to live with.

My second chance at love, my husband, most profoundly influenced the development of Solomon's character, from his black moustache to his New England dialect. Of course, I had to pair Solomon with a woman who resembles me, at least in regards to her hair color and the speed at which her baby was born. Not every reader is going to fall head over heels with this commanding character, but there'll be plenty who do. All I can say, ladies, is, "sorry, Solomon is all mine."

To see a real–life photo of my inspiration, just check out the photos page on my Web site, www.

marlissmelton.com. And while you're there, check out a preview of my next SEAL Team Twelve book, featuring the blue-eyed, baldheaded Chief Sean Harlan.

Did I mention that my husband is also bald?

Yours truly,

Marlis Melton

♥ ♥ ♥ ♥ ♥ ♥ ♥ ♥ ♥ ♥ ♥ ♥ ♥ ♥

From the desk of Elizabeth Jennings

Dear reader,

Charlotte Court, the heroine in PURSUIT (available now), is a truly gifted artist, who perfected her craft in Florence, Italy. Art is her entire life until a murderer comes after her and she has to go on the run to Baja California. That's where she meets Matt, a former Navy SEAL, a rough, tough guy, who falls head over heels for her and is blown away by her talent.

Like Charlotte, I spent a number of years in Florence, Italy, immersed in an artistic environment. My mom worked at a US graduate school of fine arts—now, alas, defunct—in a beautiful villa nestled in the green hills just below Fiesole, Villa

Schifanoia. Legend has it that this was the villa where the young Florentine noblemen and women fled to avoid the plague in Boccaccio's *Decameron*.

We lived around the corner from a fabulous international art school that was in itself a small masterpiece. It was in a 16th century deconsecrated church in the Borgo San Frediano, simply a stunning place to study art. Just a glimpse inside felt like being magically transported back to a Greek or a Roman temple.

I'm arty, but not visually gifted like the students I grew up around. I love words. At the time, I was learning characterization, hooks, and motivation, studying the masters, going over the writing again and again and again, revising and rewriting until I got it right.

I founded a writer's group in Florence that met in the basement of the American church—quite an eclectic group of people. I was the only one writing romance and it did me good to pit myself against those who had no sympathy for or knowledge of the genre. It stiffened my spine. And, boy, did I learn how to tighten up my writing.

Since I was putting myself through this intense apprenticeship, exactly as a young Renaissance artisan working in a *bottega* or the young artists in that beautiful school, I had an enormous amount of sympathy for the work involved in becoming proficient at an art.

Charlotte Court was born then in my mind, all

those years ago. A beautiful woman, exceedingly gifted and hardworking, who lives for her art. I had her study at this wonderful art school. She was alive to me—her drive to paint and draw almost obsessive, yet totally understandable.

I have held Charlotte in my head and heart all these years, and in this, my eighth book, I have finally given her life.

She is put to the test in PURSUIT. Wounded and hunted, she shows immense courage and fortitude. I like to think that her art gives her strength and grace.

Happy reading!

Elizabeth Jennings

Dear Reader,

I hope you enjoyed *Lady & the Vamp* as much as I enjoyed writing it!

If you're wondering what happens next in the Immortality Bites series—in *Stakes & Stilettos*—the story shifts back to fledgling vampire Sarah Dearly as she and her master vampire boyfriend head back to her home town to attend her high school reunion (from hell, that is).

Head on over to my Web site at www.michellerowen.com for a sneak peek at chapter one!

Michelle Rowen

VAMPIRES! FALLEN ANGELS!
SLAYERS WITH HEARTS
OF GOLD!

WELCOME TO THE
REMARKABLE PARANORMAL
WORLD OF

Michelle Rowen!

BITTEN & SMITTEN

"A charming, hilarious book! I'm insanely
jealous I didn't write it."
—MARYJANICE DAVIDSON

ANGEL WITH ATTITUDE

"Four stars! Rowen does a delightful job mixing
things up with her sassy and sexy characters.
She has her own unique spin . . . which makes
for downright fun reading."
—*Romantic Times BOOKclub Magazine*

FANGED & FABULOUS

"You can't put this book down."
—CHARLAINE HARRIS

SATAN, DARK ANGELS,
AND ROMANCE?
NOW THAT'S A HELL OF A MIX!

DON'T MISS THESE SEXY,
HILARIOUS PARANORMAL ROMANCES
BY RITA-NOMINATED AUTHOR

STEPHANIE ROWE

"Rowe is a paranormal star!"
—J. R. WARD

DATE ME, BABY, ONE MORE TIME
"A hilarious underworld romp."
—KATIE MACALISTER

MUST LOVE DRAGONS
"Snappy patter, good humor, and enormous
imagination. One of those genre twisters that [can]
make readers rabid for more."
—*Publishers Weekly*

HE LOVES ME, HE LOVES ME HOT
"A lighthearted romp . . . filled with plenty of action.
Fantasy romance fans will enjoy the latest amusing
battle of the souls (soulless?) on hell and earth."
—*Midwest Book Review*

SEX & THE IMMORTAL BAD BOY
"This outrageously hilarious series is chock-full of
sexy mischief and mayhem."
—*Romantic Times BOOKreviews Magazine*

Want to know more about romances at
Grand Central Publishing and Forever?
Get the scoop online!

GRAND CENTRAL PUBLISHING'S
ROMANCE HOMEPAGE

Visit us at www.hachettebookgroupusa.com/romance
for all the latest news, reviews, and chapter excerpts!

NEW AND UPCOMING TITLES

Each month we feature our new titles
and reader favorites.

CONTESTS AND GIVEAWAYS

We give away galleys, autographed copies,
and all kinds of fun stuff.

AUTHOR INFO

You'll find bios, articles, and links to personal
websites for all your favorite authors—and
so much more!

THE BUZZ

Sign up for our monthly romance newsletter,
and be the first to read all about it!